MISTLETOE LATTE

MISTLETOE LATTE

Ellen Mint

FREE BOOK OPPORTUNITY

Scan this QR code with your phone to receive a free book and join my newsletter!

DEDICATION

Thank you to my sweet puppy Essie-May who's crossed the rainbow bridge. She was my biggest supporter.

TABLE OF CONTENTS

CHAPTER ONE

"ARE YOU HERE for the mistletoe latte?"

The excited voice plucked Emma from her fog. She'd wound up standing before a cute coffee shop. An adorable, hand-cut sign dangled above the door — Brew 4 U. They'd even added a coffee cup to the u. It would have been a local favorite back in Portland. A soft pain throbbed at the reminder of what she'd lost and sent her driving cross-country a week before Christmas.

"I'm sorry?" Emma said to the stranger who'd stopped her.

He only looked up from his phone to take a picture of the sign. "The mistletoe latte, you know."

"Um…" She had no idea but it sounded interesting. Had she stumbled on a small-town gem by pure accident?

He plucked open the door. The toll of the shop bell sang not a cherry Christmas jingle but a death knell. While the outside of the café was bright and cheerful, the interior of Brew 4 U was as dour as a funeral. Every fixture was made of darkened wood. Copper pipes running the length of the vaulted ceiling were stained to a brown.

Emma couldn't see past the line of customers ending right before the glass door. She moved to let a woman leave and bumped into a sign. In large, jagged letters, it declared, "Do not ask for the mistletoe latte."

Strange. Maybe they were low on supplies. She knew too well the pain of facing down an irate customer who couldn't understand her inability to make the missing ingredient magically appear.

The line moved and heads parted to reveal what waited at the end. A menu board with jagged letters smudged by fingerprints laid out the bare bones options. Someone had recently wiped away the bottom part under "Pastries" to write, "No Mistletoe Lattes" in all caps.

"Who's next?" a voice boomed above the excited chatter of the crowd. A tingle shot through Emma faster than espresso. With his arms crossed and stance wide, the man didn't so much stand behind the counter as guard it. The hanging industrial lights glinted off his shorn dirty-blond hair and the day-old scruff. It struck his square jaw, emphasizing the rugged terrain. She couldn't make out his eye color, but she'd guess it was steely gray for the stone grit to his wide brow and long nose.

"Uh-huh," he boomed, tossing a pad of paper to the counter. He swiped a pencil across it to take the order the old-fashioned way. Suddenly, his detached expression knotted up. His whole jaw gnarled into a sneer.

"That's it!" he shouted, leaping around the counter like a wide receiver going for a touchdown. The customer blanched as the man grabbed him by the arm and hauled him out of line.

"Wh…what are you—?" the man stammered as the enraged owner stormed past, half dragging him. Even as Emma folded away with the rest of the line, she could feel the immovable force from the owner. It'd be like fighting a tidal wave.

He yanked open the door, flinging it against the wall, and hurled the customer into the cold. The man rebounded off the lamppost festooned with Christmas greenery. "Do you know who I am? You'll be sorry for this!"

"I'm sorry I woke up today!" the man shouted before latching onto the door and slamming it back. Silhouetted by the morning sunlight, his wide shoulders shook in unsuppressed rage. Only his jagged panting and the squeal of tools from the auto repair shop down the road filled the air.

Slowly, he drew a palm over his face and revealed a smile below. "Are you here for the mistletoe latte?" he asked, his baritone voice crackling.

The man beside Emma nodded excitedly. "Yes, I saw the article—"

He shook the man off and stopped right before her. She was wrong. His eyes weren't steel gray but ice blue and beamed with such ferocity her chin dropped to avoid them stripping her to her core. "What do you want?" he thundered.

A job.

A home.

A future.

"A coffee," Emma whispered.

"Finally." He crooked a finger at her. The powerful scent of coffee wafted off him as he raised his hands. "Everyone who's here for the mistletoe latte, will you please step to the side?"

The entire line moved, leaving Emma exposed. She knotted her fingers together and flicked the hole in her glove. He didn't grab her like the last customer but guided her to the counter. Once there, he picked up his abandoned notepad and knocked the spiraled edge on the desk three times before looking at her.

"Coffee, right? How do you like it?"

"In a cup?" she squeaked before slapping a hand to her mouth.

To her shock, his rigid sneer slipped up for a moment, and he gave a quick snort. "That's complimentary. Do you want sugar, milk?"

"Um, a little cream? Please." Normally, she didn't drink coffee without sugar, but this day was far from normal.

The man nodded and jotted it down before he hauled a mug off the pegboard behind him. It bore the logo of a local hardware place.

"Anything else?" he asked.

Emma's stomach twisted, reminding her how she hadn't eaten since the motel and that was a long car ride ago. "Do you have any…?"

His glare intensified, the pencil poised over the pad as if he'd snap it in half if she asked the wrong question. Her throat dried and she struggled to swallow. Fighting through it, she asked, "…food?"

"Yeah, I think there's a pastry or two in back. What's the name?"

"I'm Emma. What's yours?"

He meant it for the order. She realized that the second the question slipped from her mouth. He cracked another bemused grin and darted his icy eyes up. "It's Nick. Here's your coffee." He passed over the mug along with a carafe of milk.

She scooped it all into her hands. The heat had caused the yellow logo of the hardware store to melt away into a blue cartoon moose accidentally nailing his antlers to the wall. After blowing across the top, she began to raise the mug to her lips.

"That'll be three-fifty…" Nick paused in entering the order into his old cash register to look right into her eyes. "Emma."

THE WORLD HAD lost its damned mind. Usually, this was the part of the day when Nick could take his first breather. But every Tom, Dick, and jackass woke up this morning to assault his coffee shop. The usuals huddled around their tables, mugs at the ready while they enjoyed watching the calamity unfold.

"Skylar!" Nick shouted.

"What?" she screamed back louder.

He turned from the mindless horde snapping selfies to the only newcomer with any sense. She'd set up shop on the stool by Sam's and kept twirling a spoon in her mug. With a red knit cap on her light brown hair and her puffy overcoat fluffed to the sides, she reminded him of a little wren in the snow. Didn't help that she was perched on the stool as if about to take flight.

"You found the pastry yet?" Nick called to his single helper wandering in the back. "Shouldn't be more than a minute," he added to the woman when the crash of tumbling metal burst from the back.

"Sonnofa…" A blonde head popped out of the door, followed by a lanky arm propping up a plate. "This is all I found," Skylar said, not explaining the sound.

Hopefully, a donut was good enough for Emma. He took the plate and his hand flash froze. *Where the hell did she find that thing?* "What was the crash?" Nick asked.

"Don't worry about it." Skylar beamed her smile, wider than ever since she lost the braces.

He groaned and pulled on the door of the microwave. The old metal box gave in, but it wasn't until he put the frozen donut in that he remembered there was no juice. "Uh." Nick approached the woman with her mitts wrapped around her mug. "I'm afraid your 'pastry'…" He sneered at the warping of the word to fit a donut from god knew when. "…is a little cold."

As Nick placed the plate on the counter it crackled like breaking the ice on a lake. With the tip of her finger, she touched the donut. The icing shattered. Nick grimaced and reached to yank the plate away when Emma plucked up the pastry.

"My coffee should warm it." She dipped a quarter of the donut in, her brown eyes a richer hue than the chocolate frosting sliding into her drink. The smile didn't waver for a second, which usually set off every nerve in Nick's body. But Emma's smile made him want to give one back. *Almost.*

As she raised the dredged donut to her lips, Nick winced. He dashed to the register and slammed his palm to the old buttons. "Let me refund you," he said. *What did she pay?* He snatched onto a fiver and held it out to her.

Emma's coral-pink lips wrapped around the edge of the donut and her eyes closed as she struggled to take a bite. Before she could complain, he slapped the bill down on the counter. She chewed quickly, covering her mouth with her hand. "You should keep it," she said, pushing the bill toward him.

"That thing has to be freezer burnt to hell. I can't charge you for it."

"It's not too bad..." She gritted her teeth and took another bite. "And this coffee is delicious." Abandoning the ancient donut, she hefted her mug up and took a long drink. "Best I've had in...in months."

Nick beamed at her words. Even if she was being nice for the sake of appearances, he pulled the bill back and dropped it in the register. As he closed the drawer, he looked at her. "Tell you what, free refills for the abysmal donut."

She smiled wide, revealing a touch of chocolate on the side of her mouth. "Sounds like a good deal. Oh..." Her eyes fell and she fidgeted with the donut. Spinning it around and around in a circle, it took a beat before Emma whispered, "Could I have some sugar? I don't handle black coffee well."

Laughing, Nick bent under the counter and produced a whole stack of sugar packets. "Here." He added some Equal then a palm-full of half-n-half cups. "Just in case."

Her cheeks turned as pink as her lips. She cupped her hands around the bounty before he slipped away. Her fingers — one hand frozen from the donut, the other warm from the coffee — brushed his. Nick glanced up in surprise and found himself falling deep into her eyes. Everything about her was tiny—little mouth, petite nose, short body, but her eyes were wider than the moon. *What lucky sot got to dunk into her?*

"How long until our lattes are ready?"

The impudence ripped Nick from his romantic delusion. He looked to the pile of people standing patiently in line. "They're ready when they're ready," Nick said noncommittally.

The back door swung open and Skylar finally bothered to get to work. She carried the wash bin to the regulars' tables, plopping the mugs and silverware wherever they landed. The clink reminded Nick of the horror that awaited him in the back. "Gonna tell me what happened in the storage room?" he asked.

Skylar stared up, and he reared back at the gobs of black makeup smeared across her lashes. "Why? You'll find out soon enough."

"Sky…"

"Oh, sh…oot." She caught herself quickly and looked at the clock. "I've got to get to school. Here." Without pause, she thrust the wash bin into Nick's hands. He stumbled to catch it, giving her just enough time to yank her backpack up from the counter stool and make it one step to the door before he noticed.

"You are not wearing that."

Skylar, a fourteen-year-old going on twenty-five, crossed her arms over a midriff-baring t-shirt. The only thing keeping it on her shoulders were two miniature ties barely knotted together. "Unless you have time to drive me all the way back to home and then school, I think I am."

Oh, hell no. He was not having sass from her this early. Nick dropped the wash bin to the floor and kicked it to the side. He waggled a finger in her face and ordered her to stay put before walking into the back. Past the storage room was his office. Without bothering to flick on the lights, he reached into an old box and yanked up the first shirt he found while grumbling the entire time. At least Skylar hadn't left, though she was innocently picking at her nails like he was the bad guy.

Nick hurled the old polo at her head. "Put that on."

"Ew!" Skylar started to throw the shirt away, but at his glare she held it. "I'm not wearing that. It stinks of coffee and some old guy's BO."

"You are putting that on, young lady, or so help me."

"So help you what?" she taunted, waving the yellow polo like a fighter taunting a snorting bull.

He couldn't gore her, but he had better options at his fingertips. "Or you're working the entire weekend."

"But, it's the winter formal…"

Nick crossed his arms and nodded as if he remembered that all along.

Skylar's sarcastic perch crumbled. Her lips trembled in familiar rage. She hurled her book bag to the ground. "Fine!" Stuffing the old polo over her head, she kept ranting at him. "You're ruining my life! I hate you."

"I know," Nick said.

She yanked her ponytail from the wide neck hole, her skinny body properly hidden behind a large, unshapely polo. Clenching her hands as if to choke him, she gave that patented teenage girl shriek of rage. "Why are you so awful?"

"Years of practice."

Exclaiming once more, Skylar pulled up her bag and spun on her heel. Nick slipped behind the counter and began to buff the surface. She tugged open the door harder than he had and took one step into the frosty December morning.

"Have a nice day," Nick called, his voice sweeter than sugar.

Skylar gave him the glare of death. He knew it took a year off of his life, but it was worth it. She slammed the door so hard that the bell ricocheted, struck the ceiling, and fell to the ground. "Teenagers," Nick said with a shrug.

"Excuse me." One of the latte people disengaged from the pack and approached him studiously scrubbing the counter while whistling. "When are you going to bring out a mistletoe latte?"

"Never."

The man jerked in shock and looked back to the others. A titter of nervous laughter rebounded around. "But this is Brew 4 U," he said patiently.

"What it says outside." Nick jabbed a hand at the sign and spotted Skylar looking back with vengeance. *Now what?*

"Aren't you famous for the mistletoe lattes that are rumored to…"

Nick whipped his glare at the man and dug the heels of his palms into the counter. The guy had enough sense to stop talking. "I don't know what's gotten into your heads, but can any of you read? Says right there in big ass letters!" He gestured to the first sign he'd made when this madness started. "No Mistletoe Lattes."

"But the—"

"And if you're not here for a cappuccino, or an americano, or a mocha, take your damn influencer ass out my door!" Nick pointed at the horde. They'd probably pay ten bucks for a cup of burned bean juice, but he didn't have the patience to bother.

Like a flock of chickens, they bumped into each other to flee, phones flashing as if to prove they'd been bamboozled. Whoever was going around telling these people about the mistletoe lattes was a liar, and if Nick ever found 'em… He wrung his towel around his hands and looked out the front window.

Skylar met his eye and raised a mischievous grin. In one fell swoop, she tugged the polo off, dumped it in the trash, and took off down the street whistling.

"Skylar Iverson!"

CHAPTER TWO

BEING TRAPPED IN a coffee shop for over an hour hadn't been part of her plan. Having to abandon Portland and drive across the country wasn't in there either. She forgot to pencil in her car stalling on the highway outside of a tiny Michigan town called Lake Holly.

For all the things going wrong in her life, at least she was somewhere warm with unlimited coffee. It could be a lot worse. Emma picked up the mug and took a careful sip trying to not smear her lipstick.

"Good morning, Miss." A man in a winter cap with the ear muffs sewn in plopped down beside her. He opened a bag and tugged out a black box with dials on the side and started to fine-tune them.

"Hello," Emma greeted him.

"I've got a...melted can of frosting with some coffee in the cup!" Nick shouted to the throngs forced to stand next to the door. He handed it to the first person he could to run back to the counter and take the next order.

Emma shifted in her seat, growing uneasy at the rising number of people and the one man to handle it all. Four of them got up, leaving a pile of soiled napkins, cups, and used sugar packets behind. Without a thought, she slipped from her chair, gathered up the mess, polished the tabletop, and deposited the trash in the bin.

"You the new waitress?" the man in the hat asked as she sat down

"Ah...no. I only thought I may as well help while I'm here." By the time she finished, another group took over the table, scattering more sugar across it. That was the way of the restaurant—clean only existed for a millisecond of time before someone, somewhere dropped an egg.

The old man stared overlong at her.

What am I doing? No one asked me for my help. What if I made it worse?

"You've got somethin' on your cheek..." he pointed to her face and Emma winced. Out of habit, she slapped her palm over her cheek. A thousand jeers railed out of her memory. Folding in on herself, Emma turned away and lowered her hand. A dot of chocolate rested on her palm. Of course. She never forgot to cover her...

The static from the man's box crackled and an official voice said, "Officer Collins, we've got a report of a suspicious character out on maintenance road at mile marker thirty-seven. Do you copy?"

"Ooh, haven't had one of those in a while," the man in the hat said. He tossed open his notebook and hunched over it to write.

The box's static cut out again and a person, presumably Officer Collins, responded to the request. Nick looked up from the register to the man. "Sam? What'd I say about the scanner?"

"To put it away when the sheriff's here," Sam said.

Nick sighed and looked heavenward before his gaze slipped over to her. His grimace lightened as if a smile was on the horizon. Diving forward, Emma brought her mug to her lips and drank. She kept drinking until the buzzing in her head left.

Trembling hands put the coffee mug down. Nick must have read that as due to jitters from the police scanner and not the heavy dose of caffeine. He leaned across the counter to whisper to her, "Don't worry about Sam. He's weird but harmless."

"I ain't weird," Sam insisted. "Don't you know there's been an increase in crime ever since they tore down the old granary?"

"Really?" Emma asked.

Nick mouthed to her, "Twenty years ago."

"No one's paying attention, but mark my words, they're gonna want this data one day."

"Uh-huh, here, let me top you up." Nick sounded more like the patient bartender with Sam and less the surly coffee slinger of before. An ear-screeching noise yanked his grumpy mask back on, and he glared in the corner. "What are you doing?"

He slammed the coffee pot to the counter and rounded on the flock huddled by the corner. "Moving this for better light," one explained, hands clasped to a bench as he jerked his chin to the dark corner. Despite Nick's glare, he pulled again, causing Emma's teeth to clench. "You need better lighting in here."

"Did a badger shit in your skull?" Nick fumed, slamming a foot onto the bench. "Don't. Move. The furniture!" He waved a threatening finger at the four, then hauled up the hefty bench and flung it back against the wall. "And we're out of the big mugs so stop asking!"

Grumbling under his breath about the damn youths, he rubbed off another section of the menu and wrote his same order to them, then he added 'mistletoe latte' and drew a big slash across the words. This mysterious latte must be quite amazing for so many people to keep pushing for it. The people who hadn't been chased off by his growling bear act snapped pics of their orders and chatted loud enough to cover over both the vague classical music and the police scanner.

"What brings you to Lake Holly?"

"Not the latte," Emma admitted. Oh, it wasn't Nick who asked, but the friendly Sam. He peered from below his snowy eyebrows. "My car started clunking on the highway, then it slowed down. I pulled into the first mechanic shop I could find before something bad happened."

Before more bad things happened.

"Daryl's?" he asked. Emma nodded. "Good place. Reliable. Course it's also the only place in town."

"He said he'd call once he found the problem, but…" She lifted her phone to find no missed calls and the battery at twenty-five percent. The charger was in her purse, but the single noticeable outlet was mobbed by the mistletoe gang. "At least I'm somewhere warm," Emma said, shaking off the worry.

"Wouldn't want to break down out on the highway. Not in this weather," Sam said what she'd been fearing. Though, if whatever was wrong with her car wasn't easily fixed, then what?

"Dispatch, this is Officer Collins..." the police scanner piped up. Sam wiggled his gaunt shoulders and hunched closer.

Another section of the café cleared out, leaving their mugs of varying sizes precariously stacked. Emma glanced to the owner, only to find him white-knuckling a pencil as he wrote down a customer's order. If that tower fell, he was liable to blow. She dashed to her feet and caught the mug just as it began to tip. A spoon rattled inside, almost flopping to the floor.

"Suspicious character appears to be an inflatable Santa Claus stuck to a fence."

Emma spread the dishes out on the table so none would break. Nick could get to them later once he had time. It seemed the best answer when the coffee shop's door opened and fifty people rushed in. They fanned out after the choke point, filling the café. Their chattering covered over the police scanner. Sam tried to turn it up, but nothing could compete with the excitement of the mistletoe latte.

"Are there any tables?"

"Get us somewhere to sit."

"This lighting is atrocious."

The horde split off into ant trails, lines winding through the place and trying to take every available seat. More grabbed the benches by the wall. One even found an old stepladder and pulled that up to the counter.

"What about this?" A woman hooked her hand around the table and tugged, causing the cups to rattle.

Emma reached over to keep it in place and got a withering glare. "What are you doing?"

"I..." She gulped and spotted the abandoned wash basin from earlier. "I haven't finished clearing this." With a quick skip, Emma picked up the tub and loaded the plates and mugs into it. The whole time the woman glared as if she was wasting her time.

"Have a good day," Emma said as she stepped away with the washing.

"What are you doing?"

Her heart dropped at the voice not being directed at the people moving the furniture. The confused wrath was aimed directly at her. Nick uncrossed his arms and poked a pencil to the tub growing heavier with each second.

"You seemed so busy, I didn't want these to fall. Or break. Can I put them somewhere? A sink in the back?"

He reached to take the tub when the customers surged for the counter. A coffee tin collecting donations for the local toy drive hit the floor, sending pennies and dimes scattering across the tile. "You've got to be..." Nick flexed his hand, snapping the pencil in half. "Everyone, take a step back!" he ordered with such authority even Emma obeyed.

Sneering, he stopped the rolling can with his foot. Bent over, he started to shovel the lost coins in, but he kept speaking to her. "Through that door, first left."

Emma nodded that she understood and quick-stepped for the employee-only door. Another teeth-grating squeal rose through the air.

"If you don't cease moving those benches, I'll nail you to them!" Nick shouted, silencing the whine.

Before it got worse, Emma hustled through the door. She expected the back area to be nothing more than plain drywall and dirty tile, but it looked the same as the front. To the left, she reminded herself, pushing on a second door. It smacked into a tipped-over shelf tossing more boxes of paper goods across the floor.

"You, sugar and cream!"

She jerked to find Nick standing at the door into the café, his arms crossed. "I'm sorry," Emma called, "there was a shelf in the way."

"That's what she knocked over," Nick grumbled in a bass that managed to crawl along the floor.

On the far wall, Emma spotted a stainless steel sink with an overhead sprayer. A handful of mugs rested on the drying pegs above, but just as many had accumulated in the bins on the side. Emma dropped the dirty dishes in the sink and hunted for soap.

"Don't worry about that," Nick said, causing her to pause before turning on the water. "Skylar's a wrecking ball in a teenage body."

He meant the shelf. Emma smiled as she filled the sink with suds and sprayed down the mugs. The heat of the water burned against the chill of her hands, but the sensation made her smile. Even when the chef was shouting her stupid, she could always find solace in dish duty.

"What I wanted to know is…" The door swung open, struck the fallen shelf, and rebounded into Nick. "Sonnofa!" he cursed, his pale skin bright red down the middle of his forehead. He rubbed the wound while hauling up the fallen shelf and shoving the napkin boxes to the side.

Popping back up, he watched Emma hand scrub mugs and place them safely on the drying pegs. He smiled at her and she almost missed the peg. Blushing bright, Emma turned to face him as he asked, "Can I hire you?"

CHAPTER THREE

"HIRE ME?" SHE repeated.

"For the day." Nick realized how that sounded the second her face resembled a startled deer's. "As a waitress, cashier—" The din of people braying for his blood and coffee rose. Nick winced. "Anything to help me deal with *them*. If you want, I can get you a two-by-four to chase them away."

Her easy smile lifted, almost bringing one to him until the door's bell clanged like someone kicked it. "How's two hundred, no…two-fifty sound for the next six hours?"

"That's a lot of money for one day," Emma

whispered. She kept spinning the mug in her hands, one of a dozen he hadn't had time to wash in days.

It'd cost him a lot more if he was pushed to the breaking point today. Where the hell did all of these people come from? Was the winter circus in town?

"Well...?" he prompted, needing to get back to the front before the mob stormed the castle. Nick pushed open the door, mentally back into the trenches, when Emma's gaze fell. She tugged out a phone and twisted it around in her hands. As the black screen bounced back his harried reflection it finally hit him.

"You, oh, you probably had something better to do today. To get to. Forget I asked."

"No." She took a leap for him, her face gleaming with purpose. "I'd...I'd be happy to help wherever you need me." Extending her hand, she slipped on her smile. He had to be crazy but the thing felt genuine, especially the glimmer catching in her brown eyes.

Take her damn hand.

Nick slammed his palm to hers so fast it felt like a slap, but she cupped her small fingers in his, and he jerked it up and down.

"You'll be needing..." For the first time since she walked in, he let his gaze travel past her rosy cheeks. The coat had been blocking an even tinier frame than he'd first guessed. A pink turtleneck sweater hung from her petite chest and stopped somewhere around her thighs and the black jeans were stuffed into tall boots. Mystery curves for a mystery woman.

Emma gazed down to match his look that was veering into a leer. Nick snapped up and reached for the first box he found. "An apron!" he shouted, picking up a roll of toilet paper instead. "Hang on...there." This time he managed to pull out one of Skylar's abandoned aprons. It wasn't special, brown to hide the inevitable coffee spills. They hadn't even bothered stitching a logo onto it, though there'd been plans.

Nick frowned and turned away from Emma under the guise of having to hunt for a hat. It'd been five years. He'd moved on, burned it all. *Why am I even thinking about…?*

"How's this?" A sweet voice plucked him from his mad dig through stacks of sugar packets.

She'd rolled her sleeves up to her elbows, the chunky-knit sweater making her arms appear as slender as swizzle sticks. The apron string was so long that she had to bring it back around the front to tie it. Rather than a simple rabbit knot, she'd done some cute double bow. A long-buried urge bubbled inside of him to pull the fragile woman into his arms and forget all the ills of the world.

Closing his eyes tight, Nick banged the ball cap on his palms then looked at her. "For your…sweat and stuff." He meant to say for her hair, but his brain churned at the silky hazelnut tresses caught under the apron's halter. Before common sense could catch up, he reached behind her head and cupped his hand under her hair.

It wasn't until he tugged her hair free, her eyes big as saucers, that it struck him how weird that was. Nick shoved the cap at her, Emma quick to catch it, and clung to the wobbly shelf.

He had a business to keep afloat, a fourteen-year-old to keep from doing teenage shit, and the mess with his brother. Last thing he needed, last thing he wanted, was to start up *that* again. *She's just passing through,* he reminded himself. In a voice colder than he meant, Nick said, "I take it you have some experience in a café?"

"I've worked in restaurants, yes," she said.

It was an easy guess. She'd started washing dishes like it was in her DNA. There were always pots to scrub in the kitchen. Nick jerked his head to the door and shoved it open. Emma trailed behind as he led her to the front. Before he stepped out he thought of another problem. "And you're older than eighteen?"

Her startled gasp drew him to find her face shifting red. She bit her lip and looked down, the brim of the hat hiding a lot of her expression. *Am I wrong? Ah shit, she isn't a runaway, is she?*

"How old do you think I am?"

"I know better than to answer that." His thirty-five years came with some wisdom, at least.

Emma laughed with a snort. "Don't worry, I'm twenty-seven."

Way too young for him. *That's a good thing, right?*

"Ah, good. 'Cause I can't keep you for longer than four hours otherwise. I mean not keep like in, but working. You can't work more than... Do you have any questions?"

"What do you want me to do?" She bounced on her heels, her head barely popping above his chest. Damn, he could scoop her up into his pocket.

Nick winced at the stupid thought, deepening a scowl aimed at himself. "See those illiterate fools out there? Make them order anything else." Before he tried with his fists.

Emma nodded as if she'd suspected as much. He pushed on the door, then stepped to the side to let the lady through first, but she paused. "Um...may I ask why they keep requesting a mistletoe latte?"

Nick pulled his body in, slamming the door shut. "Damn if I know," he muttered. The fools had started showing up last Friday, asking and asking, then

23

growing more belligerent with every no. "It doesn't matter how many signs I put up, they keep wanting the cursed thing." Over and over, from five a.m. until closing, without a break in sight. He was liable to burst a blood vessel or stroke out at the cash register. "I haven't made one in five years."

He jerked at the words slipping from his lips. The brick wall in his memory was shuddering. For a brief moment, he could smell the hint of juniper and cinnamon. No. He wasn't going back down that road.

"Got it." She stepped ahead of him, her body turned to his as they both crammed inside the door's threshold. Nick pulled in a breath, growing aware of how much heat radiated from her lithe frame. He lost all control of his hands, clinging desperately to his thighs in the assumption that would solve everything.

Emma dipped the brim of her cap and smiled brightly. "I know exactly what to do." With her declaration, she stepped into the dim lights of the café. "Who's next in line?" she called like the kind fairy about to bestow a gift to the princess.

Nick hung in the doorway watching her barely have to glance at his old-fashioned order pad before she jumped right in. "I'm sorry, the mistletoe latte isn't currently available, but I think you might enjoy a cinnamon and nutmeg mocha?"

As she took the order, giving the man her undivided attention, Nick's lips started to twitch all on their own.

"You look like a mule kicked ya in the head," Sam said with a laugh, his ear next to the scanner.

Scowling, Nick flipped on the milk steamer and shouted back, "Put that damn thing away before I throw it through the window."

The day went smoother than he ever expected,

smoother than it had in years. Emma had flitted between the tables asking people how they were doing, then she'd return to take orders without her smile dipping for a second. Nick could only catch a glimpse of her here and there as he'd manned the espresso machine. For every one mistletoe disappointment, another three ordered something, almost always a convoluted latte with ten substitutions. But since Nick didn't have to talk to the person demanding the kiss of an orchid flower permeating their no-foam oat milk latte, the people were happy.

Infuriating as hell, but happy.

He took a quick break in the back when things died down. Nothing much, just time to cram in a bologna sandwich. Everything seemed to be in good hands, so he decided to let Emma man the storm a little longer. Woman the storm? Barely a woman, truth be told. Nick had vague memories of twenty-seven, the strongest being the third-degree steam burn down his arm thanks to a raging hangover. Emma seemed downright respectable in comparison to his wild youth. She was probably traveling cross-country to meet her boyfriend and would have a grand tale to tell about her day working in a hole-in-the-wall café.

Chasing after the scattered napkin boxes, Nick managed to get two in his arms before a third wound its way under the back shelves. The wood bowed from the hefty bags of beans, pinching in the middle. Picking up the wayward napkin stash revealed a box hiding under the shelf. The layers of dust told him it was ancient and that Skylar wasn't mopping on the weekends like she'd promised. He reached for the box when the bell jangled.

"Damn it." After rising off the floor, he tossed his apron on and didn't bother to tie it off. Didn't matter how dead the place got, the second he took a break...

The employee door swung open on the calmest Tuesday afternoon he'd ever seen. Sam was squirting mustard onto the ham and cheese sandwich he brought in regardless of what Nick said to stop it. A couple sat in the old armchairs by the window, seeming to not care about the cold draft rattling the glass. No customers stood in line belligerently shouting into their phones or screaming about Starbucks. *So what made the...?*

A soft jingle rang and he looked to the door. Balanced by the tips of her toes on top of a chair, Emma strained to loop the fallen bell onto the door joint. Her nose was crinkled as she concentrated with everything she had to reach that last inch. There was no chance she'd make it, but she wasn't going to give up without a fight.

"Hey, let me..." Nick began when the chair started to tip forward. His muscles reacted as his brain went numb. He didn't do the smart and gentlemanly thing to run forward and catch her. Instead, his meaty arms caught the chair's back and slammed the legs to the floor. It caused Emma to tumble backward towards him. She reached a hand out to catch herself and grabbed onto his shirt.

Her nails drew down his chest, yanking the crew neck into a v as she went. Nick steadied her by her shoulder. Both were left panting, Nick's neck burning at the eyes on them. Then Emma raised her gaze and the heat sank straight to his crotch.

"That..." He tried to think through a woman's nails raking down his chest and clutching his shirt. He didn't need this. He didn't want it. Nick walked back and squared his shoulders. "That was stupid."

"I was trying to —"

"I know." He yanked the bell from her hands as she

stepped off the chair. God, her barely five-foot frame made him want to laugh at her trying. Turning his back, Nick reached up and knotted the bell on. "Next time ask me. You could have gotten hurt."

"I'm sorry," she whispered, tugging her hat brim lower so he couldn't see her face. Five years with a preteen who became a full-blown teenager taught him that was a very bad thing.

"It's just...customers get touchy when there's blood on the door." Nick went for the joke and it sunk like a rock. "Why don't you take a break in back?"

She nodded sharply, still not looking up. *Good job, Nicky, you cratered that one before it could even begin.* Emma slipped around the counter and began to untie her apron. Reaching for her hand, Sam patted the girl like a wounded animal's paw. "I had faith in you," he said as if she hadn't nearly cracked her skull.

If Nick hadn't been there... "Cream and sugar!" he shouted. Emma paused and stared at him. At least there weren't tears in her eyes. "You can have whatever you want in the fridge."

Whether she'd accept his charity or not he couldn't guess, but Emma slipped away, leaving Nick to haul the chair back. As he stood up, feeling every one of his years in his sore back, Sam swiveled on his stool. "You're a regular Galavant, you know. Girl's just trying to help."

Did it count as personal growth if Nick knew he was a boor and instantly regretted it? Probably not. Skylar and her gaggle would call him problematic and tell him to check his privilege. He hefted up the cleanest dish towel and was about to start scrubbing the espresso machine when he noticed there was nothing to mop up. She must have gotten it all without him even asking.

"I wish I knew why," he whispered to himself.

Sam pipped up, "Probably just passing time until the guy she's waiting for gets here."

The boyfriend. That guy could be her knight in shining armor. Nick was a broken-down java jockey who fell asleep at eight p.m. Damsels didn't go for that.

The repaired bell jangled, and he looked up into ecstatic and unknown faces. One began to speak, but he interrupted, "Before you ask, no, we don't have the mistletoe latte. Order something else."

CHAPTER FOUR

"EXCUSE ME, SIR!" Emma picked up a scarf that had slithered out of the customer's coat. He patted his pockets even as she handed it back to him.

"You've got quite the eye, Miss," he said after taking it back. Winding the scarf around his neck, the last customer slipped out the door. Emma used the momentary break to check her phone. It was nearly three and there was no sign of the mechanic.

"Next time you should keep it."

She jumped at the voice behind her ear. Spinning on her heels she came face to face with Nick. Emma placed a calming hand to her chest and pulled in a breath.

"Isn't that stealing?"

Nick shrugged. "Nine-tenths of the law. How do you think I was able to pay for this place?"

His entire demeanor was dead serious, leaving Emma uncertain how to respond. Nick bent over to pick up a brooch that must have tumbled under the table. "See," he said. Emma was about to reach to take it back when he turned and placed the jewelry in a lost and found box. For a brief moment, the edge of his lips lifted in a smile, and she pulled in a sigh. Laughing under her breath, Emma plucked up a spray bottle and spritzed the table.

"You mind if I ask what other restaurants you've worked at?"

It was the first question he'd directed at her since her folly with the bell. She glanced up to watch him carefully place mugs upside down on the espresso machine. "I don't mind. I was a hostess for a steak joint."

"Fancy." He whistled as if her being trained to carry menus, defuse angry customers, and fill out reservations required SEAL team level training.

"And a waitress at a diner during most of school."

"Not a barista though? I'm surprised. You took to this like a fish addicted to caffeine."

Modesty mingled with a growing flush, and she cast her gaze down to focus on the handful of crumbs. "There was an espresso machine at the restaurant where I was a—"

The bell jangled, stopping their conversation dead. Both looked to the new customer, a teen girl staring upward. "You fixed it. Since when do you fix anything?" she asked Nick while tossing her book bag to the ground. It struck with a loud thud, and she massaged her shoulder.

"It wasn't my idea," Nick said and Emma's heart crumbled. She was only trying to be helpful but shouldn't have overstepped her bounds.

The teenage girl squinted at her from across the room. "You hired someone. Great! Guess you won't be needing me to help close…" She hauled her bag up, but Nick caught it and laughed.

"Nice try. Emma's just here for the day. And she's dealt with enough riffraff today without you adding to it."

"Riffraff?" the girl repeated. "How old are you?"

With a shake of his head, Nick said, "Emma, this is Skylar. Skylar, don't drown her in your sass."

"I'll save all my sass for you!" Skylar said with a smirk as she saluted.

Nick groaned at the teenage ribbing, then he pointed to Skylar's shirt. Instead of the same midriff-baring blouse from before, a plaid flannel covered her chest. "What are you wearing?"

"Clothes," Skylar scoffed. "This isn't a nudist coffee shop."

"Uh-huh. School make you put that on?"

"No, I wanted to. That damn place is freezing all the time. I swear it's older than you."

Nick smiled wide as if he'd won a game of chess. "Maybe you should have thought of that before heading out half-naked in December."

Her response was a dramatic eye roll and a shove against his chest. Skylar stomped for the back room, but before going she looked to Emma. "How can you stand him?"

"It's not that hard when she's actually pleasant to work with, unlike someone I can name," Nick shouted in the direction of the swinging door. As it made one last rotation a hand with a raised middle finger shot out before Skylar vanished.

Emma did not want to get in the middle of this teenage rebellion. She remembered the chaffing yoke of her parents but had also spent years of her life cleaning up after kids that thought stacking cups filled with ketchup and syrup was cool. Bowing her head, she focused on the last of the trash left by the windows when the bell rang again.

"Daryl, the usual?"

"Nah, I'm looking for a woman. Name of Emma."

She spun around at her name and recognized the man in a blue shirt with grease on his hands. Giving a little wave, she hurried the trash to the bin and wiped the sticky coffee off of her palm.

"It's you? You're the one she's…" Nick muttered.

"Soul, right?" Daryl bellowed.

Her cheeks blushed as if her Kia Soul breaking down was all her fault. Maybe it was. When did she last change the oil?

Nick was kind enough to slip away, leaving them alone to talk. He busied himself behind the counter moving the mugs around as Emma waited for the news.

"I hope your smile means it's fixed?" she asked.

"Fraid not. Been backed up to the moon lately. Thanks to Kenny going and having a baby. Just got around to checking your vehicle out and thought you'd want to know. Nice of Nick to let you stay." He raised his voice for the last sentence and waved to the man.

In a craggy groan, Nick grumbled, "I'm a real sweetheart."

The mechanic chuckled while Emma checked her bank account. "What's the damage?" she asked, staring at far too few numbers to cover a big problem.

"It's the catalytic converter. Went kablooey from the engine heat, and that took out some pistons and connecting rods."

Emma winced. Whatever that was sounded really bad. "How much will it cost to repair?" Regret bubbled in her for not demanding back the rent money she'd already paid. But the idea of confronting her roommates after they'd kicked her out made her legs wobble. Even though she needed it, Emma couldn't have asked.

"Dunno," he said, scratching his chin. "Gonna have to send away for the parts. Don't see many Kias around here."

"They'll get here in…a day?"

"Anything's possible. I'll call in tomorrow. Part shop's closed by now. Hope you got somewhere warm to bunker down."

She didn't. Her sister's place was two states away, and the way Emma's life was going, she feared if she left her car she'd never get it back. The pain must have shown on her face as Daryl reached over and patted her shoulder.

"Sorry, Miss. Everyone's making their holiday trips, so by the law of chaos, everything's breaking. Wish I could tell you better."

"Thank you…for looking at it. And coming to tell me."

"I wouldn't be against a coffee to go. Nick, you prickly pear, what you got on tap?"

Emma flicked through her phone, trying to will an answer to appear. Her finger shook around the screen and a picture of her in her chef's whites opened. Closing her eyes, she dropped her phone into her pocket and stared upward.

What am I going to do?

DARYL? REALLY? HE was expecting some ex-college football player or high-powered lawyer to waltz in and sweep her off her feet. Not the mechanic with the kind of face some would unfavorably compare to a pug.

Nick fiddled with the espresso machine, pressing buttons to run water through in an attempt to not eavesdrop on their harried conversation. It was a terrible cover, causing him to only get the occasional word and phrase drilled into his ears. Emma looked unhappy, her tiny body curled in tight as her head kept drifting lower and lower. Did she just find out that her coffee shop hunk had a wife? Daryl reached a hand out toward her and Nick glared at the movement. He perched on the tips of his toes, leaning to the side to watch the mechanic land his palm on Emma's...

"What are you doing?"

Nick leaped into the air, smacking his knuckles on the hot machine. "Jesus...!" The curse words were bit down along with the pain. But he focused all his ire on Skylar, who watched the two afternoon lovers without a care.

"I found that mess you made and didn't clean up," Nick said. He picked a mug off of the top and queued up a tea pour. Not that he wanted it, but his hands had to do something.

Skylar shrugged. "You told me I wasn't supposed to be late anymore."

"Uh-huh." He couldn't decide if it was patronizing that she didn't think he knew she caused that racket, so he wouldn't stop her from going to class with her belly out. Or she wanted him to catch her so he would miss some other scheme she had brewing. Nick didn't remember signing up to house a super-villain all those years ago.

"Who is she, anyway?"

He shrugged, not having gotten her life story during the horde rampage. "Some girl in town."

"Some girl you can't stop staring at."

"I am not." Nick craned his back to them so fast his ankle popped. "I was watching for customers because I'm running a business here. Now, are you going to help out, or should I ship you to the orphanage?"

"Ha ha."

"Put a sign around your neck. 'One teenager to a good home. Warning, constant eye rolls and sass.'"

Skylar didn't respond to his long-standing and toothless threat. She was nose deep in her phone like every damn teen. Swaying back and forth, she said in a sing-song voice, "You get rid of me and you won't learn why everyone's beating down your door for a crusty old latte."

"What?"

"Here." She passed him her phone and Nick's jaw plummeted. On one of those social square things was the image of his mistletoe latte. He'd taken that picture, struggling to pour just the right cup for the online menu. She'd kept racing back to the kitchen to get him another...

His scowl deepened, and he scrolled. The lingering happy memories combusted on the spot as he read the drivel caption from whoever stole his old pic. "'Once a staple of Lake Holly, a quaint town in the UP, this latte was believed to be as elusive as Nessie herself. But I hear it's back at Brew 4 U. Even better than the fabled nutty and intoxicating flavor, there's a legend that if you drink a mistletoe latte—"

"Nick, you prickly pear, what you got on tap?"

The mechanic's request threw him off, but he read the closing order to the sycophant's cultists. "'Get there quick, caffeine addicts, before the magic runs out.'" Great, so some damn influencer was making shit up about him. "Skylar, who wrote this article?"

"Posted. It's a post. Your bones must be dust." She took back the phone as he poured a to-go cup for Daryl. "Says the account's owned by a Miss B."

"Who's that? Why isn't there a picture up in that circle there"

"Because the account is anonymous," she said. Nick kept glaring at her, waiting for her to do her teenage magic. They were more terrifying than Big Brother at tracking down the latest persona non grata. Skylar gasped and clasped her phone to her chest. "I'm sorry, do you want me to…dox them?"

Nick groaned. "As that's probably a bad thing, no. Can you just figure out who it is?"

Skylar rolled her eyes and walked away, muttering under her breath, "Were you born before coffee was invented?"

"You're a big help as always!" Nick shouted to her before he capped off the cup and handed it to the mechanic.

"See you tomorrow," Daryl said with a tip of his finger before taking a long drink.

"Sure," Nick muttered. He had to find whoever that Miss B was and get them to take down their post before the 'followers' started getting more insistent.

It wasn't until Daryl said, "And call you tomorrow," to Emma that Nick was yanked from his vague revenge plans. She smiled at him but didn't chase after. Some romantic rendezvous to make her wait all day, talk for five minutes, and run. Damn it, her shoulders were hunched, and she'd dipped the brim of her hat down. He had to do something.

"You okay?" Nick asked. He approached her tentatively, ready to offer a hug or run out and hogtie Daryl to drag him back.

"Yeah." She put on a happy face he knew was a bald-faced lie.

He ran out of ideas on what to do and looked to Skylar. But she glared back and jabbed her thumbs at Emma from behind her. Did he tell her it'd get better? That there were other fish in the sea? Less mummified ones.

His mouth opened without him knowing what to do when she said, "It's my car."

"Your car?" Sweet lord. Nick nearly slapped himself in the forehead. Mechanic. Car. Of course.

"It sounds bad. Something about a catalytic comforter, I think. He won't know the state of it until tomorrow, so I have to find somewhere to sleep tonight. Hope for the best the next morning."

"Wait, he left you waiting here all day just to tell you that?"

"He said he was busy." Emma offered up an excuse for Daryl, a man she didn't even know. He couldn't tell if she was that naive or too kind for her own good.

"He ain't that busy. Maybe it's time I call in his tab if he's got so much business."

"Please don't punish him on my account." In pleading for her jailer's life, she caught Nick's hands in hers. He stared at her skinny fingers gliding back and forth over the tops of his, his brain buzzing and throat falling numb.

"You should stay at our place."

Nick yanked his hands back at the same time Emma dropped hers, both adults turning to the teenager wearing a Cheshire grin. Skylar waved a hand to Emma. "Sounds like she saved your ass today. It's the least you can do."

"I am paying her. I...I should go get that." Nick kept jerking his thumb to the cash register even while walking backward to it. Emma's cheeks flushed, and she stared at her fingers twisting up. It took him three tries to remember the code before he could pick up enough cash. With two-fifty in hand, he looked up to find the tip jar damn near crammed to the top.

"Here," he said, holding the bills out. "I couldn't have survived today without you."

"You're welcome, and thank you for giving me a good distraction while I waited." She carefully folded up the money and placed it in her purse.

"Ah, and...you should take this too." Nick snatched up the tip jar and handed it to her.

Emma's eyes went wide. "The whole thing? No, I... that's. It's too much. I couldn't."

"Believe me, you earned all of this. Most days, all I get are some saver coupons and a Chick tract."

"Or that mouse trap," Skylar chimed in.

"Sam thinks he's a cut-up. Please. You worked for this. I mean, you put up with me for six hours. Think of it as hazard pay."

"Thank you, it'll help with my car."

Or getting her a motel for the night. Though, if it was the catalytic converter and probably worse, she'd need all those Canadian pennies just to drive out of here. Emma carefully removed the bills, counting each one before placing them into her purse with the rest. Once she was done, she returned the jar to the counter where the cobwebs could sprout again.

Then, to his shock, she picked up the broom Skylar was supposed to be pushing. "You don't need to do that," Nick said before pointing to his wayward ward. "She is." At Skylar's face, he added, "Or do you want to skip your winter ball altogether?"

"Fine!" Skylar snatched up the broom and smacked it onto the floor. At least the dust was moving.

"So I should…" Emma pulled off her hat and handed it to him, then she slipped the apron off over her head. With a finality, they landed in his arms. This angel that had no doubt kept him out of jail was returning to wherever she came. "Thank you, again, for your kindness."

She put her coat on, hooked her purse to her arm, and walked to the door. He would never get to see her again, and he was going to leave it at that? A couple of hundred bucks and some trite thanks?

"Hey," Nick shouted. Emma paused with one foot out the door and looked back. "Why don't I make you dinner?"

CHAPTER FIVE

A TUFT OF snow tumbled off the a-frame roof, splatting on a wrap-around porch. They drove around the house toward a little garage at the back. A net-less basketball hoop hung off the side of the house while an old grill was chained to a post without a fence. Nick put his truck in park and announced, "We're here."

Emma let go of her seat belt, realizing how tightly she'd clung to it on the drive. Round about a hundred feet from the coffee shop she'd realized no one knew where she was, and she had no idea how to get back. But the house that'd fit into any family sitcom calmed her fears. At least it wasn't the middle of the woods.

"Yeah, no shit," Skylar complained. She popped up from the back and pushed on Nick's seat. "Can you get out before my legs are impaled through my rib cage?"

The beleaguered man sighed and opened his door. Lightning quick, Skylar leaped out behind him. "Watch it!" Nick shouted, weaving to the side to avoid her flying book bag. The girl didn't even pause at the near beaning, already running for the front door.

Emma slipped to the cracking driveway and stared up at the second story. "Almost got knocked out by biology," Nick muttered, rubbing his chin as he came up beside her. "This is the place."

"It's nice."

"It's four walls and a roof," he said as if most people wouldn't kill for such a house. She'd lived in a thousand-square-foot apartment with three roommates. This was a mansion in comparison. "We should get inside before we freeze to death." He jerked a thumb to the door to make sure she knew where it was, then began to walk. "This winter's been a brute."

"Oh?"

"They say there's gonna be even more snow. Some chicken ate the red corn instead of the blue. How do you argue with that?" Nick paused at the door and stood to the side to hold it open for her. He wasn't even in a coat, just a flannel shirt, and Emma tried to shoo him in first, but he remained steadfast.

Pumping her short legs as fast as she could, she clipped onto the porch and dove into the house. The heat struck her first, gushing from nearly every side and warming her bones. She stopped on a rug and banged her heels together to try to dislodge the snow. "Should I...?" she pointed to her shoes as Nick closed his door.

"Ah, sure. Or not. Whatever you want to do." He

raised his head and spotted a trail of wet prints dashing inside. "Seems some of us think tracking snow into the house is a good idea!"

"Are you talking to me?" Skylar shouted back from deeper inside.

Nick grumbled under his breath, then he turned and caught Emma struggling to get her shoe off. "Here." He held out a hand and balanced her until Emma stood in her socks. "How about a tour? This is the...I don't remember. Side room? Entryway. Used to be a mud room when I was a kid, but I guess my mom wanted a foyer. That's what it's called."

"You grew up here?"

"Inheritance," he said and she winced.

"I'm sorry."

"Don't be. It was a long time back. Things happen. Anyway, through here is the kitchen..." Nick waved a hand from behind her past the archway. Emma peeked in and was greeted by a farmhouse kitchen. A border of tiny chickens rimmed the top of the room and a silver plate with an embossed rooster decorated the far wall. A single dining room table of distressed wood sat below. Two of its chairs were pulled out and the last one had stacks of boxes on the seat.

The stove was designed to look like the old wood-burning ones, though she'd guess the microwave beside it did most of the work. Next to that was the fridge, an older model with the freezer on top. It was covered in scraps of receipts, magnets for local repair services, and a handful of child drawings.

"Ooh, I've always wanted a farmhouse sink." Emma dashed to it and peeked down, finding some plates deep in the basin. She could wash cherries for pies in it, and dunk all her pots and pans in one go.

"Really? A sink?" Nick flipped on the faucet, spraying warming water across her hands. "You'd need a stool to reach to the bottom," he said and Emma gulped. She slipped her hands back, her ears ringing with his rightful chastisement from earlier.

"You're probably right," she said slowly. The tops of cabinets were a quagmire for her. That she wanted a hanging pot rack in her future kitchen sounded as ludicrous as the farmhouse sink.

"You're just, I mean…" Nick roughed his palm over his cheeks, and he slammed a hand down on the faucet. A handful of droplets scattered onto the plates like rain. "Skylar! What are you doing?"

A great commotion broke from the room beyond before the girl poked her head inside. "Putting my shit away. Like you always tell me to."

"Sure. Give Emma a tour while I start dinner."

"She doesn't have to. I'm sure she has important things to do." Emma didn't want to impose.

Nick pulled a spatula out of the rooster-themed canister and wielded it at Skylar. "There's always your homework—"

"I'd love to give you a tour!" Skylar shouted in excitement. "This is the kitchen. It's where he set the toaster on fire."

"Because you crammed a Lego inside."

"And through here is the sitting room…where he set the rug on fire." Skylar leaned closer and stage-whispered to Emma, "Don't let him have any matches."

"I'm selling you to the zoo, assuming they'll even take you."

She knew she shouldn't, but Emma couldn't stop herself from laughing at the exasperated father-daughter routine they'd perfected. She'd been wondering all day where the mom was in this trio. There weren't any pictures on the fridge, nor a calendar jam-packed with activities by the door. Maybe there were portraits in the sitting room.

"Come on, I'll show you the bathroom." Skylar waved her on. As Emma walked into a quaint room with a furry white couch facing a fireplace, the girl leaned into the kitchen and said, "Don't burn dinner."

All Emma could hear was Nick grumbling as the girl danced back on her toes. She moved with a hyperactive grace that Emma would kill to have. "Here's where we sit when Nick thinks we need to have 'screen-less' time. Through there's the office slash TV slash whatever doesn't count as family time. It's full of boxes of café shit he says he can't throw out because of taxes. Ooh, this is the downstairs bathroom. It's nice 'cause it's for guests." She flipped the light on fast, revealing a flash of white tile and blue towels before the room went dark.

Taking her hand, Skylar pulled Emma around the small sitting room to a staircase. "Up here are the bedrooms. Mine's on the left."

Emma clung to the banister and gazed at the multitude of pictures on the wall. The black and white wedding portrait probably held his parents. There were more taken from the eighties of two boys racing each other in Big Wheels. At the fifth stair was a picture of a gangly Nick in a tux with a carnation boutonniere. She hunted for the mystery woman. There certainly were quite a few pictures of Skylar from a chubby infant up to a precocious grade-schooler. But the only picture of a woman that wasn't a kindly grandmother was a wedding portrait with a man who wasn't Nick.

"Can you believe that hair?" Skylar snickered, pointing to the mystery woman.

"Are there any pictures of your mom?" Emma asked out of pure curiosity, no other reason.

"Yeah, right here. With the electrified poodle look. Why?" she asked, folding her arms. The teenage glare caused Emma's gaze to drop. "Oh! Do you think Nick's my...?" Peals of laughter echoed off the picture frame, Skylar's entire body shaking before it snapped on a dime, and she leaned closer. "Are you hoping he's single?"

"No!" she cried out, Emma's cheeks burning red-hot at the teenager smugly smiling.

"Kay," she surmised and pointed to a door down the upper hallway. Emma scurried up beside her as she said, "That's the second bathroom with the good shower. There's my room. And that..." Skylar smacked her lips and bounced on her heels. "That's *Uncle* Nick's bedroom. In case you need to find it later."

A string of giggles broke from Emma, at first laughing ludicrously, then growing more strained from the rising panic. She was leaving in a day once her car was fixed. Why would she need to know where he slept? It was just dinner.

Skylar slapped her hands together. "That's the tour. Better head back before the whole kitchen goes up in smoke." She leaped down the stairs, taking them four at a time while Emma eased her way after.

At the landing, Skylar wrapped a hand around the top of the banister and swung in a circle. "He's not married. Never been. If you're curious."

"I'm not. I was just..."

"Asking to see if he had a wife," she filled in fast.

"Who has a wife?" Nick asked, startling Emma out of her socks. The teenager smirked while Emma struggled to look at him without melting into a puddle. After a beat, Nick pointed to Skylar. "I need your help in the kitchen."

"Of course you do." She sighed dramatically and took a bow before rushing for the kitchen.

Nick took a long time turning to follow, keeping one eye on Emma as she breathed a sigh of relief. The matter seemed to have slipped his mind, thank goodness. Smiling at him, she followed after Skylar.

"Chop the veggies," Nick ordered to the teenager who stuck out her tongue in disapproval.

"Can't we get pizza?"

"No. It's meatloaf night." He put his verbal foot down and took up the counter beside Skylar. While she toyed with a carrot, he mashed the hamburger mixture together with his hands.

"Uh-huh." She dropped the paring knife and turned to him. "And did you ask our guest if she's a vegetarian or vegan?"

The back of Nick's neck turned red and the bowl clattered. "You're, um…" He glanced over his shoulder at her and gulped. "I think there's some rice—"

"I'm not," Emma interrupted, "though I could chop the veg if you'd like."

"You don't have—"

"Please!" Skylar said, nearly throwing the knife at her. Emma snagged it fast, slipping in beside Nick as the girl fled.

She almost made it out of the door, when Nick calmly asked, "So…whose wife?"

Skylar froze, her head cocked as if she was about to ask what. But that wouldn't stop the line of questions, not if he kept bringing it up. Putting on a smile, Emma chirped up, "I thought that Skylar was your daughter, and she corrected me. I can't imagine the tragedy you've both suffered." The second it slipped from her, Emma winced. People didn't like being reminded they were supposed to feel sad.

"Tragedy?"

"Oh!" Skylar laughed and waved her hands around. "My parents aren't dead."

They aren't? Then why is she…?

Nick opened the fridge to grab the ketchup bottle. "To make a very long and boring story short, my brother found a job further south. But this one here didn't want to leave her friends, and the schools are better, so… It's not a big deal."

He banged the bottom of the bottle, barely dislodging more than a drop onto the loaf. "If she works for me in the shop I'll keep her fed."

"In school, we learned that's called indentured servitude," Skylar said.

Nick sighed and stared at the ceiling. "Only four more years before I'm free of this curse." He snickered at the idea and shook the ketchup bottle just for a huge glob to plop all over the loaf and counter.

"I'm not cleaning that up," Skylar called as she vanished out of the door.

Emma picked up a kitchen rag and wet it under the faucet. As he took it with a silent thanks, he said, "I'm doing it 'cause…I mean, what's the alternative? That girl would run circles around my brother without even trying."

"Well." Nick wiped off the last of the wayward ketchup and pushed the meatloaf into the oven. "We've got an hour to kill. What do you want to do?"

Her cheeks turned bright pink and Emma nearly sliced off her pinkie.

CHAPTER SIX

HE DIDN'T THINK any of this through. The house was in as bad of a state as his storage room. Even worse, he couldn't blame it all on the wrecking ball in leggings. Without the mind-numbing work of grinding, packing, and pushing buttons, he had no damn idea what to do with his hands. *Why does it take an hour for meatloaf to bake?*

After rinsing the carrots, she stepped up to the counter and shook her sleeves back.

"Do you need an apron?" he asked. Her sweater looked expensive...and soft.

She stared up at him, her big eyes blinking slowly as

she raised a carrot. "I think I'll be okay."

"You really don't have to do it. Skylar's supposed to…she's meant to help. Used to love helping. Now it's like juggling flaming chainsaws just to get her to pick up her shit."

"She's lucky to have you looking out for her."

Nick snorted at the idea. "Don't say that to her face unless you want her to rip it off." Okay, she wasn't a bad kid. There hadn't been any run-ins with the law. He hadn't found boys, booze, or worse in her room. A few of her teachers even liked her. But he couldn't stop worrying that if he let up for a second, she'd slip the same as the rest of the Iverson clan. That fall didn't have padded floors.

A pile of carrot skins had built up on the side of the cutting board. Nick blinked, realizing she'd already peeled all the carrots. Damn, that was fast. Emma pushed back her sleeves and lined up the first carrot.

"Skylar should be learning basic cooking so she doesn't starve. Skylar!"

"It's okay. I want to. It's nice to get to cook in such a wide-open space." She glanced around the kitchen which was a handful of counters and a stove.

"I keep thinking an island would be better, but unless there's a construction fairy I don't know about…" He rubbed the back of his neck so fast that when he touched the stove's door handle, a spark launched through him. *What am I doing? The meatloaf's fine.* He shouldn't be looming over her shoulder while she held sharp objects.

It wasn't that it felt weird having a woman in the house. It was weird how normal it felt. He'd taken the rag from her without question, as if he knew it'd be there. Nick needed a distraction, then a drink. "Skylar!"

"What. Do. You. Want?" she shouted, pushing the kitchen door to match each word.

Nick didn't rise to the bait. "You got homework?"

Her childish antics withered instantly. "It's...it's nothing. Just some worksheets. And we have a guest. Isn't it good manners to entertain her first?"

Crossing his arms, Nick glared down at the wayward teen. "Homework comes before good manners."

Her eye roll could have caused a tsunami.

"Why don't you get your books and study at the table? That way you can both entertain our guest and not flunk out of school dooming yourself to a life of riding the rails. How's that?"

She clenched her jaw and rocked back and forth, but couldn't find a loophole. Slapping the door, she slipped off to get her books. With that problem solved, Nick returned to the matter of dinner. Meatloaf and a few carrots wouldn't exactly...

Holy shit! The knife moved so fast all he could see was a silver blur, then a pile of julienne carrots. She wiped the blade off and placed it on the cutting board. "Any chance you have some bell peppers, brussels sprouts, or cucumbers?"

"Uh..." Nick's mouth ran dry, and he blindly swatted for the fridge. "Let me look."

As he dug through the crisper drawer that had more pizza rolls than veggies, Emma said, "I was thinking of whipping up a simple balsamic slaw salad. Nothing too elaborate, but the brightness might work well off the meat."

"That sounds way better than anything I'd had planned." Boiled carrots and peas were good enough after a long day. He pushed aside a carton of strawberry yogurt and spotted a single produce bag. "I think all we have is this broccoli stem."

She took it with a smile and broke a tiny tree off the bigger branch. To his relief, it made a snap instead of a soggy plorp. "This can work."

"All right, all right, I'm here, doing stupid math. Is that satisfactory for you?"

"Depends on what you got on the last test," Nick said, slipping closer to stare over Skylar's scattered sheets and textbook. He only spotted a handful of numbers and words and hated to admit it was all Greek to him.

But as the girl caught his eye, he came back with a, "Hm?"

"A seventy-eight, which isn't that bad. One of the kids got a ten."

"Skylar."

"I don't get the point of this. Where in the real world will I have someone ask me to prove this is a circle? Look, it's round. It's a circle. Stop giving it an existential crisis, geometry!" She slammed her book down in frustration.

"You need to get good grades so you can—"

"Get into a good college," she said in her 'stupid adults are talking' voice. Suddenly, Skylar turned on a dime and asked in a sweet voice, "Did you get 'good grades' Uncle Nick?"

He knew he shouldn't lie to her beyond the little ones, but if he told her he scraped by with a C-minus average, it'd blow his platform. Nick stepped back and looked to his only salvation. "Emma?"

"Hm?"

"Did you get good grades in school?"

She smiled and waved the broccoli stem around. "Ah, yes, a bit."

"And did they help you get into a good college?" he prompted, watching the fury rise on Skylar's face.

"Well, sort of. The CIA doesn't worry about a high GPA as much."

The...what?

Nick stared at the perfectly sliced-up carrots, her knife moving so fast he couldn't see. *Who did he let into his house?*

"You're a spy? Sweet!" Skylar shouted.

"Oh," Emma's face burned bright. "No, not that CIA. The Culinary Institute of Arts."

"You're a chef." Nick sighed in relief. No wonder she knew her way around a kitchen. It all made sense.

Skylar however leaned forward. "That's exactly what a spy would say." She could only maintain her serious glare for a second before breaking into a fit of giggles. Emma was quick to join in. The rare ring of laughter echoing through the kitchen brought a smile to Nick.

The hour passed faster than he'd feared. Skylar put a dozen questions to Emma about chef school instead of answering the half dozen on her homework. Every time he'd tried to redirect his niece's attention, she'd think of something new to ask the poor woman. It wasn't until he plucked dinner out of the oven and stared at the molded tomato and hamburger loaf that it hit him. A real chef was going to eat his food.

She smiled brightly at him and asked, "Plating time?" All he could do was nod, and Emma pulled her reducing balsamic glaze off the burner. "Plates are...?"

"That cupboard," Nick said, pointing to one above her head. Damn it, did he forget to grease the pan? He tipped the loaf upside down over the cutting board, but gravity failed him. Giving it a shake didn't work either, so he started to bang a knife against the bottom of the pan. A tiny struggle like the cry of a mouse cut in between his hammering.

Poor Emma had one hand pressed to the counter as she hopped up into the air and reached for the plate. "Almost…" she whispered. Nick slipped in behind her before the whole cabinet came tumbling down. She stilled in her leaping and his hand grazed her retreating one. Her hair brushed down his chest as he picked up a serving platter for her.

"Sorry about that," he muttered. "Skylar likes to put them way in the back."

"Since when?" she countered, but her voice faded to a background whine.

Emma turned around and took the white plate in her tiny hands. Clasping it to her chest, she looked up at him through her eyelashes. Her pink lips pursed like a wry strawberry, and she said, "I should bring a stool with me."

"Don't worry about it," he whispered, realizing his hand wrung the edge of the counter right next to her body. "I like helping." She beamed her big brown eyes up at him and pressed a single white tooth deep into her lip.

The loud scoff of a famished teenager was the only thing to puncture through to him. Nick turned like a ringmaster introducing the clowns, letting Emma escape from where he'd pinned her in. He hadn't meant to, he was…out of sorts. "Dinner?" he asked, needing an auditory reminder of what he'd been doing.

"Finally!" Skylar shouted. She leaned over and, with both arms, shoved all of her homework and books. "Table's cleared."

After pulling down three plates, Nick rolled his eyes. "You know you'll be picking it back up again." He stabbed at the meatloaf, managing to cut free three crumbling sections. Good enough. He loaded up his forearms like he was working at a diner and walked to the table.

It was Emma who held up her serving platter with adorable carrots and small broccoli sprigs carefully laid out. Brown and red sauces were expertly dashed across, then formed a ribbon on the white plate. He'd never seen anything so fancy he was supposed to eat in his life.

"I hope this is good enough," she said as if he wasn't facing utter humiliation for his weeknight whatever dinner.

Skylar launched up and took the vegetable platter out of her hands. "I don't care. I'm starving."

With a wave of his hands, Nick guided Emma to the table. "Bon appétit."

EMMA LAY HER fork on her plate and settled back in the chair. "That was really good."

"You don't have to do that," Nick insisted, his gaze darting over the rim of an Oktoberfest stein before he tipped it back.

She blushed brighter than her rosé and reached for it for help. "I thought the meatloaf was good."

Finishing his stout, Nick banged his thumbs on the top as he stared around the table. "It's fine. Nothing up to the standards of a spy chef though. I mean, you pulled off a miracle. You got a teenager to eat a bunch of veggies that weren't deep-fried or covered in ranch. That deserves a Nobel prize for cooking."

"I don't think they have those," Emma said, growing hotter at the attention.

"Beard." Skylar darted up for a second from her phone. "It's a Beard award. Don't you know anything?"

"You caught me. I'm dumb as a post and twice as ugly." He stared his niece dead on, but she only snickered and returned to her scrolling. With a sigh, he focused on Emma as if Skylar wasn't there. "You're a miracle worker. I've never had broccoli that wasn't rubbery and limp."

Skylar gave a loud cough, unsettling both adults who looked at their hands.

"Dunking it in ice after steaming helps to stop that from happening," Emma explained. She stared at her nearly drained glass of wine, feeling each bubble race up her spine. Maybe she should have had a half glass instead.

"Know any tricks for making the meatloaf better?"

"You call Gino's and ask for the large," Skylar chimed in.

Emma laughed at the momentary tic across Nick's face before she shook her head. "I thought it was perfect as is."

"Now you're blowing smoke up my ass." He leaned back in his chair. She'd think him annoyed if it weren't for a little smile dashing across his stoic face.

"I swear, I liked it," Emma insisted, though he didn't seem to believe her. "It's nice to have someone else cook for me."

He sat forward, the hanging light casting an orange halo off his hair. "You don't have anyone else in your life? To cook for you. You probably have men. People. In your life."

"Smooth," Skylar whispered.

"Not as much. Work took up all my time, and now…" Emma bit her lip and glared at her hands. They did as she told them, prepping and dicing at a speed that could take off fingers. But it was never good enough. "Truth be told, you're better off asking another chef about your meatloaf problem. I never worked the meat station."

"Did you do veggies? Do they have one of those?"

"There's a lot of prep. I'd do whatever I was told by the chef that night. But most of my training was in desserts."

That perked Skylar up. "Really? Can you make a chocolate cake right now?"

"No, she shouldn't. She's a guest, which is that thing where people don't do work for you just because they can."

Emma glanced over her shoulder to a dusty flour canister. She could probably do a lava cake while blindfolded. There were a lot of those, crème brûlées, and layer cakes day in and day out without change. She missed the rare days off when it was just her, an oven, and a dozen test recipes at her disposal.

"Where, um, where are you headed once your car's up to snuff?"

"Maine, to my sister's." Who wasn't happy about clearing out a room for her, but Emma was out of options with barely a penny left to her name.

"That sounds difficult, going cross-country in December." Nick placed his hand on the table directly across from hers. Only an inch of space separated their fingers. Worry knotted across his lips and scruffy jawline.

"Hey Nick, you're trending."

He yanked his hand back and turned to Skylar, who

held up her phone. "For what?" He reached for her phone but she pulled it back.

"The hashtag Mistletoe Latte is blowing up…locally. Oh, there's a video of you throwing some guy out. Here."

She pressed play on Nick shouting, "We don't have no mistletoe lattes!" before the voice warped and began to harmonize with sleigh bells set to a man stumbling out the door.

"What the hell?"

"It's already got a hundred thousand views. Nice."

"That's it, I'm banning all cell phones in the café until this madness ends."

"Not sure that'll work…" Skylar dramatically paused, her scrolling fingers flipping wide like she was spinning slots at a casino. "They've found the legend and, oh, there's a challenge to get the first latte of the season."

"The legend?" Emma asked, fully lost. She understood not having the ingredients on hand and customers insisting he perform magic for them, but he'd sounded downright offended every time someone ordered it. Now there was a legend?

"It's a load of hooey," Nick said, but Skylar peered to the side to meet Emma's eye.

"They say if you drink a mistletoe latte, the next person you kiss is your one true love."

Emma gulped. "That sounds—"

"Like bullshit, because it is." Nick stormed to his feet and yanked open the fridge. She expected him to grab another beer, but he started to rearrange the food while ranting.

"What about the Thompsons?" Skylar asked.

"Those fools were already dating before they ordered

one. That doesn't count." He pulled the aluminum foil roll off of the top of the fridge and ripped a jagged edge off.

"Jerry and Teresa?" Skylar asked, her voice rising higher with each couple.

"They come in every day for coffee. It was bound to happen eventually."

"Roger and Joe?"

Nick froze in mummifying the leftover meatloaf in rolls of foil. "Okay, that one was weird. But it was a coincidence. It's one of those things where you make something happen, then act like it's fate."

"Self-fulfilling prophecy?" Emma asked. He pointed a finger to her and nodded vehemently.

"Fake. All of it. Just bullshit made up by people with nothing better to do. And why in the hell do you know about this? You were just a kid." Nick stared at Skylar who hid behind her screen.

"Because," she said, her voice wobbling. "People like to talk in town. They miss it, and people online are talking about it too."

"Great. I can't close the café until this rolls over."

"They're not gonna be happy until they get a mistletoe latte," Skylar taunted.

"They should get used to disappointment."

She sighed and slammed her phone down. "Why don't you just make them again?"

"Don't you start too." Nick gritted his teeth and red sprouted over his forehead. "You know full well that…!" His rant faded, and he looked at Emma who was trying to stay out of the argument she didn't understand. "I'm not gonna give in to peer pressure. And neither should you…for drugs and stuff."

Skylar snorted and rolled her eyes, but she resumed

her death scrolling rather than face her uncle. Nick took to rounding up the plates, his outburst calmed.

"Why don't I help?" Emma offered, gathering up the silverware. She feared he'd argue her away, but Nick stepped to the side with a laugh, leaving her in charge of the sink.

"You, put the phone down, and get back to your homework."

The teenager grumbled but did as told. Though she was careful to lay her phone to the side just in case she needed to check it again. Emma rolled her sleeves up and reached into the soapy water. After rinsing the knife under the faucet, she handed it to Nick who buffed it with a towel.

"Okay, do you know a secret for washing dishes faster?"

"Yes," Emma said, nodding deeply. "Hire an intern."

He laughed hard at that and a warmth spread across her chest. She held onto one end of a butter knife and Nick clung to the other. Neither let go, the flimsy metal warming from their combining body heat as he stared into her eyes.

"I'm glad you walked into my café today," he said, his voice nearly growling from how low it dropped.

"Oh?" She swallowed deep, her heart pounding faster as she'd swear he moved closer to her.

"Cause otherwise I wouldn't have…" Nick's fingers caressed the tips of hers, and he blinked. His hand slipped back, and he took the knife from her. Vigorously rubbing the towel over it, he muttered to the side, "…managed to deal with the latte crowd without breaking a nose."

"You." Emma bowed her head, watching the soap bubbles pop across the surface. She was leaving in less than a day. His turning away shouldn't hurt at all. "You're welcome."

By the time all the dishes were done, they found themselves in the sitting room. Skylar took up the armchair, her legs crossed and books scattered over them. It left Emma perched next to Nate on the couch with her second untouched glass of wine on the coffee table. They stuck to polite and distant conversation, the uncle trying to push his niece to study harder with questions about Emma's time in college.

"I fear I'll be paying off loans until I'm dead," she said and added a laugh to punctuate the grim reality. The government would take her pennies for the ferryman if she skipped out early.

"See," Nick said, jabbing a finger to the disinterested teen. "You've got to get a scholarship."

With a sigh, Skylar closed her hand around her finger and stared him dead in the eye. "And how many scholarships did you get, Uncle Nick?"

He gulped, looking toward Emma before focusing on his niece. "This isn't about me," he said when her phone buzzed.

Skylar leaped to her feet, tossing her homework to the floor. Nick reached over to gather it up, chastising her, but she held her screen to him while saying, "It's dad. Hi, dad!" The sour teenager sweetened as she dashed up the stairs.

Instinctively, Emma watched her until she vanished down the hallway. A heat prickled up her arms and over her neck as she realized she was alone with Nick. She swiveled her gaze and found him looking back at her. Startled, she reached for her glass the same time he went for his mug. Their hands bumped, nearly scattering coffee and red wine to the carpet.

"Sorry," she said, slamming both hands over her rotating glass and keeping it pinned.

"My, uh…" He gulped, jostling his coffee back and forth like a carousing pirate. "This is weird, right?"

"Extremely."

"Not that it isn't nice to have you. Here. It is. Nice, I mean. To eat dinner with instead of the sullen groans and sighs from Skylar."

As she looked to him, Nick tipped his head back to take a long drink of coffee. The skin under his whiskers heated up, turning the blonde scruff red. "Though, you'd probably rather be anywhere else."

She was supposed to be in Maine being berated by her sister, not sitting in a near-stranger's living room trying to not blush to death. Out of all the places for her car to have broken down, she couldn't have asked for nicer. Emma opened her mouth to explain as such when the light caught on his barely pursed lips and glistened. "It's a comfortable couch."

Oh, my goodness.

He chuckled as if she'd told a joke and glanced at a cuckoo clock hanging above the fireplace. "Ah shit, it's already eight? I… This is gonna sound pathetic, but I try to get to bed by nine. Early morning cattle call and all. Um…"

"Oh? Oh! You…" Emma fumbled to her feet, realizing he wanted her to ship out. "I should…get out of your hair. Thank you for the meal. I could order a car or…" She checked her couple of ride-share apps, but they didn't show anything for a hundred miles. Apparently, small towns didn't rely on the side hustle market. "Or you could drop me off back in town and I'll figure it out from there."

Nick rose too, towering above her. She had no idea

what to do or where to go, leaving her feeling like a mouse in the presence of a giant. "Listen, it's cold out. Gonna get colder, and you should stay here."

"Oh…that's a generous offer." He wanted her to stay in his house, sleep in a bed somewhere under the same roof. Emma's brain panicked at the idea. "I couldn't burden you further after all you've done."

"It'd be a bigger pain to drive you to a motel. Really. Just, stay here. So I don't worry about you navigating the mean streets of Lake Holly on your own in the dead of winter." He lifted his eyebrows and his eyes pleaded with her to say yes. "Unless it's weird. It's probably weird. If you don't want to, I can take you back to your car."

The moment the nervous energy crackled from him, Emma wanted to ease his burden. She placed a palm against his arm and said, "I'd be happy to stay."

Nick's grumbling faded and his blue eyes gleamed. "I'd like it. Oh…uh, wake-up's at four in the morning."

She laughed. "I don't mind."

"Got to get to the café before the regular zombies roll in needing caffeine. And it takes an hour to drag Skylar out of bed."

"Really." She pressed her fingers to his arm to get his attention, but the biceps hidden behind an expanse of flannel caught hers. Forgetting to let go, she held on to his muscle flexing harder and sending a flush down her spine.

Nick peered at her from below his brows, and she dropped her grip. "I kept a lot of strange hours working in the restaurant business. Four a.m. is no bother."

"Good. I mean, I should show you where you can sleep. It's up here."

"Skylar gave me a quick tour earlier," Emma said as

she followed him up the stairs.

Nick paused at the top and sighed. "She's going to be insufferable about this." He banged his fist on the first door covered in warning tape and Korean pop singers.

"What?"

Poking his head in, Nick revealed a sliver of Skylar's room. The furniture and fixtures looked like they were meant for a young girl—all pastel purples and fluffy clouds. But the piles of clothing, angsty posters taped to the walls, and cork board of various quotes told a different tale.

"Emma's gonna be staying with us for the night." A huge grin rose across Skylar's face at the news, but Nick cut her off with, "Don't."

She held up a hand before looking down the hall. "You know we threw the spare mattress away when the mice got into it."

"Ah…shit. I forgot." He tossed his head back and groaned.

Emma didn't want to be a problem. "This was a kind offer, but—"

"Come on." Nick didn't even hesitate, only waved her on.

"Shut the door!" Skylar shouted before doing it herself.

Even without a mattress, she could still sleep on the floor with a couple of blankets and a pillow. It didn't matter as long as there was a roof. Emma put a smile on, prepared for whatever mouse-infested room awaited her when Nick pushed open the door at the end of the hall.

He flicked on a light and said, "You can sleep here."

A queen-sized bed with a navy and cream duvet took up most of the master bedroom. To the side was a flat dresser with a handful of shirts and socks on the top. A military trunk sat at the foot of the bed, the latch lifted but not the top. This was clearly his room. He wanted her to sleep…in his bed?

Oh, she couldn't.

Could she?

Walking past her panic, Nick picked a pillow off of the bed, then a blanket out of the closet. Maybe he was going to give them to her, let her sleep on the floor.

But he kept on walking and pointed to the door handle. "There's a lock on this. It's a bit tricky, but holds."

"You…where are you going to sleep?" she cried out in concern.

He paused and stared at her in surprise. "The couch. Don't worry. I sleep there a lot lately. Good for the back, and catching any teenagers who want to try sneaking out." Nick assured her all was fine, but Emma gulped.

"This is too much," she insisted, but he kept carrying on as if she'd said nothing.

"There's a toilet through that door attached to the bedroom. The shower is by Skylar's room so good luck fighting her to get in. Need anything else?"

She couldn't stay here, take his bed from him, not after all he'd given her. Emma tried to will up the courage, her head dropping, when Nick winced. "You probably left all your luggage in your…um." He dashed past her and dug through the shirts on the dresser. After sniffing a few, which he then tossed to another pile on the floor, he handed her a gray T-shirt. "You can sleep in this. I'm pretty sure it's clean."

It surprised her how soft it was. Emma rubbed her thumbs over the fabric as she clutched the T-shirt tight. "Thank you, for all of this."

"Yeah, well…" Nick shrugged as he backed out of the room. He didn't turn but kept looking at Emma as he went. At the threshold, he glanced down the hall. "You can thank Skylar. It was her idea."

Oh. Of course. "Then I'll be sure to thank her too."

He nodded, still keeping his gaze away from her when Nick suddenly looked back. "Goodnight, Emma."

For some stupid reason, she gave a little wave. "Until four a.m."

Laughing, he pulled the door closed leaving her alone in his bedroom. She breathed in to steady herself, but the scent of musk, sandalwood, and coffee radiated off the shirt he'd given her. Clutching it tighter to her chest, she readied herself for a long night.

CHAPTER SEVEN

CLINGING TO THE ratty blanket and single pillow, Nick sighed to himself. "You're a damn fool." He hadn't acted this stupid for a pair of pretty eyes in… A shiver of regret and anger shook his body at the memory. They'd said with time it'd lose its stink and only be rose-scented. But after five years, he couldn't even think her name without wanting to kick a wall. *It's all this damn latte's fault.*

What was he doing tying himself into knots for a woman who'd vanish in twelve hours? She was so tiny, his shirt would probably reach to her knees. *Bare legs below a tattered hem and the fabric so threadbare there'd be an outline of her nipples poking from the –*

"What are you doing?"

Nick jerked so quick a spasm shook his spine. He slammed a hand to the wall to steady himself and glared at Skylar holding out her phone. Gritting his teeth, he twisted his hips fast enough to crack his back.

Her interest in his going's-on died quickly. "Here." She handed him her phone. "Dad wants to talk to you."

"I have a few things to say to him."

"But it's so hard to hear anything he says on that old thing." Skylar launched a nuclear hint right at his head. Then she went for the kill. "Wouldn't it be good for my safety if I got a new one."

Ignoring her gift suggestion Nick placed the neon pink phone to his ear before pausing and glaring at his niece. "Shouldn't you be in bed?"

She rolled her eyes. "I'm the only god damn teenager with a freaking bedtime."

"Welcome to the real world, population everyone's out to get you specifically and no one else."

His thick sarcasm earned him a dramatic sigh. She walked slowly to her room, taking care to just about – but not entirely – close her door.

"You there?" his brother asked, but Nick didn't say a word until he'd gotten down the stairs.

Tossing his bedding to the couch, he finally said, "Yes. And there's something we need to talk about. Christmas is coming up – "

"Yeah. About that," Peter interrupted. Nick could hear him clawing at his forehead, causing the phone to bounce into his skull. "I'm not sure if I'll be able to send you the money for gifts – "

Nick shook his head. "I already got her Christmas presents…including the ones from her loving father."

"Oh. Great. How much?"

It didn't matter what Nick said, they both knew the gesture was empty. He heard a creak up above and, cupping his hand over the phone, glared at the staircase. There was a blind spot where a certain girl could hide to listen in. He waited a few more seconds, hearing no noise, before saying, "Don't worry about it. Skylar would never eavesdrop on private conversations. She's too smart to risk a grounding for a week."

He pretended he didn't hear a small gasp, then the flap of feet hitting the floorboards. Girl thought she was Einstein and James Bond rolled into one most days. Good thing he knew all the tricks as he'd pulled the same as a kid. Still, it was better to give himself more distance. Slipping on his coat, he took the conversation outside.

Cold bit his drawn cheeks. Nick huddled into the collar of his jacket. "Are you coming home for Christmas?"

His brother sighed the same way Skylar would whenever Nick asked if she'd finished cleaning the bathroom. "You know I'd love to if I could, but it's a long drive, and the traffic…"

"They've got these things called airplanes. Might want to look into it."

"Funny. Even if I had the money for a ticket, I can't go back to Lake Holly. Don't ride my ass about it." The pleading switched to anger in a heartbeat, piquing Nick's interest.

"Okay, then how about she spends winter break with you?"

"No!" Pete shouted fast, before softening to his smooth-talking sales-pitch voice. "That doesn't seem like the best idea. My roommate situation is perilous and—"

"She hasn't seen you in years." Every year Skylar got her hopes up that her father would visit for Christmas or her birthday. Every time he'd find a perfectly fraudulent excuse. Nick was sick of it.

"I know," Pete whispered. "I'd be there right now if I could."

"Would you?"

"Nicky…"

The wind shifted and the ice cracked on the pond. He used to swing Pete around by his arms on it when they were kids, never once fearing they'd fall in. Now, it felt like he was drowning with the surface just above him. No matter how hard he swung, his fists couldn't puncture the ice. "This is stupid. Just tell her the truth. She's old enough."

"You don't understand."

"I'm the one who's keeping her clothed, fed, and out of most trouble. What are you doing?"

His brother sighed. "You're not a father."

Nick jerked at the patronizing comment. His fingers clenched so tight around the phone the volume shot up. "So what?"

"So you don't get it. If she finds out she'll lose all respect for me. A daughter cannot handle that. It'll warp her."

"You think it's better she only gets the occasional phone call from you instead? We can't keep this up forever. She's not an idiot, despite her parentage."

"You've got the same genes, bro," Pete taunted him, causing Nick to grumble. "Look, this isn't a good time for me. Next year, I'll finally be out of here with my own place. We can have a proper family Christmas. I'll cut down a real tree."

That's what he said last year, and the year before that. Rather than call him out, Nick pulled in a breath. Ice stung his nose, the frostbitten winter rallying for another bad year. As much as he hated it, Pete was right. He wasn't Skylar's dad, just the man keeping her safe. "Fine. But next time…"

"I'll do the whole thing right. I promise. So, um…you think you could wire me some cash? Nothing huge, just a little to get by…"

Nick managed to get out of that conversation having to only Venmo his brother a couple hundred. It wouldn't help Skylar if her father starved. When he went to return her phone, the lights were off and a lump rested under the covers, so he ignored the halogen glow still radiating from the recently-turned-off bulb.

Between feeding himself, a teenager, and her dad, the money was stretching to the breaking point. Maybe he should just give the horde what they wanted? As Nick eased down the stairs, the light caught on a picture frame. The old photo was of him with his arm around someone that couldn't be seen because he'd put a picture of nine-year-old Skylar over her.

Clenching his fists, he vowed he wouldn't make another mistletoe latte over his cold, dead body. They could eat ramen for Christmas—Pete included. With heartbroken rage keeping him warm, Nick sat on the couch, twisted around to sleep, and lay the blanket over him. His feet stuck out off the edge, the chill biting his toes.

Nick only closed his eyes for a minute when the tell-tale creak of the door sent him shooting up. The hazy streetlights softened the silhouette of the girl in big trouble. "Ah-ha! Where do you think you're going?"

Skylar flipped on the overhead light, burning his retinas in the process. While he blinked, feeling a sticky pull between his lids, she spun his set of keys on her finger. "Warming up the truck. It's four-thirty."

"What?" One foot struck the ground and an icy chill shattered up his calf. Nick stared at the weird clock which he knew had been on the eight hand. But, sure enough, that damn hour pointed to four. That couldn't be right. He'd barely slept more than a few minutes. Did Skylar change the clock to...?

The creak of the stairs drew his attention to the woman in her full outfit, her hair tamed by a headband. As Emma's soft hand glided down the banister, fractures of his dreams returned. Those same fingers had slipped into his mouth then trailed down his chest, nails scratching along the way.

She paused, her eyes dark as espresso. The harsh streetlamp lit up her pink sweater until it glowed like angel wings. Another snippet of his dream returned— that same sweater had been piled on the kitchen counter, her thighs straddling his waist as he dripped honey down her naked breasts and bent over to lick them.

"Morning," Emma called, her voice showing only a hint of grogginess. Both of the girls were dressed for the day while he was in nothing more than a ratty shirt and sweats.

"Damn it," he cursed himself and rose to his full height. "Give me five..." Nick was about to run for the stairs when his pants tugged on the raging erection. He mentally shrunk to a fifteen-year-old that just spotted his crush's bra strap. Hunching down, he snatched up the pillow and blanket then draped both in front of his crotch. He had no choice but to lumber past Emma, who'd paused at the foot of the stairs to watch him curiously.

If she knew what he'd been dreaming about, how pink would those cheeks of her turn?

Oh, that was not a smart thought. His libido leaped from a cute blush to her buttocks glistening in his hands. All the blood in his body pumped into his enraged cock. Facing them, Nick took the stairs backward, one hand slapped to the wall for balance, the other hiding his vengeful shame.

"Ten minutes. Give me ten to get dressed." At this rate, he'd need one to solve this and nine for clean-up.

Skylar sighed and spun the keys on her fingers faster. "We're gonna be late."

Away from her eyes, Nick bolted to his room and dashed for his clothing. He managed to tug his sweats down past his hips, freeing his cock. The chill of winter should have calmed the thick crown pulsing on its own, but he glanced to his bed. Instead of resting against the headboard, the two pillows were positioned vertically in the middle of the bed as if she'd wrapped her entire body around them to sleep.

The last of his dream returned, of naked breasts and hard nipples pressing against his back and her warm breath caressing down his ear before she bit the lobe. *Oh, fu-u-u-u...*

Nick slapped a hand over his mouth to keep the groan internal. His other was busy trying to catch the mess before it dripped everywhere.

"Fifteen!" he shouted, struggling to contain himself. "I'll be ready in fifteen minutes."

CHAPTER EIGHT

THE AIR SMELLED of snow. She'd missed the crisp bite right before a tumble of flakes. In Portland, it was a melancholy scent when heavy sleet rained instead. The street, in fact the whole world, was silent. Only a single streetlight blazed through the winter darkness.

Nick turned the key in the door, and Skylar blew past him. Emma waited more patiently, not as freezing as the socially dressed teen. He finished tugging back the door's lock, then held it open for her. She blushed at the chivalrous move. In walking around him, the scent changed from bright and sharp snow to a heady, masculine musk that made Emma's eyelids hang low.

She'd spent the night wrapped up in that, his smell embedded into the sheets. When she'd woken to find herself entwined with the pillows, breathing deeply of him, she was so glad that Skylar banged on the door and not Nick.

As she walked into the back room of the shop, the scent of coffee grew so strong Emma could taste it on her tongue. She wasn't enough of a connoisseur to pick up on the blends radiating in the air.

"Skylar, start grinding the dark and medium roasts."

"What do you think I'm doing?" the girl asked. Before Nick could answer, the sound of machinery and cracking coffee beans overpowered them.

Nick said something. Emma could see his mouth moving, but all that came out was a whisper under the grinder.

"What?" she shouted, trying to protect her ears with her shoulder.

To her shock, he took her hand. His wide fingers swept across all of her palm, protecting and shielding it. Nick tugged her past the stockroom where Skylar sat in the only chair with her feet on the sink. Eeriness radiated through the café, the single light source catching on the upside-down chairs resting on the tables. They poked through the air like naked trees stripped of their branches.

She didn't realize she was clinging to his hand until Nick let go and raised the lights. The illumination chased away the unsettling feeling of an impenetrable forest in the dead of winter.

"That damn grinder is loud, even out here," Nick muttered. He booted up his espresso machine and checked the water levels.

"Should you let Skylar get so close to it?" Emma

asked, fearing for the girl's ears.

Nick waved it off. "It's quieter than the music she blares out of her headphones."

Without a thought, Emma pulled the chairs off of the tables and placed them on the floor. Nick looked up a moment and nodded in thanks before he tended to his equipment. Remembering what she'd put away last night, Emma returned the stacks of coffee accouterments to the counter. "This shaker could use a top off," she said, lifting the powdered creamer.

She was already walking to the back storeroom when Nick bent down and hefted a large box onto the counter. "Don't tell anyone I use the generic stuff," he said.

"I won't, I promise."

The smile winding about his lips caused Emma's heart and hand to jerk, scattering generic coffee creamer across the counter. She blushed. He was about to clean it up when Nick's grin knotted into a frown. Emma gathered the spilled powder with her hand to scoop it into a napkin when she realized he wasn't glaring at her. Past the darkened windows stood a line of people waiting for the proverbial rope drop. A pulsing vein rose from the side of Nick's neck as he faced another day of mistletoe latte madness.

"Here ya go," Skylar announced, slamming a container of grounds to the counter beside Nick. "Enough to get you through the early rush."

Nick shook out of his dour turn to shout, "We still need—"

"Can't. I've got homework to do. Didn't you say grades mattered most?" she called to him before vanishing into the back.

His grumbling made Emma smile in shared

frustration. "I could run the grinder if you'd like."

"Ah, no. It's...it can bite. I'll set it up." Nick slipped away from the growing fans freezing outside and walked to the back door.

Uncertain, Emma gazed around the quiet café. "Where do you want me?" she asked, rolling up her sleeves.

Nick froze in the doorway. A passing car's headlights lit his face a chalk-white before it rolled on. "I want you... You should sit there. Take it easy."

"Sit here?" Emma wrapped her fingers around the stool. "But I can—"

"It's not your mess to fix. You'll be leaving soon."

She opened her mouth to argue, but there was nothing she could say. Once the mechanic got the part, she would be hitting the road and never see him again. Nick turned away, methodically prepping for the day without talking to her. Not wanting to get in the way, Emma sat on the same stool as yesterday and texted her sister to let her know what was up. She didn't expect a reply.

"Time to face the gates of hell," he announced in a voice brimming with dread.

Putting on his customer service frown, Nick approached the front door, undid the lock, and shouted, "There's no damn mistletoe latte today!" The groans began immediately from people who'd been standing in the cold for God knew how long. If they'd thought coming early would get them a coveted latte they were sadly mistaken. Nick let the door start to close and turned. His gaze landed on Emma. "But...there's this holly mocha you can try instead."

"Will I like it?"

"How the hell should I...? Yeah, you'll love it." He

ushered them in with a wave of his hand. Most followed after, no doubt doing the math and realizing any warm drink was better than frostbite. "Get in line here," Nick growled, jabbing a finger to the spot behind the cash register.

A woman in a beret hustled past the others who gawked and took pictures of the unfinished ceilings and walls. "Give me a—"

"Wait." Nick held up a hand to stop her and leaned over the counter to look at Emma. "Cream and sugar?" he asked.

She blushed at the thought and nodded.

"Coming up. Okay, your turn."

By the time he got through the first glut, a second round arrived who were just as annoyed about the lack of the mythical latte. The lines were backing out of the door as Nick raced from machines to registers. Emma was about to slip to the floor and help when Skylar joined him.

She did better with the customers than the grouchy owner, though Emma could swear she heard her tell them to ask for the mistletoe latte tomorrow. After her second cup of cream and sugar coffee, the tourists died down. A few regulars walked in, dressed in factory fatigues and barely opening their eyes. They grunted their orders and Nick handed the cups over before they finished.

It was nearing six-thirty and Emma had run out of ways to kill time. Feeling like a waste of space and time, she opened her purse and pulled out her ratty notebook. The cover was pink pleather with a unicorn sticker on the front. Inside were the mad ramblings of a some-time chef.

Cracking it open, Emma frowned at the last recipe

she had for a beef cheek bourguignon and herbed ricotta. If she closed her eyes, her ears rang with the chef's screams about the sponginess of the cheek. Emma turned the page, then another two more to a fresh blank sheet.

What should I work on? What about a Christmas pudding but as a trifle?

"I'm sorry, but we don't have a mistletoe latte," Skylar said sweetly before rolling her eyes.

He couldn't actually put mistletoe in there, so what would he add? Hm, a coffee base over ladyfingers. No, a chocolate and coffee reduction for drizzling over fruitcake. Oh, that's even worse. Emma scratched at the whole mess, but she wrote mistletoe and circled it. There was something to the idea if not the exact poisonous flavors.

"You know, there's this one thing you should do before you leave."

Nick appeared with another pot of coffee. Without her asking, he filled her cup and tipped in the fresh cream from his pitcher. As she stared up at him, his stern glare softened to a secretive smile. The round drop to his bottom lip entranced her. His top lip vanished even when his face was neutral, but the bottom one bulged as if it was made to be nipped on.

Is it kiss you?

Emma tried to ignore the silly thought dancing in her head, but she couldn't pull her eyes off of him. Would he be as stubborn and certain in kissing her? Or would a tender sweetness hide below his gruff exterior?

"Oh?" she asked, trying to sound coquettish.

"There's this book shop at the end of main."

He wanted to get rid of her, of course. She was leaving soon. Emma dropped her head and started to gather her things up. All she said was, "Okay."

"It's not very big, lots of people miss it, but it's got some...um..." Nick's voice stumbled so low it faded away. He scratched his forearm, no doubt getting uncomfortable that she hadn't moved on to the bookstore. He needed the space for other customers.

"Hey, Daryl!" he exclaimed to the door, turning Emma around. Sure enough, there stood her mechanic rubbing his grease-stained hands and nodding.

"It's colder than Satan's taint out there. I saw a squirrel with his nuts stuck to a pole," the mechanic shouted. He didn't look at Emma but strode for the cash register. "Give me the biggest, hottest thing you've got."

Nick nodded, but his eyes cut over to her. After taking Daryl's money and putting a thirty-two-ounce cup on the counter, he jerked his head to Emma. "Aren't you forgetting something?"

"No. I'm driving the Beasly's car, got to listen for a thunk."

"What about her?" he pointed right to Emma. She wanted to thank him for remembering but also frowned at how readily he wanted her gone.

"Oh, the Soul. Yeah, I was gonna call you after I filled my gas tank. Where's the joe, Nick?"

Emma slipped to her feet and slung her purse over her arm along with her coat. "How long until you can fix it?"

"Hm?" He swirled his black coffee, then ripped open ten sugar packets. "It'll take a week."

"A week?"

"To get the part. You know how Leo is, always backed up, especially this time of year."

She couldn't spend a week here. Renting a hotel would empty her measly bank account in a night, never mind seven days. And food... Maybe if she left her vehicle here and got a ride. Emma took a quick glance at the cost of an Uber to the only bus line that went near Maine and her heart stopped.

"I'll be sure to call once it's in," Daryl said to her before he cradled his coffee and sauntered off.

Every bad decision that led to her being stranded came roaring to life. Every failing was shouted at her by a man in chef's whites. If she'd just planned better, or... if she hadn't gone down this path in the first place. They'd warned her she couldn't cut it in a kitchen, but Emma wanted to prove them wrong. Instead, she'd proved every cruel voice right.

"Here."

She blinked, trying to fan away the tears on her eyelashes. A hand held out a brown cap. She traced up the wrist and forearm to find ice blue eyes and a determined frown.

"You're gonna need it," Nick said. "And this." He handed over the same apron from yesterday.

"But I thought..." He'd wanted to get rid of her. Emma weighed the two pieces of hope in her hands, fearing they might float away.

He nodded once and slipped behind the register to take the next order. Working fast, Emma put on the apron and bundled her hair into a ponytail to slip through the back of the cap.

"Things are hectic now, but around ten they'll slow. Then you can get your things from your car."

This was too much. His sheltering and feeding her for a day was kind, but an entire week? She dashed around the counter to his side. Lowering her voice, Emma dropped her hands into the apron's pockets. "You don't have to—"

"I can use the help," Nick said over her. "And you seem competent. So…" He stepped aside and waved her to the customers.

Smiling wide, Emma walked to the counter. "What can I get you?"

CHAPTER NINE

AFTER HANDING A no-fat praline latte to the customer, Emma turned to find Skylar behind her instead of Nick. "Where's—?"

"So you're staying for a whole week?" the girl asked, looking more like a sly jewel thief than a fresh-faced fourteen-yeah-old.

"I'll be helping out, yes," Emma said, uncertain of what the arrangement would be.

With broom in hand, Nick swept by and looked at Skylar. "You'll be working too."

"Ah, come on… What do you need two of us for?" she whined. Nick nodded to the growing line of customers.

He handed her the broom and caught Emma's attention. "Most of these are locals, I can handle them. Why don't you make sure the pouting princess here actually cleans up instead of shoving all the trash into a corner?"

"I did that once," Skylar shouted at him. She locked both hands to the broom and began to push.

"Two months ago," Nick said before catching the next customer's eye. "Usual?"

"Without cream, trying to cut back."

Emma slipped past to gather up the scattered wrappers and napkins. While slapping the broom's head under the bench as loud as possible, the girl glared at her uncle, but he didn't rise to the bait. When that didn't work, she sighed just as Emma passed.

"What are you gonna make for dinner? The carrots were good, but broccoli's blech. What about pizza?"

"I don't know…"

"Pizza can be fancy and have veggies on it."

"That's true." Emma tried to keep her hopes low. "I don't think I'll be with you for dinner."

"Why? Is he making you work through dinner? *Viva la revolution!*"

"You're not a French peasant, and I sure as hell ain't a king," Nick grumbled before greeting the next customer.

"It's not that. Your uncle's been very kind and… pleasant." Emma's voice drifted away as she watched him serve regular after regular by calling out their order before they could. How could he be so nice to someone he barely knew?

"By pleasant you mean…?" Skylar prompted, elbowing her in the side.

Blushing, Emma shook the thought away before Skylar pried worse from her. "I shouldn't impose on you both. I'll look for a rental place or a cheap room."

"I wouldn't if I were you. Anyone renting out a room in Lake Holly has bodies inside the walls and under the floors."

"You're kidding."

Skylar gripped her shoulders and twisted Emma around. "Why do you think Sam keeps listening to the police scanner? It's so he can run if they find the victims."

Feeling the stares, Sam turned from his hobby and, rather than wave, shot finger guns at both of them. Emma jerked in her arms and Skylar smiled wider. "It's best to stay with us. There's no room to hide anything in that house."

While she appreciated the sentiment, Emma knew better than to impose on her boss so personally. Maybe he knew of a room or...? Nick, with his square jaw gritted and lips in a sneer, caused her legs to wobble. Maybe it'd be better if she looked on her own.

"One mistletoe latte, please."

The growl managed to rumble over the chatter of the patrons and Emma braced herself. Nick slapped a hand to the menu board, pointed to the sign, then asked the customer behind him for her order.

"I don't know why he doesn't just make the damn thing again. They aren't gonna stop," Skylar said.

Despite not knowing him for even a day, Emma doubted he was the type to give in easily. Stubborn as a mule would be the impolite way of saying it.

"Hey." The girl passed over her broom and eyed up Emma. "Why don't you ask him? I'm sure he'd listen to you."

She scoffed at the idea. "He doesn't know me from a hole in the wall."

"Mmm-hmm," was all the girl said. Skylar transformed into a fifty-year-old pack-a-day gossip hound with just two syllables. So maybe Emma enjoyed the touch of his hand on hers, and she had leaned a bit closer than necessary when they'd washed dishes. But that didn't mean Nick thought anything of her beyond an extra pair of hands for the breakfast rush.

Right?

Skylar looked up from sweeping the dirt into a dustpan, her eyes twinkling with mischief when the bell jangled. A bright flush stampeded across her face. The dustpan clanged to the floor and the broom slipped. Emma caught it before it smacked the window while the girl raced to hide behind her hands. She risked a quick peek between her fingers at a young man standing in line.

With wavy hair daringly grown past his swooping jawline, those fine glass features that didn't threaten a teenage girl, and a full set of pouty lips it was no wonder poor Skylar was melting. Emma always preferred the more silver fox grizzled type, but even she could sense the golden charisma radiating off of the boy.

"*Buongiorno.*"

Oh no, he had an accent. Skylar was screwed.

"Yeah, what do you want?" Nick asked the young man, incapable of being swayed by the Italian charm.

"Oh my gosh, oh my gosh." Skylar faced the window, only risking the occasional glance over her shoulder to make certain the boy hadn't vanished.

Emma chuckled at the painfully familiar feeling. Leaning closer while watching Nick take down the precise order—his sneer growing—Emma whispered, "What's his name?"

"Antonio." She practically sang her response, Skylar mid-sigh when the boy shifted his head towards her. "Crap. He can't see me here. Not in this!"

That must have been who the midriff shirt was for. Emma gave a little wave to Antonio who seemed curious about the young girl crumpled on her shoulder. "Why don't you say hi?"

"Because he's a junior…from Italy."

"None of those are reasons you can't greet him," Emma said.

All Skylar could do was eep and yank her cap down. She shook her head and turned her back on the boy who listened intently to Sam explaining the police scanner.

"He seems like a nice young man."

"Skylar."

At her uncle's bellow, the girl gripped tight to Emma's shoulder, her body shaking.

"We're out of lids. Get some more."

"No!" she shouted, her voice pitched high and ending in a squeal.

Nick slapped a hand to the counter and glared at her, drawing everyone to see what caught his wrath. "Why the hell not?"

The poor girl chattered her teeth while staring in dreamy terror at her crush. Emma patted her hand. "I'll get them," she said, walking crisply to the storage room door.

"That isn't your…" Nick began, but she already stepped into the back. It didn't take her long to find them.

Carrying a stack of the lids as long as her arm, Emma

emerged into the coffee shop to find Nick glaring, Skylar shaking, and Antonio completely unaware. Nick pointed to the line of steaming cups, and Emma quickly capped them off, calling out the orders. But for Antonio's, she took the cup in both hands and walked it to him.

"Are you Antonio?" she asked.

He smiled the kind of blinding grin that'd give girls heart attacks in algebra. As she handed him the cup, he said, "*Grazie.*"

"Do you know Skylar Iverson? She ground these beans special just for you." Emma turned to face the girl whose face was redder than Saint Nick's suit. But when Antonio looked, she melted and gave a little wiggle of her fingers.

"Thank you, Skylar," he said then took a quick sip. He smiled brighter at her after the drink, wrapped his thin scarf around his neck, and vanished out the door.

Barreling over, Skylar nearly head-butted Emma. First, she watched Antonio in his tight jeans and fashionable coat waltz down the street. Then she glared. "What did you say to him? Why did he thank me?"

Emma shrugged. "It should be a lot easier to say hi now that he knows your name."

"Oh my god. Antonio knows my name." She squealed and shook her hands back and forth as if a dance was about to break out. "Addy!"

A stylish forty-something woman trailed by a teenage girl stepped into the shop. It was to the girl Skylar ran, both speaking and squealing at lightning speed about the previous events. Addy seemed even more excited about the Italian heartthrob learning that Skylar existed.

Smiling to herself, Emma slipped away. She knew far too well the nervous agony of wanting to talk to someone who was too handsome, knowing he'd never look twice at her. It felt like a lifetime ago that she'd been the teenager sidling next to a boy and thinking that'd somehow make him ask her out. She looked up from the table to find Nick rolling his sleeves back and her heart flipped. A little squeal built in the back of her throat as he wrung a palm over the scruff of his jaw.

She took a step closer when the woman who came in with Addy reached across the gap and touched Nick's arm. Her cheeks were flushed, her smile perfect, her skin flawless. She brushed back her coiffed blonde hair and giggled at whatever Nick said.

The handsome coffee shop owner and the beautiful businesswoman in a steamy relationship—it made perfect sense. Why'd she think for a second he'd look twice at a washed-up…? It didn't matter.

"Excuse me, miss?"

Emma abandoned the flirting to focus on a customer.

"This isn't what I wanted."

Me either.

Shaking away the pain, she smiled. "Let me fix that for you."

SKYLAR WAS ACTING like a fool again, and he didn't have time for it. At least Emma swooped in to save her butt and his. Nick spotted his savior gathering up the crumbs on the table. The apron string pulled at her sweater, lifting it as she reached. It exposed a line of bare skin just above her jeans with a hint of lace that had to be her…

"Addy!"

The shriek of his niece saved him from having to hide himself by pressing against the counter. All the damn hormones in the air were messing with his brain. "What'll it be…? Ah, Mrs. Wilkins."

"Good morning, Nick." She sidled up next to the counter and nearly leaped onto it.

"How are you?" he asked on default. The espresso machine beeped, and he gathered up the finished pour. "Americano, sprinkle of cinnamon!"

Once the customer took it, he returned to the cash register. Mrs. Wilkins beamed at him. "A lot better now," she said.

"Coffee'll do that," Nick answered absently. "What do you want?"

"Why don't you surprise me?"

Great, like he wasn't already behind. Taking a mug off the top, Nick tried to think of a good flavor combo. *Maybe hazelnut and caramel with a sprinkle of nutmeg?* He pressed the button and let his robot do the work.

"I see you've hired new help," Mrs. Wilkins said, staring at Emma. "I didn't know you were looking."

"I wasn't. But seems she can't get enough of the place."

A loud laugh, then a handful of giggles escaped from Mrs. Wilkins. Nick scratched his head, uncertain what was funny, when she reached over and patted his arm. He looked at her fingers. Rather than slip away, she clenched tighter before releasing.

"It's been a challenge, the first Christmas since the divorce."

"Uh-huh."

"This time of year must be so trying for you. And poor Skylar with her father—"

"We get by just fine," Nick interrupted. Luckily, his

niece was deep into conversation with her friend and didn't overhear, but he couldn't let her find out from idle gossip. "If you could stand to the side…"

He pointed to the counter for Mrs. Wilkins who moved without taking her eyes off of him. The last of the coffee hit the cup and Nick snatched up the first bottles he found. Adding a dash of amaretto and too much hazelnut, he topped the whole thing off with a sprinkle of powdered sugar and handed it to her.

She kept staring at him without leaving, so Nick said, "Enjoy."

"I know I will. Oh, did you hear about the ice skating party this weekend?"

"No." He didn't skate, but Skylar did. Or she used to. Weird she didn't mention it to him.

"You should come. While the kids run around we can sit together, sip hot cocoa. It'd be a perfect opportunity for the two of us to talk."

"Uh, yeah…" When was the last time Skylar put her skates on? It couldn't have been last…no, two years ago. Nick frowned. "Sounds good," he mumbled, focusing on his niece.

As Mrs. Wilkins sipped her drink, Skylar and her friend chatted together. There'd once been a time when she'd have told him all about a skating party. What else was he missing?

"Skylar?" He called to her while glancing at the calendar.

"Yeah?"

"It's delivery day. I need you to come to the café right after school."

Her shoulders slumped and she groaned. "Are you serious?"

"We could get pizza after…?"

"I'm going dress shopping with Addy. Remember?"

Nick scratched his head, his thoughts fuzzy. "But I need you here to help." Without another pair of hands, the delivery guy was as likely to leave their stock in the parking lot.

Skylar crossed her arms. "I asked you like a week ago and you said it was fine. Or do you want me to go to the dance naked?"

He winced at the threat and shook his head. "Don't even...that's not funny. Fine. Get your dress, then get back here as fast as possible."

"You know." Skylar reached over the counter for her book bag. When it landed in a heavy thud, she stared him right in the eye. "You're not alone anymore." With a deliberate swivel, she directed him to the young woman pushing a pencil behind her ear. A strand of her chestnut hair had slipped out of her ponytail and kept brushing against her slender neck.

"Eh?"

He clenched his hands, shaking off the thought of curling her hair around his fingers, and caught his niece bouncing her eyebrows. "Get your ass to school," he growled.

CHAPTER TEN

THE DAY WENT quicker than the last one. When the customers had died down, Nick had called her over to teach her how to use the espresso machine. There'd been so many cycles, Emma had to jot them down next to her half recipes. Then he'd stepped back and left her to try.

She'd feared it would be a disaster, but when the first cup came out dark and rich, the liquid stopping right at eight ounces, Emm danced in a circle. Nick snickered and lifted the cappuccino. "Do you get this excited about everything?" He ripped open two packets of sugar and dumped them into the mug followed by the cream.

"What's wrong with celebrating?" Emma asked before slowly drinking the fruits of her labor. "Maybe you should do a little dance every time you finish a cup."

"I'd probably lose ten pounds." He slapped his stomach which only resounded with a hard thud of muscle.

Lowering her lashes, Emma tried to focus on the coffee percolating from the system and not the flush running through her body. The scent of sandalwood drifted off her hair. It'd followed her the whole day thanks to his pillows, causing her to blush every time she smelled it.

"Can you see me dancing?" Nick asked. He pulled the order tickets and tossed them into a box under the counter.

"Only if it's the apocalypse," Sam quipped, then cracked a smile.

Emma shooed him away. "I bet you dance wonderfully."

"Ha, sure." Nick crumpled a receipt and turned to her. "Wait until I break a toe and smack your stomach with my elbow."

They stood so close when he swung his arm around it nearly brushed her waist. Nick held onto the menu board and leaned down. She shifted on her toes, doing a small jig in a tiny square. He swayed back and forth with just his hips, the two of them proto-dancing together. *He raised his hand...for where? To hold my shoulder? Take my hand? Or cup my waist?*

The spoon in her mug rattled like a grasshopper. She moved to catch it when Nick took the whole cup and saucer. "Sounds like the delivery's here. And no Skylar, of course. Are you up for moving sacks of coffee beans?"

"No problem," Emma said. He placed her half-full coffee on the counter and a cold breeze blew between them. She wanted to call it common sense. He was her boss, sort of, and she'd be leaving in a week. Doing anything to mess that up would be the dumbest thing she'd done in, oh, five days.

"Usually I lock the front when taking a delivery, but..." Nick pointed to the old man happily jotting down a case of a missing cat found in the owner's bedroom. "Sam, can you mind the fort?"

"Not a problem!" he said.

As Emma walked with him to the back, Nick explained, "We get in a hundred-pound bags..."

"Woof," Emma exclaimed.

He chuckled. "Don't worry. You don't have to carry them. Just hold the doors for me and maybe push the dolly."

They slipped into the parking lot and the freezing December wind cut straight through Emma's sweater. Her teeth chattered and she rubbed her arms for warmth.

"Hey, Rob?" Nick called to the idling plain-white delivery truck in the middle of the back lot. The driver's side door swung open and a man dropped to the cement.

"Got the usual for you, Iverson," Rob said. He nodded to Nick, then bent over to undo the latch on the back.

Nick glanced at Emma fighting off the shivers. To her shock, he wrapped both his hands around her arms and vigorously rubbed them. "How's that?" he asked.

The winter cold burned away thanks to the heat

building on her cheeks. "Better," Emma whispered.

A rat-a-rat-a-rat drew her attention to the truck's back door flying up. Rob hopped to the edge and reached in, undoing a strap. "Two bags medium roast, one dark."

"I hope so," Nick said. Rob grunted as he picked up one of the giant burlap sacks and tossed it at Nick. Emma flinched, but he caught it without pause and hoisted the bag onto his right shoulder.

"Number two!" Rob called, launching the second into the air. That one gave Nick more trouble. He balanced two hundred pounds on his shoulders. Sweat beaded on his forehead, and he leaned on his heels before catching himself.

"Mind getting the door?" he asked through obvious strain.

Emma dashed back and pulled it open so it eclipsed her. Nick waddled past, his shoulders bulging so wide from the bags he had to turn and duck to make it inside. Once she was certain he was past, Emma risked peeking in. Only a steady shuffle, then a loud grunt of exertion escaped.

"Hey, girly," the truck driver called, waving her over. Emma let the door close and stepped toward him. "You ain't Skylar. Are you new or something?"

"Something," she said. The town seemed small enough for gossip to spread faster than chicken pox, but they didn't all need to know her life story.

"Well..." Rob lifted the bag and tossed it in the air.

Oh no! Emma dived for it, unprepared for the crushing weight of a hundred pounds to slam into her forearms. She nearly hit the pavement along with the sack. Digging her fingers tight into the straining burlap, Emma hefted the bag higher. She managed a couple of inches, the bottom of the sack slamming into her shins as she waddled away.

"Good luck with him, Something," Rob called as he slammed his truck door closed. "You're gonna need it."

Moving like a penguin with vertigo, Emma wobbled for the door. Her palms ached from the scratchy burlap abrading her skin. But if she stopped to adjust, there was no way she could pick the bag up. Staring intently at the beans, Emma didn't realize she'd reached the door until her toe smacked it.

Now what?

Maybe if she hugged the beans she could open the door. Emma hunched even lower, wrapping her entire arm around the sack. She was about to let go for the handle when the door swung for her. In a panic, she half waddled and half fell backward.

"Same as next..." Nick said. He caught her struggling to lift the bag.

She put on a smile. "I've almost—"

The beans defied gravity, growing weightless and rising into the air. Emma followed them, her arms grateful for the release. Nick swung the bag over his shoulder.

"You should have waited for me," he said, his biceps cradling the bag like a fireman would a fire victim. The muscle's strain warped his sweater's waffle weave to the limit, revealing the hard lines below.

"Sorry." Emma winced at herself for noticing. "He just..."

The truck pulled away, blasting hot air as it went. Nick sighed. "He does that." After opening the door, Nick walked the bag down the hall like it was no big deal while Emma wandered behind. "Skylar's used to his tricks, but...I'm guessing delivery trucks didn't throw crates of vegetables at you."

"Not usually. We'd carry them off the truck. When we were on the chef's bad side." Which was every day for her.

Nick nudged open the storage room door with his foot and heaved the bag to the floor. "Aren't you professional chefs supposed to be living the high life? Tasting the sauces, giving orders, calling people donkeys?"

Emma barked a laugh at the idea. "Maybe the head chef for the entire chain, but the rest of us put in the twelve hours prepping and cooking for each service. This has been a vacation in comparison."

"I know a fourteen-year-old that would disagree with that. Loudly. There's a can back there by the wall. Can you get it?"

"Sure." Emma had to slip around him, Nick already ripping open one bag and rolling the excess burlap down to expose the beans. Stacks of cardboard boxes stood in the way, but she spotted a metal cylinder. Emma squirmed around two shelves and reached for the canister shoved against machinery covered in a tarp.

"So…what do you like?"

Emma's fingers scraped straight down the can, and she looked back to the man exertion-sweating from carrying three hundred pounds worth of coffee beans like they were pillows. *Don't say gruff café owners.* "In?" she asked.

"Cooking. You said something about desserts but also veggies and…"

"Ah." She was silly for thinking he'd want to know what she found attractive. "I prefer to work in chocolate. In my intern days, I got to help make chocolate sculptures for fancy hotels and weddings. There were so many swans."

"Because marriage is just like a large, angry bird that can break a man's arm. Well, come to think of it…"

Emma put on a smile at the familiar dismissal. She knew she couldn't make elaborate chocolate sculptures all the time, but most people…most men found it completely worthless.

"Did you find the can?"

"Yes. Sorry. Working on it right now." She got a hold on the handle and tugged the quarter-filled canister forward. Except a rivet must have snagged on the tarp, as it yanked off whatever it was protecting. "Oh my goodness. Is this a…?" A commercial oven and smaller deep fryer sat against the wall, both as pristine as the day they were made.

"Hm?"

Emma jumped as Nick's head, then the rest of him appeared in the narrow gap between shelves. He had to stand in an awkward position to fit, his stomach sucked in and one leg on the shelf. He looked to her hands, then slowly trailed the fallen tarp up to the hidden bakery. "Oh. Those."

"This is a nice oven." Not as big as the one she'd used back in Portland, but surprising for a small café that seemed to only sell hot drinks. Instinctively, Emma pulled on the oven's door handle. It didn't plummet but slowly descended. She shivered at the idea of baking in a near virginal oven. "Does it work?"

"It should. I think the gas is still hooked up 'cause getting it capped would have cost more."

"It's beautiful. I can't believe you aren't using it."

Her glee faded as she realized there'd been a note of dread in his tone. Nick wasn't looking at the oven like a long-lost treasure but with a wary eye. Slowly, she closed the door and pulled the tarp off the bolt that'd caught it.

"The original plan was to do food in-house. My partner…" Nick winced and ducked away. "Thought of it."

"Your business partner was the baker?"

"Eh. I wouldn't go that far. But that didn't work out, so I tried bringing in food."

Emma frowned thinking back to her frostbitten donut. While it was edible, she couldn't imagine trying to sell that while there was a perfect fryer right here. "You know, I could… I'd be more than happy to make something for the café. Donuts, or pastries. Cake pops, people love those."

He shook his head hard as if he wanted to wash his hands of the whole thing. "I don't think that's a good idea. People are used to what's on the menu. Best to not."

"Oh…" She hid her disappointment and put on a smile. "Of course."

"Here." Nick picked up the canister and slipped out through the gap. After giving one last pat to the oven, Emma tossed the tarp over the potential of fresh pastries and donuts.

The sound of the can dragging across the floor was followed by a sifting tumble of beans. Emma eased through the gap to find Nick dropping a bucket into the giant bag of new beans to transfer them into the can. "You know, this part's…I was gonna say easy. Okay, it's easy but tedious. You can go do whatever. Do you need a break? That's a thing people do. Take breaks."

He had both his sleeves rolled up, revealing the veins on his forearms sweeping around the rising muscles. The hot burn of his blue eyes landed on her and Emma scrambled. "It'll go faster if I help." She found a giant measuring cup and used that to scoop up the beans.

At first, they scooped and dumped in silence, only the assuring shush-shush of falling coffee beans filling the air. "Since you're gonna be staying the week, I should probably do the paperwork. Don't want the government coming after you."

"Right. Yes. That's a good point."

"And I'm realizing I don't even know your name. The full one. For the paperwork and all."

"Emma Belmont."

Nick grinned. "That's a pretty name."

"I think my family paid to get a crest in Scotland once," she said out of hand.

"I'm Nick Iverson, though you probably figured that out."

His gruff cheeks burnt as red as an embarrassed school boy's, and she snickered. The beans were running low. Emma reached deep into the bag—filling her smaller cup—just as Nick plunged his bucket in. Their arms bumped and she dropped her scoop. Surprised, she found Nick had bent closer to reach the bottom. She couldn't look away from the distinguished nose with a bump on the bridge, the lines of life crinkled beside his eyes, and the tiny dimple in the middle of his wide chin. It wasn't until he blinked that she realized she'd been staring into his eyes, the blue irises fracturing into a green-gray around the pupil.

The bag shifted under her, nearly tossing Emma onto her back. Nick rose and hefted the beans into the air. "It's easier to pour the last bit out." He did just that, creating a caffeinated cascade while she tried to make herself busy. That was always the best distraction.

"Does the other sack go in there too?" she asked, spotting the two medium roasts he'd brought in himself.

"There's a bigger can for those here," Nick said, slapping a trashcan-sized canister beside himself. Perfect. Emma worked her way around behind the large sack, stooped down, and wrapped her arms around it. Putting all her strength into it, she stood up as fast as possible. The bag jerked, but she fought it off and was able to get it into her hands.

She smiled at Nick. He grinned in response, and she took a careful step closer. The beans shuffled in her arms, the tumbling sound increasing. Emma's toe knocked into a wayward bean. She kept going, only to kick more. Nick's smile dropped and he waved his hands.

"Stop!"

"What is…?" She tried to look down even with the giant bag in the way when a dozen small beads bounced against her foot. *Oh, those aren't beads.*

"The damn thing's ripped!" Nick leaped for her, arms outstretched to take the bag, just as the bottom gave out. Slippery coffee beans gushed across the floor. Emma dropped the bag far too late and tried to flee onto a rising ocean of beans. They cracked and popped under her feet, rolling her ankles. She realized she was falling just as the shelf went rushing past. Emma reached out to catch it and herself, but something else beat her to it.

An immovable force pressed against her back, hauling her back to her feet. She tried to steady herself and found it was Nick's hand holding her safe. The two breathed a sigh of relief, which pressed her chest into his. Somehow, she'd slipped her leg in-between his, her thigh nearly brushing against his crotch. Emma tried to not think about the weight of what was almost caressing her leg when Nick's hand dropped lower.

She gazed up at him, unable to escape the hard press rising over her leg. Nick bent closer and their fight against gravity failed. He cried out a shortened "Fu—" before falling to his back and taking Emma with. She landed on top of him, his head smacking the floor.

"Are you okay?" she cried out, terrified he'd suffered brain damage.

"Just...peachy. My ego on the other hand." Nick moved as if to sit up when he suddenly jerked and laid back down. "Back's not happy either. How about you?"

Emma placed her hands astride his shoulders and found her knees had straddled him too. The coffee beans cracked like bubble wrap, but the little buggers were still slippery. Her palm skidded, causing her cheek to fall to his chest. "This is going well," she said, laughing at herself until fingers toyed with her ponytail and scooped down her neck.

Blinking, she looked up into Nick's face to find the gruff scowl replaced by a tender smile. "I could think of worse ways to hurt myself." His hand slipped down her back, pressing her tighter instead of away. Emma tipped her head, her eyes closing in anticipation.

"I'm back, so you can stop..."

Both adults panicked at the loud shout of a teenager. Emma flung away, skidding on the floor. She managed to wedge herself in the gap. Nick scrambled on the beans, groaning hard and clutching his back. All the while, Skylar watched. "You seem to be having fun. Maybe I should come back later."

"Ha." Nick managed to hook a hand to the canister and hoisted himself up. "One of the damn bags ripped, again. If you'd been here..."

"I could have stopped Rob from using cheap sacks?

I'm more powerful than I thought."

Nick groaned, first from Skylar, then as he rubbed his back. "There's beans everywhere. Clean them up."

"Can't." Skylar held up her phone. "It's six. You know what that means."

"Damn it. We'll clean this up in the morning. Here." Nick extended a hand to Emma. She wasn't certain if she should take it with the way Skylar was watching, but refusing would make it look so much worse. Emma placed her fingers in Nick's palm but used the shelf to guide herself out of the coffee bean avalanche. She didn't need to fall a second time.

"What about dinner? I'm starving," Skylar whined.

"When aren't you a bottomless pit?" Nick wiped off his hands, then looked at his niece. "Did you find a dress?"

"Yes."

"Can I see it?"

"No."

Emma left the two of them to bicker over a rite of passage as she checked her phone. All of her messages about renting the cheapest places in town went unanswered. The motel was full. There was a fancy hotel with vacancies but the rooms started at two-fifty and only got worse from there. What was she going to do?

"Cream and sugar?"

She shook out of her funk to find Nick gazing at her. When she glanced at him, he smiled. "What do you want on your pizza?"

CHAPTER ELEVEN

EVEN AFTER A second night on the couch, Nick felt more refreshed than he had in weeks. If he wasn't tone-deaf, he'd have whistled a happy tune while scooping the scattered coffee beans into the trash. At least most of the bag was salvageable. He left the girls in charge of the front while he cleaned up the mess. The bad thing about beans was their tendency to roll. A pile of them had made it clear under the shelves, which he fished out until the broom struck cardboard.

That damn box. Dropping to his knees, he hefted the shelf up and slid the box out. It'd once been white but dust had turned it a muddled gray. Strange, he couldn't remember it at all. Nick tried to lift off the top, but it stayed stuck. Even shaking the box didn't free it. He hooked a finger into the gap and started to wedge the lid away.

"Oh, Uncle Nick!"

That wasn't good. Skylar only used that sing-song voice when she was facing a suspension or worse.

Leaving the box on the floor, Nick stood up and called, "What?"

"Your adoring public is waiting for you."

"My...?" He wiped the crushed coffee grounds off of his hands while walking through the door and nearly stumbled back. Bright lights blazed from every inch of the café. It took him a second to realize that was because someone had replaced the bulb in the dark corner he kept meaning to get to for...a year. An uptempo jazz version of Sleigh Ride played under the sound of gushing steam and happy customer chatter. He looked to the source of the change and found Emma with one hand on the counter. The rest of her body was strained as she placed a piece of pink chalk to the menu board.

She'd erased his threat to not ask for the mistletoe latte and changed it to 'Please ask about the holly latte and the praline mocha.' Her lettering was gentle and looped in a cute cursive. She ended her addition with a simple drawing of a cup of coffee and a sprig of holly.

When Emma dropped back to her feet, her ponytail swung in a circle. Cheerfully, she greeted the next customer while Nick stared in awe. Even at five in the morning, Emma was a million bucks in a form-fitting red sweater. She belonged in an upscale coffee shop while he looked like a trapper that wandered in out of the Yukon.

At least he put on deodorant. *I did, right?* Before Nick

could even do a half-sniff, Emma finished with her customer and turned right to him. The way her eyes gleamed under the full lights pulled him back to the night before. They'd wound up on the couch again, Skylar stomping up to her room to complain about the jacket he said she'd have to wear over her dress. Sitting right next to him, Emma's eyes had sparkled and her lips all but begged for a kiss.

"What are you doing?" Skylar practically shouted. Nick didn't leap, but he clasped a palm over his ear to still the ringing. "He's over here."

"Who is?" Nick knew he asked the wrong question the second he spotted the stylish coat and scarf combo.

"Good morning, Mr. Iverson. I'm with Foodie Gems. We're a growing podcast of—"

"No, thank you."

The instant dismissal threw the man. His eyes widened like one of those old cat clocks, the pupils darting back and forth from Nick to Skylar. "We're a media empire devoted to..."

"Don't care. If you're here about the mistletoe latte..." He paused, watching the man nod expectantly and reach for his phone. "We don't have any. Either order the things on the board or get out." Nick waved to the menu, forced on a gritted smile, and walked away.

"But your niece—" the man exclaimed.

"Is not in charge. No matter what she says. Order or get out."

The podcaster gulped, all the color draining from his monologue. "Ah, yes, the praline mocha sounds most interesting."

Nick left him in Emma's care and caught said niece typing on her phone. "Why did you do that?"

"Help you get free advertising? Can't imagine why I'd think that would be helpful." She rolled her eyes and returned to her screen. He wanted to yank the damn thing away.

"All this mistletoe mess was finally slowing down."

"About that." Skylar swung her phone around to reveal a new article from that same Miss B. Nick skimmed quickly, his heart dropping with each word. Whoever it was leaned heavily into the damn legend, even interviewing people who claimed to have found their one true love after drinking his cursed brew.

"Wait. If she's talking to the locals, does that mean she's here?"

"There's this thing called the internet. People use it to communicate instead of the tin cans on strings from your day."

Nick glared at his niece trying to be cute. He noted Miss B's promise to suss out the ingredients in the mistletoe latte. *Over my dead body.* This woman was going to give him an aneurysm.

The bell jangled and he frowned deeper. Assuming the customers didn't give him a heart attack first. "Great. It's the snob," he muttered to himself. The kid that had peppered him with questions and demanded he not burn the coffee beans strode in. Nick was happy to leave him to Emma's tender touch when he noticed that Skylar's texting had stopped. She turned redder than a baboon's ass while staring at…

"No. Oh, hell no."

"What?" Skylar squeaked. The snob glanced over at the sound, and she yelped, hiding behind her phone. Nick fumed harder.

"Skylar?" The thick Italian accent floundered to the floor as the boy slipped out of line. "The girl that grinds the beans."

Was that some kind of euphemism? Nick glared at his niece who only had eyes for the boy.

"H-h-hi, Antonio."

"And you are...?" He focused away from Skylar to Nick and stuck out his hand.

Crossing his arms, Nick raised his chin. It unnerved him that the snot-nosed brat was nearly as tall as he was. What were they feeding kids? "I'm the slack-jawed American that can't roast properly."

"Ha. Of course, that is all Americans. You don't understand *un caffè*."

Nick's ancient years spent in the Marines came railing back as he stared at this anti-American jackass. "I'm also Skylar's uncle." There was no reason to snap this toothpick in half to teach him a lesson. He looked like the wind would do him in.

"Ah, yes, I can see the resemblance," the kid said.

Skylar full-palm slapped Nick on the arm. "Thanks!" she snarled at him before turning to Antonio. "You, uh, do you like coffee?"

Dear lord, that's her opener? Nick knew he had nothing to fear, when the damn Italian reached over and whispered near her cheek, "I love it."

Jail time be damned. Nick cracked his knuckles and calculated how quickly he could yank the snob off of his feet by his collar.

"I have a long-pull espresso to go." Emma's announcement pulled the kid away before Nick did anything stupid. He took his coffee with a jolly smile, pried off the lid, and sniffed it. After that passed his basset-hound test he took a little sip. Nick caught the tiny wince, but the kid looked to Skylar and gave her a big thumbs up before walking out the door.

He didn't even let her finish sighing before putting his foot down. "No. That whole…thing is not happening."

"You can't tell me what to do," she argued back.

"Like hell I can't. That kid's what? Sixteen?"

In a tiny voice, Skylar said, "Seventeen."

"That's almost eighteen. That's an adult."

"No, it isn't. It's not even four years difference." Skylar stomped off, slamming her foot down with each step.

"You are not…" Nick began chasing after her when Skylar turned her back to him. Every damn alarm bell was clanging hard. He grabbed her arm and spun her around to face him. "You are fourteen years old. That is way too young to date guys that drink espresso."

"God! Stop it!" She flung him off and ran to the office, scooping up her backpack.

Nick followed, trying to think of a dozen reasons why a kid that could be a senior was bad news for messing around with a freshman. But Skylar dashed for the backdoor. Just before she ran into the parking lot, she shouted at him in tears, "Why do you keep trying to ruin my life?"

He took a step to chase after, and his shoe hit a bean. It cracked and sent him skidding, allowing Skylar to flee. By the time Nick reoriented himself without falling on his face, she was gone. *Damn it.* She was too hopped up on hormones to see the dangers that he, a once seventeen-year-old boy, knew were coming. Scowling, Nick pulled out his phone and started to text his niece.

He's trouble. He'll use you. He won't care if he breaks your heart.

* * *

Skylar would ignore every sentence. Erasing them all, Nick typed, "You better be going to school," and pressed send. She left him on read.

EMMA ADDED A drizzle of dark chocolate over the praline mocha and passed it over. The customer's eyes lit up as she twisted the cup around and took a quick pic. Her 'thank you' was quickly silenced by a drink.

The storage room door flung open and Nick stepped out. He'd been in the back cleaning for over an hour since Skylar ran off. Luckily, there hadn't been any major misadventures for Emma, but she grew worried as the line stretched to the door.

"Getting busy?" he asked, the bags under his eyes more pronounced. Nick pinched the bridge of his nose and shook his head as if to scatter whatever was bothering him. Instead of a comforting smile, he wore an off-putting grimace. All the better to terrify the indecisive customers with.

When he barreled to the cash register, Emma dropped her fingers to his arm. "I can deal with the ML lot if you'd like."

"The ML…? Oh." He snorted once at figuring out her code but shrugged away her offer. "It's okay. I've dealt with them before. I can handle them now."

It didn't take Sherlock Holmes to figure out he didn't approve of his young niece's fondness for a teenage boy. Having once been a love-struck fourteen-year-old herself, Emma understood all too well the dramatic pain of crushing on the cute, impossible boy in class. But she'd also been the naive nineteen-year-old told by men ten and twenty years older than her how she was mature for her age. It was everything she'd wanted to hear, and they'd used it to walk all over her. Of course, nothing said Antonio acted like that. He could be a total sweetheart.

"What do you want?" Nick barked at the next customer, who slapped a wizened hand to her chest. She looked prepared to launch a 'well, I never' but he stampeded over it. "If you don't know, step aside for someone who does."

"An Americano. Please."

Emma dashed to the espresso maker to start the drink at the same time Nick ambled over. Both reached for the same cup. Her thumb caught through the handle first, and she couldn't get it out. Nick kept staring, causing her blush to rise. Pulling again caused Nick's hand and the rest of him to lean closer. The thick scent of coffee was eclipsed by sandalwood and Emma melted.

"I can let you do it," she said, uncertain how to get herself out without losing a thumb.

He breathed in, the lights glinting off of his peppery scruff. Nick sighed and released the cup. "Go ahead. You know what you're doing."

She placed the mug under the drip. Scrolling through the menu buttons, Emma said softly, "Only because I had a good teacher."

"Ha. You have any idea how many times I burned my arm figuring that thing out?" He raised his forearm as if to show off the scars, but the buffalo check flannel hid away his skin. Rummaging a hand through his hair, Nick turned away. "I bet you think I'm an ogre. Or whatever horrible thing Skylar's called me."

Steam burst from the machine and Emma watched the last drops of the espresso hit the cup. Picking it up, she walked over to the counter and dropped it onto a waiting saucer. After the woman took her coffee with a sour look, Emma said out of the corner of her mouth, "I think you're doing the best you can."

"Chasing customers away, terrorizing the foodie community…whatever the hell that is."

"I can't blame you there. We didn't have a service where an influencer wouldn't come in and demand free food for exposure."

Nick sputtered a laugh. "If I didn't know any better, I'd say you don't much care for them."

Oh, dear. Emma's cheeks burned and she scratched her ear. "I'm capable of disliking people. On occasion."

"Yeah?" Nick dropped an elbow to the counter and placed his chin in his hand. "What about now?"

God save her, in that pose all she could see was a gruff cowboy flirting with the barmaid before he won a duel at high noon. To taste that pouty, taunting lip, run her hands through his salt and blond hair, feel the rush of his peppery scruff against her thighs…

"What was the question?" Emma stuttered, burning up inside her sweater. She tugged on the neckline, hoping to cool herself off, but the apron fought back.

Nick laughed and waggled a finger at her. "You're too nice for your own good."

All of her old teachers reared back at her at once. *You're too weak, too tenderhearted. You'll never make it as a chef if you don't toughen up.* None of them believed in her. Emma had been certain she'd find her inner strength and prove them all wrong. In less than a year, she went from working up the ladder to abandoning her dream. She was the one who couldn't harden her skin and tough it out long enough to become head dessert chef.

Ducking her eyes, Emma slunk back to the machine and fulfilled the orders as they came in. It was easier for her body to slip into auto mode while she kept silent. It was the only way to keep the tears at bay.

Addy's mother appeared, flirting even harder than before while Emma made her coffee. Tossing her blonde hair back like a fighter enticing a bull, she said, "The divorce is going to be finalized soon, and I can't decide how to celebrate." The air thickened with tension, demanding Nick respond to cut it.

He took the cup from Emma and capped it. "Wine and a fire?" he said.

She brightened at the suggestion. "Sounds romantic."

"I was thinking more cathartic. I guess the size of the fire depends on how much of his shit is still at your house." Nick reached over to pick up a bar towel when a cart loaded with boxes labeled for canned green beans rolled in through the door. Instead of shouting, he smiled and waved to Emma. "Hey, this one's for you."

Confused, she walked around the corner as the younger man in a red polo stopped at the counter. "Got your order here. Ten bags of flour, sugar, baking soda, baking powder, a bunch of spices, and a five-gallon jug of fry oil."

"Oh my goodness!" Emma clasped her hands in shock, then she peeked at the pile of baking goods. "But you said...?"

Nick finished signing the bill. "I thought it over, and you're right. Seems stupid to leave that oven sitting idle when it could be put to better use. May as well do something with them."

Tears sprang in her eyes. Luckily, Emma was able to blink them away before ruining her mascara as she hefted the box into her arms. Nick reached over. "Do you need any help?"

"Nope! Oh, what should I make? Can I bake now? Or should I save it for tomorrow?"

He laughed and waved her on. "Go ahead. I can deal with this riffraff. Hi, Sam."

"Hi!"

"As for what to make..."

Emma froze, her back against the door, her arms bulging with possibilities.

With a smile, Nick said, "Follow your heart."

CHAPTER TWELVE

THE LUNCH RUSH was dying down when the back door opened. He smelled it first, a heavenly temptation of sugar spiraling in the air. It drew every head in the café. Some staggered to their feet. Nick half expected a few to float like cartoon characters when Emma emerged with a tray.

"What is that?" Sam asked, his life's work to catalog every potential crime in the county abandoned.

Her cheeks pinked and she hefted the wide tray higher. Poor thing looked about to buckle so Nick swept over to help. He got a hand under while Emma said, "They're nothing special, just cake donuts. There wasn't time to let the yeast rise so I tried for these."

Nick's fingers glanced against hers as he took the weight of the tray, and she looked over at him. A spot of white had stuck to her cheek. "You've got a bit of…" He moved to help wipe it away, forgetting the pile of donuts in his care.

Thank god she had enough sense and caught the tipping tray before all her hard work wound up on the floor.

"Christ, man, you nearly gave me a heart attack," Sam said as he reached over to take a donut.

"These are the cinnamon sugar ones, and those I glazed." She sounded so proud even Nick felt a smile tugging on his lips.

Without pause, Sam snatched up a glazed one and bit down. His eyes rolled back and he sunk into his chair. "I've never had anything so good, especially here."

"Hey." Nick reached over and caught Sam's hand before he could snatch up a second. "You've got to pay for it."

Sam blinked slowly and stared behind Nick. "I don't see them on the menu, which means I don't have to pay. Them's the rules."

"No, it…" Nick realized he was losing this argument fast as the horde abandoned their drinks to pick out a donut. A good two dozen quickly whittled down to nothing but crumbs. "You can only take one."

"First one's free, eh? Gotta get 'em hooked so they keep coming back for more," Sam jibbed even while reaching for a second. At Nick's withering glare, he had enough sense to drop back and fiddle with the knobs on his scanner. Though he kept staring forlornly at the tray.

The café filled with the sound of happy chewing,

every corner echoing with pleased comments. "I can't believe this," Nick said in shock. "You shut them all up."

Emma snickered. "That hadn't been the plan, but maybe next time I'll make a peanut butter and jelly donut."

He laughed at the idea of the ML twerps all struggling to unstick peanut butter off the roofs of their mouths. Emma slipped the lighter tray to one hand and picked up the last cinnamon sugar donut. "You should try one. See if it was worth the investment."

Nick already knew it was by the greedy eyes hunting for more. But he was curious, and his stomach growled in hunger. With a smile, he accepted the donut and was about to bite in. Emma placed the empty tray on the counter, only crumbs remaining. "Here." Nick broke the donut in half and passed her the left side. "So we can both try one."

She laughed and took the half. Gently, she nibbled a small end, her red lips pressing into the sugary crust. Nick gulped, so enthralled with the cinnamon sugar coating her mouth he forgot about his donut. When Emma darted her tongue out to lick away the sugar, he stuffed the donut in his mouth to keep from doing anything stupid.

God. How did he forget how amazing fresh donuts were? The spongy cake crumbled with the cinnamon and sugar, all of it slipping down his throat. He lost himself in the surprise flavor lurking below. "Is there nutmeg in here?"

"I saw some on a shelf. Is that okay?"

"It's brilliant. And good. Very good. Think you could make them for tomorrow? Once I add it to the menu." His comment only caused Sam to hunch closer to his scanner.

Emma nodded. "Yeah, no problem. Maybe I could do pastries as well, if I make the dough tonight." She rocked back and forth on her heels, causing the light to catch on the white spot.

Without thought, Nick placed his thumb over the spot, and her big brown eyes gazed up at him. The warmth of her skin danced up his, causing the whole of his spine to tingle. It was like plucking a sweater out of the dryer but in a good way. Slowly, he brushed his thumb over the apple of her cheek. It rounded as she smiled. Her lips glistened with a sprinkling of sugar like diamonds.

"You…" The bell jangled, and a cacophony of young voices bounced around the café. Nick dropped his hand, revealing her cheek was wiped clean. "You had a bit of flour."

"Oh." Emma cupped her palm over where he'd touched her. "Thank you. I should check on the next batch." Blushing, she picked up the tray and slipped into the back room.

"Yeah, you…next batch?"

Before he could even ask, the Junior League of Explorers not in any way associated with the Boy Scouts stampeded to the counter. "What'll it…? Oh. Nope. No, thank you."

"Mister. We're selling these beautiful Christmas trees," the head boy who barely fit into the hunter green shorts spoke up. He waved a hand to the kid behind him and, like clockwork, a four-foot pine tree was pulled through the front door and passed hand to hand.

When it landed, the sap-covered trunk slammed to the once-clean floor and Nick shook his head. "Don't need one."

"And I couldn't help but notice your place of business is without a real tree." The kid kept going through his spiel without listening to a word Nick said.

"I quite like it that way. Last thing people want to deal with are needles falling into their coffee. Get it out of here."

"But we carried it all the way here, through the snow."

There was at most a quarter-inch of slush on the sidewalk. Nick steadied his shoulders for a long fight when Emma appeared, and the Explorers went wild. Tiny hands already covered in pine goo and who knew what else lunged for the donuts. Nick stepped in the way. "Those are for customers. And seeing as how you're here to exploit me…"

"Is that a Christmas tree? It's adorable."

Oh, no. Emma placed the tray of donuts on the counter, still in range of the children who could somehow reach eight feet when they weren't supposed to. Her eyes glistened like new-fallen snow and her cheeks ruddied like a bowl full of cherries as she gazed in wonder at the tiny, shedding tree.

"Yes, it is, ma'am." The leader found his opening quicker than a prisoner with a shank. He sidled up to Emma and raised the pathetic tree. "Our troop is selling it for poor children who might not have a merry Christmas."

"Uh-huh, and what's the charity exactly?" Nick asked.

"The League of Explorers charity fund," the kid came back with. Meaning all the money would go into buying them spray paint cans and Swiss army knives.

He rolled his eyes, ready to hustle the kids out. But when Emma cupped her hand under the branch and drew her fingers back with such a delicate touch, he knew he was screwed. At his look, she pulled away her hand and dropped her gaze. "It would help make the place more festive."

"You don't have anything Christmasy, mister. What do you have against Jesus?" one of the boys with the least badges shouted at him.

"I don't have anything against…it causes a mess. And." There was no winning. Nick let himself get walked into a trap. With a resigned sigh, he went to the cash register and opened it. "How much for the tree?"

All business, the head boy slapped his hands to the counter. "Forty-five."

"Dollars? I can get an eight-footer for that down at the hardware store."

"But do they hand-deliver?" he offered, earning him a slow glare. "It's for charity, mister."

"Fine. For charity. But I'm going to need a receipt."

"Not a problem," the boy called as he pocketed the money then whistled for the others to haul up the tree. He jotted down the gist on a scrap of paper with a grocery store coupon on the back.

Nick didn't care. He was too busy watching Emma excitedly carry the tree to the unpainted corner. She nearly danced in place, fussing over the branches to make it look as perfect as possible. He knew he'd pay a lot more than forty-five bucks to see her smile like that.

"Hey, mister. How much for the donut?" The boy flush with cash stared at the tantalizing treats.

Snickering, Nick beckoned them all closer. "Forty-five dollars for a dozen."

* * *

WHAT WAS SHE going to do with the tree?

Emma didn't mean to adopt the little Christmas tree. She just found it adorable. Now it leaned against the wall, needing a stand to keep it upright. Nick finished with the boys that had brought it in and joined her by the tree.

"What now?" she asked, slipping the needles through her fingers. This one was soft, and waxy, and smelled like a winter forest.

"You decorate it, I guess," he summed up, leaving her adrift.

They both heard the back room door swing open and looked to find Skylar. She caught the donuts first and snatched up two.

"It's not even one o'clock. What are you doing out of school?" Nick chastised her.

She rolled her eyes and crammed her cheeks with donuts. "Half day," she said, took a big swallow, and finished. "Like I already told you."

"Uh-huh, and you're not skipping school out of some misplaced rebellion."

"Right, 'cause the cool thing to do is skip school in order to clean up coffee shits in the bathroom. I could leave if you like. Seems as if you've got everything in hand. Or should I say hole?" Skylar lifted a third donut and peered through it with just her eye.

Nick groaned and swiped the donut away. "That's for customers, thanks to Emma."

"Well, you sure as shit didn't make them," Skylar said. She glanced over to Emma who was trying to slip out of the conversation. For a moment, Skylar nodded as if in gratitude when she jabbed a thumb at her. "Why is there a tree?"

Her uncle shrugged and moved to clean the espresso machine. Skylar laughed and slapped her palm on the counter. "Holy—"

"Skylar…"

"Poop."

Nick groaned at the swearing swerve. Entertained, Skylar popped a hand to her hip. "She got you to get a Christmas tree? Really?"

"He bought it for charity," Emma chimed in, growing more uncomfortable being the subject of the niece and uncle discussion.

Skylar snorted. "Sure he did."

"Do you know how to get it decorated? Or standing?" Emma asked, trying to deflect from the teenager's knowing smirk.

"Yeah, there's a box in the back. Or am I, a fourteen-year-old—a mere child in this big, scary world—allowed to go into the office to look?"

Nick crossed his arms, uncrossed them, and sighed. "For the love of… Can you just...? Help her, okay?"

Skylar jerked her head at him then beckoned Emma over. Before joining her, she watched Nick grumble but resume his cleaning. The poor tree needed all the help it could get before those needles turned brown. Holding the door open, Skylar pulled Emma into the back room, then took the lead.

She hadn't spent much time in the back office, only a quick lunch, and filling out the official paperwork. Emma tried to not look too interested in the handful of picture frames across the desk she doubted Nick used. Skylar opened a closet, then tugged on a cord dangling from the ceiling. A small ladder plunged down.

"There's a mess of stuff scattered around here." She clomped up, not bothering to take a flashlight. "I still can't believe you got him to buy a tree. He hates Christmas." A cardboard box slipped down the ladder. Emma raced to catch it and was surprised at the weight. The bottom sagged, and she had to scoop her hands under to keep whatever was inside from breaking free.

"Is it the customers?" she asked, placing the box on the ground.

Another followed, this one a plastic tote with what looked like papers and garland inside.

"Customers. Music. Joy. We celebrate at home, but here it's holiday non grata, ya know." Skylar appeared down the ladder and dusted her hands off. "Can you help me get this back up?"

"Sure." Together, they folded up the ladder and shoved it as hard as possible. It rose into the ceiling and both of them dashed away. Luckily, it didn't fall again.

Skylar laughed at their good fortune and bent over to pick up the lighter box. "There's more around in the storage room. Any box not labeled 'coffee shop junk' is probably decorations."

Staring at the hefty box, Emma closed her eyes. How thin of ice did she accidentally walk on? "Should I try to give the tree back? If he hates Christmas…"

"He doesn't hate Christmas, he hates… a lot of things. But it's good for him. Isn't that what this time of year is about? Ghosts scaring the shit out of you until you appreciate the season. Or whatever that ancient movie was going on about."

Emma pursed her lips at the idea of the Christmas Carol being ancient. She used to read the book every December, usually under the covers while her sister made spooky noises to scare her. A little bit of Christmas cheer would help the café's business as well. Putting people in mind of jack frost nipping at their

nose had to sell more coffee. It made sense to her, and —
with Skylar's blessing — she decided to keep going. With
the heavy box secure in her hands, Emma followed after
Skylar out of the office, when the girl suddenly stuck
her head back in.

"Just don't mention Rachel."

"Who?"

"Exactly," Skylar didn't explain. "Hey, Uncle
Scrooge, we found the decorations."

Emma couldn't make out Nick's response, only a
good-natured grumbling. Skylar was able to get to the
café floor faster without the heavier box. What weighed
down Emma more was the question of who Rachel was
and why Nick didn't want to hear about her?

After discovering the old stand in Emma's box, it
didn't take the girls long to get the Christmas tree
upright. Skylar found a string of lights that half worked.
She tossed the whole ball onto the branches which
caused Nick to grumble and yank them off. With the
lights in hand, he vanished to the back office, leaving
the two of them to dig through the big box.

"I believe I've hit the garland mother lode," Emma
said. She tugged out the silver and red tinsel like a
magician pulling the scarf trick. The garland kept
coming and coming, so she twisted in a circle, winding
it around her body. Skylar dropped the clothespin
reindeer she'd found and rushed over.

Just as the end finally plopped out of the box, Skylar
lifted a metal star from the staging bench and placed it
on Emma's head. "All done."

"I see you two are having fun." Nick emerged from
the back with an extension cord around one arm and
the lights on the other.

"Come to ruin it?" Skylar shouted back, causing him

to frown.

He raised the lights. "Here. They should work now." The bell jangled and Nick tossed the fixed lights into Skylar's surprised arms. "Finish up without making a mess."

"Aye aye, Captain Salty."

It took a few restarts for Emma and Skylar to untangle the lights then drape them across the branches. Tiny bulbs of white, red, and green twinkled off of the tree illuminating the entire corner. They had to push the tree right up to the window to get them plugged in, which made adding the garland a challenge.

Emma weaved under Skylar, then Skylar would throw the tinsel back. One it was done, both of them stepped back to admire their work. Lights clumped at the bottom where they thought they'd have lots to work with, then grew sparse at the top. The garland didn't so much hang off the branches as twist around them like a ball of yarn tossed at the tree. It wasn't perfect by any stretch, but it was pretty.

"It needs something," Skylar said.

"What else was in the box?" Emma tipped it closer with her finger, and a stack of construction paper plummeted out. At the top were paper snowflakes cut from every color of the rainbow. She began to set them out one by one when she revealed a picture at the top of the stack.

It was a crayon drawing of a tall skinny man in a red coat with twelve stick fingers. A smaller person with pigtails, probably a child, stood beside a tree made out of a kid's handprint. Emma lifted the drawing to put it to the side when a hand caught it.

Nick spun it around and a smile rose. "Hey Skylar,

look at this."

The girl's face turned red, and she jerked away to stare at the wall.

"It's the picture you drew for me. Remember?"

"What are you talking about? That isn't mine." She tried to swipe it away, but Nick dodged.

"Sure it is. Got your artist signature right there. I like the scarecrow in the back myself."

"That's a reindeer," Skylar muttered before she yanked the paper out of his hands.

"That's fine," he said, shaking around the box and revealing even more child's drawings on the bottom. "There's a butt load of your stuff in here."

Besides the drawings of Santa and his elves, a bundle of grade school crafts rolled out. Emma picked up red and green construction paper chains and held them out. "This will look great on the tree."

"No, it wouldn't," Skylar scoffed, before looking over at the branches, then down at her old creations. "Would it?"

"It isn't Christmas without them. What do you think?" Emma glanced away from the tree to Nick. She expected him to still be smugly grinning at finding a way to cut down the teenager. But he wore a doleful smile as he stared at a more detailed drawing of a man in red and green plaid holding a coffee mug the size of his head. The drawing was dated to five years ago.

He carefully folded the picture up and stuck it in his back pocket. "You know what, it's not a proper tree trimming without cocoa."

"We're doing this properly?" Skylar asked in confusion as Nick slipped back to the counter to heat a pan of milk. "Hang on." She tossed the construction garland at the tree, then dashed to the back room. In a few minutes, music rose over the speakers, Sinatra crooning about a White Christmas.

"Now it's proper," Skylar declared.

As the classic songs of Christmas filled the air, Emma dressed the tree in the cute, often lopsided, poorly glued, and googly-eyed crafts that Skylar handed her. They covered the tree in almost no time and started to branch out to the rest of the café. Garlands and popsicle stick stars were perfect to hang off of the windows and the door. When Nick handed out the mugs of cocoa, he caught what they were doing.

Emma paused, worried he'd ask them to stop schmaltzing up his place. But he snickered once, ripped off a long piece of tape, and stuck Skylar's Santa and scarecrow drawing dead center in the middle of the door. Everyone who walked into the café couldn't miss it.

"Nick!" Skylar shouted and hurled the tape at his head.

He ducked and laughed as she tossed a balled-up napkin. "Your adoring public can bask in your masterpiece."

"That's not funny!" she called, giving chase.

"Then why are you laughing?"

"Because I hate you," Skylar cried back even as she kept giggling. She picked up a wad of sugar packets and reached back to hurl them. The only remaining customer stood up, stopping both niece and uncle. He gathered his things slowly, giving the stink eye to them.

Skylar shoved the wadded-up packets back into their holder while Nick busied himself at the counter. Just as the man walked past the tip jar, the soothing rat pack Christmas music pivoted. High-pitched squeals demanding a hula hoop reverberated through the café.

Skylar burst into laughter and tossed another napkin. The customer pulled his coat closed one-handed and stomped out, not that any of them cared.

"What is this trash? Get rid of those damn rodents!" Nick shouted, chasing after her.

"You love them. Can't get enough. Have to listen to the singing mice every Christmas."

"Skylar..."

She rolled her eyes and abandoned her attack. "Fine. I'll skip the CD ahead. Yeah, you heard right. He's so old the café uses a CD player."

It was obvious the last part was yelled at Emma, who busied herself with the decorations. Only the colorful snowflakes remained, the rest of the box empty. She taped the red and green ones to the window, added the yellow just above the bench, then spotted a gaping hole. It was at the top of the window and would be perfect for a blue snowflake with cutout hearts on each side.

Steadying herself, Emma reached to get the snowflake in place, but she was a foot too low. *Curse these short legs.* She looked for a chair to stand on when she remembered the near folly with the bell. "Nick?"

He looked up from his cleaning.

Emma wafted the paper snowflake back and forth. "Would you mind helping me?" She then mimed putting it in place.

"Sure. I mean, no. Yeah, I'll help." He walked over, and she turned to face him to hand him the snowflake. Nick blinked, then he bent down and wrapped his arms around her legs.

Before she knew what was happening, he lifted her into the air. She started to tip but clung a steadying hand around his shoulders as he guided her to the window. "How's this?"

In his arms, it was easy for her to place the snowflake against the glass. She slapped a piece of tape, then two more so it wouldn't fall. Nick kept a protective hand around her hip so the bottom of her ass sat on his forearm. The hard, strong-enough-to-lift-her-into-the-air forearm.

"Good," Emma whispered. *It's so good.* "I think I've got it up."

She didn't know what to expect, maybe for Nick to drop her like he had the sack. It certainly wasn't for him to slide his arm up. His hand caught her side, then turned her around. Her chest pressed against his, and she fell at his command. Nick's fingers tumbled under the back of her sweater, the whole of his palm spreading across her naked skin. She stared first down, then up into his eyes, barely noticing when her feet hit the ground. All her attention was on the warm hand caressing her back and her palms winding their way across his shoulders.

When Emma's fingers met at the nape of his neck, Nick brushed her cheek and raised her head. The moment her eyes slipped closed, his lips touched hers. Gently, he swirled the heat of his body across her mouth. Nick ran his fingers under the hollow of her jaw, and he tipped his head. The kiss deepened from a stolen moment under the mistletoe to something scandalous. Emma parted her lips, and he slipped in his tongue. The richness of the hot cocoa lasted only a second as the taste of him, rough and tender at the same time, filled her. A tingle zipped from her panting lips down her spine to her core.

She took in a breath, and both stepped back. Nat King Cole asked for chestnuts roasting on an open fire. A thousand thoughts swirled through her mind, but what she wanted most was to ask for another kiss.

"I found this other box—"

The two adults shoved off of each other, Emma banging her heel on the window. Nick almost smashed into the tree, but he rounded fast and started to jog towards Skylar. "You did what?"

"It was in the storage room, and I thought..." She placed the beat-up white box on the counter then looked up. In the window's reflection, Emma spotted how pink her cheeks had turned. She tried to cover them over with her hand, but the longer the girl stared from her to Nick, the worse it got. "What were you two doing?"

"What'd you find?" Nick asked fast.

What were they doing? It was a good question. One that Emma should be mulling over instead of if it could happen again.

Skylar hunched over to tug on the box's lid. As she did, Nick glanced back at Emma. She gulped in uncertainty until he smiled and ran the tip of his tongue over his lip.

"This was sitting in the room, and I thought we could use..." The lid slipped off the box with a loud whine. Skylar dug in and lifted up an apron like the other café ones, but this was navy blue with a name embroidered on the front.

"Oh, shit," Skylar muttered.

Nick's eyes went wide. With a low growl, he slapped the apron back into the box, then slammed the lid on top. It didn't close, but he put so much brute force into it, the entire box collapsed. "We've got a business to run. Get the rest of that mess cleaned up, and shut off that god damn music."

With a sneer obliterating his smile, Nick stomped into

the back and silenced Nat King Cole. He didn't once look at his flinching niece or Emma. Not wanting to cause a scene, Emma began to pack up the few boxes as quietly as possible. She didn't have a clue what just happened, but she'd swear the name on the apron was Rachel.

CHAPTER THIRTEEN

HE SHOULDN'T HAVE kept putting it off.

The tips of Nick's fingers burned as he swung the ax. Rather than split the wood, the head of his ax lodged inside the log. Grunting, he tried to shake the barely cut wood off of the blade. While he looked like a right ass whipped the trapped ax around, the log remained stuck. Growing more enraged by the second, Nick slammed both of his frost-bitten fingers into the narrow gap and pulled.

"Come on you stupid, son of a…!"

A crack shot through the frozen air, but it came from his back instead of a split log.

The rage didn't vanish, but it dripped down his spine as he crumpled a fist to his cutting stump and tried to not fall to the ground. He glared at his breath spurting into the air like a vengeful bull. "Oh, god." In his worthless body, it was more like a mad tea kettle.

He managed to slam a fist to his back and wrenched his torso up. Another crack told him he could either stand up again, or he'd broken a rib. Breathing didn't hurt, so it was probably the former.

The light at the back door rose, but he ignored it. Kicking away the obstinate log, Nick grabbed a smaller one.

"You gonna stay out here all night?" Skylar asked.

"We need firewood," was his response before he swung and split the log right down the middle. Nick bent over, but a seizing muscle told him to crouch down instead. After dumping the logs in the pile, he dusted off his hands.

"So your plan is to stay out here and pout until, what, your nose falls off?"

"I'm not pouting." He grunted, swinging the ax. It clipped the side, flinging the firewood until it smashed into the grill. "Fu…" Nick bit his tongue hard to keep the curse down. "I'm fine."

"You spent all of dinner glaring at your mashed potatoes. That's not fine."

"Since when do you look up from your phone to see what I do at dinner?" Nick turned all his venom on the girl because the one he wanted to yell at was long gone. He knew he was being a bear at dinner, and on the drive home, and while cleaning up the café. Didn't mean he could stop feeling like he wanted to maul some campers.

"I don't even know why you kept her shit," Skylar

less than helpfully chimed in.

"You think it's smart to use that word around me?"

She picked up one of the logs and cocked her head. "I'm not made out of wood."

Nick wrenched it out of her hands and placed it on the stump. "I forgot it was there. It was all…a long time ago."

He thought he'd moved on. He did. Five years was way too long to carry a torch for anyone, much less *her*. But the mistletoe latte, Christmas music, and that damn custom apron sent him on a spiral to murdering-logs town. Nick swung the ax, not caring what it hit.

The door opened and a soft voice called out, "Do you need any help?"

Guilt socked him in the gut. He stared at the stars while Skylar shouted to Emma, "We're good. He's just chopping helpless trees for fun."

"Don't…" Nick tried to silence her, but he got a knowing look instead. His niece didn't know as much as she thought she did, but it was enough to make her incredibly annoying.

Though, that was probably true of all teenagers.

"It's getting late, so I was going to turn in," Emma said.

She wanted him to come in. He should talk to her. Sit on the couch and try to awkwardly explain away that stupid kiss that gave him butterflies in his stomach, floating feet, and every other cliché Hallmark sold to people. Nick swung the ax instead.

After a time, Emma said, "Goodnight," and closed the door.

"You can't keep ignoring her. She's sleeping in your bed."

God, he did not need that reminder. That morning

he'd caught Emma slipping out of the bathroom. Not an unusual thing, except she'd been in the shirt he'd given her. The way it swam on her body, how her bare legs were exposed under the low hemline messed with his head all day. That had to be why he acted like an idiot.

One week. Not even that. Her car'd be fixed in five days, and he'd never see her again. Only a damn fool would fall for that...again.

"I'm not ignoring her," Nick said, a bald-faced lie Skylar laughed at. "What do you care, anyway?"

She shrugged. "I like her."

Me too.

Nick eyed her up, certain that wasn't the real reason. "Don't you start up your matchmaker phase again." There wasn't a single woman in town who hadn't had his business card slipped to them by an entrepreneurial eleven-year-old. They'd ranged in age from eighteen to eighty. That was the hardest Nick had ever put his foot down. Skylar needed to stay out of his love life, for both their sakes.

Her eyes twinkled with mischief, and he knew he'd hit the mark.

"Emma is...yes, she's very nice. And sweet."

"You think she's cute," Skylar taunted him.

"But..." *She's leaving soon. She wants to be a fancy chef. We barely know each other. Why can't I stop thinking about her?* "She's way too young for me."

Skylar crossed her arms. In her puffy pink coat, she looked like a pastel Michelin man. "How old is she?"

"Twenty-seven."

"That's no problem. She passes the half plus seven rule."

Confused, Nick zeroed in on his niece. "The what?"

"You know, half your age, then add seven. That's

how young you can date. Everyone knows that."

He'd never heard of it in his life. Nick started to do the math, but Skylar beat him to it first. "You can go as young as twenty-four and a half."

Jesus! He'd overhear the young college kids blathering on about their profiles and bitcoins at the café, and it made Nick feel older than dust. "How come you can't do geometry that fast?"

Skylar smiled wide and shrugged.

Twenty-four...really? No. She had her whole life ahead of her. Lots of time to screw up, start again. A busted-up vet running a coffee shop would only slow her down.

Wait. Half of seventeen plus seven was...? "Fifteen and a half!" Nick shouted.

Skylar frowned and shook her head. "What?"

"That's how young a seventeen-year-old can date. Fifteen and a half by your whatever rule. You're too young for the Ant guy."

Fury erupted across her face. "That isn't the same— It doesn't work that way for boys. Girls mature faster."

Nick sneered at that familiar line he'd heard too much...and used in his stupid youth. Rather than wade into that can of worms, he smugly slotted a log on the stump. "That's your rule, not mine. You're too young for a kid that can grow chest hair."

"Ew!"

Boy was she too young. Nick had hoped she'd stay that way, but if she was already getting knock-kneed around a gangly kid with an accent he didn't have long. Was *that* talk something he should leave to his brother? The thought of Pete having to responsibly explain anything, much less what could lead to him becoming a grandfather, sounded impossible.

Nick's cheeks burned red hot at the thought of having to talk to Skylar about all of that. They'd both jump out of a window to avoid the subject.

"Why are you so mean?" she shouted, shifting back to the young girl he'd watched grow up. Absently, Nick touched his back pocket and the drawing Skylar had made on her first day in the coffee shop. Most of the bad memories had faded from the crayon doodles.

In a fury, she smashed her foot into the frozen ground. Nick winced, certain it had to hurt, but Skylar's rage kept her moving. "Why do you have to ruin everything?"

Dropping the ax to the ground, Nick breathed in the cold air. "Maybe I'm trying to protect you."

"Protect me from what?"

He wrung a hand over his forehead, surprised to find ice instead of sweat. Maybe he had been outside too long. Nick sighed. "From making the same stupid mistakes I and your dad did."

"I'm nothing like you. You're a coldhearted asshole." After her venomous flurry, Skylar ran inside. No doubt she'd be crying big fat tears into her pillow while she told her diary how awful he was.

Nick kicked aside the log at his foot and picked up the box it'd been holding down. They were gonna wear blue and red aprons with yellow embroidery. He'd even had a local artist mock up a logo. It all went to hell before he'd finalized the menu board.

Placing the apron and hat on the stump, Nick raised the ax. Winds that smelled of snow buffeted his face. More of his sweat turned to ice as it stuck to his cheeks. He made his choice long ago and didn't have time to regret it. With one fell swing, Nick sliced apart the hat, then he cut open the apron. More swings, more tears—

that other life he nearly had ripped to nothing but thread and strings in the December wind.

"You're right," Nick said, dropping the ax. "I am."

"WHEN ARE YOU getting here?"

Emma rocked back and forth on her feet, wishing she'd 'accidentally' turned her phone off. "Soon. In a few days."

"Cause if you don't get here soon," her sister said, not listening to a word from Emma, "I'm gonna rent this room out. Where are you?"

"In a little town called Lake Holly. It's near—"

Her sister buzzed it off. "You can afford a week's stay? But you tell me your account's in the red. I'm not running a charity here."

"It's a little complicated. Someone was kind enough to give me a place to sleep."

"So you're not too good to crash on a cot in bumfuck corn country, but you demand a bed from me."

Emma gulped and glanced at her reflection in the mirror. Instead of the polished and professional young woman, a worthless girl covered in pockmarks and acne scars stared back. She hated when she had to take off her makeup, often turning all the lights off and leaping into bed to avoid the mirror.

"I'll be there soon, I promise. Please don't give the room away."

"All right," her sister sighed. "But you better have a job by the time you get here."

"I will," Emma promised despite having no idea how. She was two days' drive away with no way to get there for an interview. Any good restaurant would expect her to at least cook for them. Not that she deserved a good restaurant. It'd just be the same all over again. Men's faces turning red while screaming obscenities, her shrinking deeper into her chef's whites as she struggled to get everything to plate.

She didn't even want to work on the line anymore, but her heart ached from knowing she wasn't good enough to do it. Muttering her goodbyes, Emma ended the call and placed her phone in her bag. Her luggage was clumped up against the dresser. She kept placing her purse on his trunk without thinking.

Another loud thud broke the night. Emma slipped to the window and glanced down at the silhouette raising an ax above his head. He didn't say a word, swinging the blade down with another grunt. When the ax head stuck into the stump, Nick wrung a hand under his chin and up his cheek.

They were softer than they looked. She'd feared it'd be like a bottle brush scrubbing her face, but his scruff only left an invigorating flush to her cheeks. Emma jerked, realizing she'd been tapping her lip with her finger.

It was a mistake. She knew it the second the kiss ended. Well, not right after. Her mind was too busy floating on cotton candy clouds to realize how badly she'd messed up. But his reaction after… Forgetting she'd put it away, Emma picked up her phone. Her latest batch of requests for a room all waited to be answered. It was in her best interest, in everyone's, if she left tomorrow.

Sweeping through the room, she gathered up her clothes. There wasn't much—the pink turtleneck, the reindeer sweater. Her fluffy socks she wore while sleeping. After folding each up, Emma put them in her bag and zipped it shut.

With one last look for her things, her gaze landed on the pillows. She'd never slept so deeply in her life as she had cuddled around them. Maybe it was the size, far bigger than any she'd had back in Portland. Or it could be the density, worn and packed from years of use. *It's probably the scent of his body weaved into them.*

She shivered at the tiny voice jumping straight to the worst option. How was she going to get through tomorrow and the day after? Pretending the kiss didn't happen sounded easy, but if he caught her staring at him like a lovelorn school girl, she'd die on the spot.

A sharp gasp followed by wailing broke through the air. Emma touched her cheeks, fearing she'd broken down without realizing, but they were dry. Another round, then angsty cursing came from down the hall. She poked her head out of the door and, sure enough, heard Skylar screaming that her life was over. It wasn't her place to get involved. They'd be rid of her soon enough.

Emma looked at her bag, remembering she left her toothbrush in the communal bathroom. A hard sharp gulp, like a girl at rock bottom sucking in air, plunged into her heart. Hustling across the cold hall, Emma came upon Skylar's door and gently knocked.

"Go away!" the girl shrieked.

"It's me," she tried, prepared to scatter. To her surprise, the lock pulled back and Skylar stuck her head out. The poor girl's normally bright eyes and cheeks were a mottled red. She swiped at her nose, then grabbed Emma's hand.

"Get in here," she said, tugging her inside and slamming the door.

The posters, the music, and the printed-out quotes were different, but a dagger of nostalgia plunged into Emma. She felt like she'd been dragged back into the soup of hormones that boiled the brains of every fumbling teenager. Skylar slumped into her clamshell chair and slammed her laptop shut. Only a vague purple and blue light radiated from her bed, the rest of the room dark shadows. A woman screamed a heavy metal rage out of the speakers, dampening nearly every sound outside of the room.

"Are you...okay?" Emma asked, uncertain where to begin.

"He's going home for Christmas!" Skylar wailed.

"Antonio?" She asked, though who else but a girl's high school crush could obliterate her to dust?

"Abby just found out. He's returning to Italy, and he's not coming back! The god damn Bensons are getting a Brazilian exchange student for the next semester. It's not fair!"

Ah. It was even worse than Emma feared. Instead of the unobtainable boy failing to notice the girl in love with him, he was going to be snatched from her by a twist of fate. It was the kind of drama that'd seem almost laughable in five or ten years, but in the moment was worse than death.

"Wh-wh-what do I do? He just learned my name and now he's leaving?" In her state, poor Skylar looked as fragile as a china doll. Emma reached out and stroked her head. The girl leaned into it, needing a mother even though none could be found. Telling her it would pass wouldn't help. It'd be as useful as telling someone with a foot in a bear trap to walk it off.

"Have you talked to him?" Emma asked.

Skylar jerked away and Emma pulled her hand back.

With pursed lips, Skylar shook her head hard. "Not yet. I was gonna. I thought he'd see me in my dress at the dance and..." She sucked in her tears and glared at the floor. "I'm a fucking idiot."

"No, you're not." She wanted the princess moment, where the crowd stills and the handsome prince finally realizes the one he's wanted is standing in the spotlight. "You're a brilliant, passionate young lady."

The teenage glare almost sent Emma dashing for the door, but she kept on. "One day, boys will realize that, and then you'll have to beat them off with a stick." Or a certain uncle will chase them with an ax.

"How do I get him to figure it out now? Before it's too late?"

Emma frowned. She could tell the girl to move on to a local boy who was closer in age. But that was the surest way to get her to dig her heels in. "Well, he likes coffee, seems to have an opinion on water temperature, and you know a lot about coffee. Why don't you talk about that?"

"Just walk up to him, say, 'Boy those dark Sumatra blends sure are potent.'"

Emma laughed. "Something like that. Make a joke about Starbucks."

At that Skylar pulled a face. "It tastes like burnt paper."

"There you go. Ask him about Italy, how they celebrate Christmas. Boys love to talk about themselves."

Gruff men on the other hand...

The girl rocked back and forth, tapping a finger on the desk. "That...that's not a bad idea."

Emma stood up. "I'm talented at mediocre ideas and so-so plans." She reached for the doorknob when the girl launched herself around Emma and hugged her tight.

"Thank you, for, uh…" Self-consciousness took over and Skylar dropped her arms. She twiddled with her blonde hair, slapping it against her collar bone. "I'm just glad you're here. He'd only make it worse."

A pain struck through Emma at how easily she dismissed her uncle. "He's trying his best."

"Wow, if that's true, it's really sad."

"I can tell when I'm bested by a quicker wit." She raised her hands in surrender and opened the door. It rattled into a quiet, empty hallway. He was probably still outside chopping down half the forest. Emma slipped out and Skylar followed.

She expected the girl to slam her door and lock it, but she shoved her head out through the gap. "You're good to talk to. I'm happy your car got busted."

Emma appreciated the thought, though the reminder of how stranded she was stuck deep. As Skylar closed the door and the music dipped, Emma floated in the quiet of the house. She still needed her toothbrush from the bathroom. Shaking off the foolish thought that anyone here would even miss her, she reached for the doorknob.

CHAPTER FOURTEEN

THE COLD FINALLY bit through his stubborn armor. Nick shivered against the wind and realized he wasn't going to be able to ignore it anymore. With one final swing, he embedded the ax into the stump and wandered back inside. When the heat struck his fingers, they ached like he'd reached into a fire. Grunting at himself for not putting on gloves, Nick ignored the mess of dirty plates on the table and pots in the sink to trudge up the steps.

Skylar let out a dramatic wail and slammed her door. Nick waited on the second step, wondering if she'd run after him in a screaming fury. After thirty seconds, he risked it. No one was in the hallway.

Whew.

He didn't like to think of himself as a coward, but he did not have the energy to go another round with a lovesick teenager. *What does she even know about love? She's fourteen. She'd been brushing plastic pony hair a few years ago. Now she wants to throw herself off of a cliff because she can't date a boy. When did I get so damn old?*

The door to his bedroom had been left open just a sliver. Was that an invitation? To talk or...

Turning his back, Nick stumbled into the bathroom. He gripped onto the medicine cabinet and glared at the bloodshot eyes of a man who hadn't had a drop of alcohol. "You are a coward," he said and the cabinet started to vibrate. It bounced against the wall from Skylar's music cranked to eleven. The tiny bottles of mouthwash and aftershave jostled on their shelves.

He should tell her to turn it down before she went deaf, but she'd just have some smart-ass remark that cut him to the core. No one told him that one day the cute kid who was easily bamboozled by adult logic would learn to twist a sentence into a scalpel. Nick rifled through the medicine cabinet looking for a razor blade that wasn't covered in rust, but each throb of the angry-teenager beat thumped up his legs. Pain answered in kind. The aches were in his arms from the ax, in his legs from walking twenty miles on linoleum, in his brain from doing battle with Skylar. And in his heart from the deepest wound of all.

The only answer was a hot bath. He flipped on the spigot, letting the porcelain tub fill as he shrugged off his shirt. Hm... He didn't remember so much of his chest hair being blonde, or was it white?

Jesus, he was old. Too old for a teenager's woes, too

old to fight over a damn latte, and too old to be feeling foolish for a twenty-seven-year-old girl. He drew the tips of his fingers over the scar tissue. Men with shrapnel in their gut couldn't get butterflies.

Stripping down, he kicked his jeans to the wall and tossed his socks on top. Steam percolated through the bathroom, beckoning him into the unknown. Nick swiped off the mirror and glared at the weary face in it. Gray hair in his scruff, grit to his skin, and wrinkles that became trenches the longer he stared. He looked ready to be put out to pasture.

Another twinge caught his back, and he abandoned his pity party. After testing with his toe, Nick slipped one foot into the water. The heat lapped up his calf without scalding it, so he added the second leg and slumped down. There was a washcloth somewhere and a bar of soap. He should be scrubbing, then getting to sleep to wake up and face another day of the same.

But as the heat soaked into his bones, his muscles began to unknot. Nick lay the base of his skull on the lip of the tub, and he stretched. A deep crack snapped his spine back into place, and he groaned. It was nearly orgasmic to be free of that pain.

He drew a hand up his thigh, trying to get another knot. As he held onto his hairy leg, he thought of hers instead. She'd nudged her inner thigh against the side of his chest as he'd held her up. It took everything in him to not wrap her legs around him and put her ass right above his cock.

Fuck, that soft curve of her buttocks spreading over his forearm as he held her…

Nick rolled his eyes back and moaned as he gripped the erection popping out of the water. The memory of Emma sliding down his body hit him hard. He tightened the clamp to the base of his cock and thought of her cute breasts gliding down his chest and her round hip pressing into his thigh. The supple skin below her shirt made him flick his thumb over the crown. He'd nearly brushed over her bra band, and the idea caused the inner teenager inside of him to moan.

He raised a leg to dangle off the tub's edge, and jerked his hips, thrusting his cock into his hand. Her lips pressing to his, her mouth parting in an invitation… His wild imagination ran straight to her on her knees, opening her mouth for him.

Nick was so blinded by the thought of Emma's lips and the pounding of his heart, he completely missed the bathroom doorknob turning.

THAT'S STRANGE. EMMA slipped into the bathroom to find the lights on. Though, Skylar may have forgotten to turn them off. On the sink was her pink toothbrush, the bristles turned to face the wall. A larger gray one lay behind, playing the big spoon to hers. She walked closer toward the sink and the tub eclipsed by the towel closet.

Why does it sound like lapping water? Is that the pipes…?
Nick. Naked.
Wet.
And naked.

Head tipped back, his Adam's apple pointing skyward as he parted his lips and gasped. His shoulders glistened from the water that splashed through his virile chest hair. One leg dangled outside the tub, naked toes pressing against the tile. The rim of the porcelain bath pressed into his thigh, the muscles straining as he jerked a hand…

"Oh my gosh!" Emma cried. She slapped a hand to her eyes and tried to spin away.

"What the…?" A great splash erupted from the tub and Emma moved to hide. Her foot slipped on the spilled water, sending her plummeting to her ass.

"Sorry. I'm sorry. I didn't know—"

"I forgot to lock the— What are you—?"

She tried to stand up, but the flurry of emotions sent her plummeting again. Still, she kept her back to him, terrified of what he'd find on her bare face.

"I thought you were outside," Emma tried to explain, her heart thundering.

"I thought you were sleeping," Nick shouted back.

"I'll just…" She dropped to her hands which were far steadier than her feet and started to crawl across the floor. "Leave you to…what you were doing."

Away from the steaming tub, she could get her bearings. Pressing her back to the closet, Emma took in a breath and looked up. The mirror caught Nick with a soaked towel slapped around his waist as he stood in the tub. He clung to the shower curtain above, a jagged vein circling his biceps like a python.

What are you doing?

"Sorry," she called once more, scrambled to her feet, and leaped out of the bathroom. She didn't stop running until she got into the bedroom and locked the door.

Her heart pounded in her chest. She clasped her hands across it, trying to dampen the sound even as she listened. No wet footprints prowled the hallway. No one called out to her or moaned her name. He must have returned to his bath and…

Even knowing she was safe, Emma's heart wouldn't

calm down. Her legs wobbled and, for the second time, her knees hit the ground. She tried to shake away the memory of what happened, tying it up in a box for not polite things. It wasn't going without a fight. The way he'd tugged on his hair. How his lips slipped from a hard snarl to a soft o. The strength of his leg digging into the floor. The hard cock bursting from the water as Nick stroked his thumb against the widening crown.

She scraped her nails across her inner thigh. That strong forearm had cupped her buttocks, the same one bulging as he jerked himself off. Emma rose up on her knees and pulled back the edge of her panties. Her breathing grew erratic, pulling in more air along with the scent of him. The entire steaming bathroom smelled of coffee and the musk of a man. She'd been sleeping in that scent for the past two days.

The thought of him wrapping his hand behind the back of her head and kissing her lips sent her thumb plunging inside. The forearm that'd held her up became hands massaging and slapping her ass. She danced her finger over her clit and began to thrust onto her thumb. He'd bury his face in her neck, then plunge his cock into her as his lips formed that little o.

"Oh…" The orgasm hit hard and fast, steamrolling her. Emma clamped her lips shut, terrified of the sound she'd make as she pitched to the floor. Pressing her trembling clit to keep the ebbing pleasure rolling, she listened to a set of footsteps outside.

They paused just beyond the door. Would he call out to her? Twist the knob? Break the lock and take her in his arms?

She bit her lip, her body wound tight. Slowly, the feet turned and shuffled away.

What am I doing?

Emma sat up and tried to adjust her soaked panties. She was leaving, going to Maine to restart her life. Not waitressing in some small-town café. Not providing advice to a lovesick teenager. Not fantasizing about fucking the salty fox next to the espresso machine. She wanted...

Shaking her head, Emma tried to banish the question without an answer. It didn't matter what she wanted because she was leaving, and no hot coffee man could change that. With an uncharacteristic grit, Emma piled her luggage next to the door to make it easier. No turning back now.

Steady legs walked her to the bed, certain arms pulled back the covers. But as she slipped under the sheets, her body curled around the pillows, and she breathed in Nick.

CHAPTER FIFTEEN

THE NEXT MORNING, Emma grabbed her toothbrush. With it, and the rest of her clothing zipped up in her luggage, she greeted Nick by the door. He tousled a hand through his hair and met her gaze. In that moment, Emma didn't know what she'd do if he asked her to stay. As his eyes slipped down, his body froze. A single soft, "Oh," fell from his lips. He jerked straight up, all emotion stripped from his face. He could be a stone soldier guarding a cemetery for all Emma could glean from him.

A thousand excuses flooded her mind.

I'll be leaving soon. You don't owe me anything. I can

make my own way. Forget it even happened.

"Okay," Nick said. He fished out his keys, the wad of them clanking together as he reached down to pick up her bag. "Skylar!"

"I can still work for the day. I just don't want to get in your way, your life." Emma had to talk through the pounding silence. The only sound was Nick stifling a groan as he hefted her bag off of the floor.

"Okay," he repeated, the emotion gone. "Sky—!"

"Yes, I'm here. Just had to…" The girl stampeded down the stairs and stared at the bag on Nick's shoulder. "What's going on?"

"Get in the truck. We're late." Nick looked back to the girl, hiding his face from Emma. To her surprise, Skylar didn't complain. She tugged her book bag closer and nodded. It didn't take them long to get outside, though frozen ice pelted her cheeks.

"Fuck, it's cold," Skylar shouted, dashing headlong for the truck. She yanked open the doors and leaped inside. Emma watched Nick carefully undo the tailgate even as his skin was blasted by sleet.

"You should get inside before you freeze," he said, cranking the strap tighter so her luggage wouldn't fly out. No discussion, no questions. He stood against the bitter cold to lock down her things so she'd leave his life.

She needed to say something, to cut through the tension and convince everyone it was for the best. But there was no opening. Nick closed his tailgate, and they slipped into the truck. Skylar kept talking, complaining about how freezing her toes were, how she dreaded her finals. Emma tried to reply, but each word felt pointless. As for Nick, he silently drove, his eyes never leaving the road.

HE WASN'T SURPRISED. If anything, he was surprised she'd stuck around for as long as she had. Three days was a damn near tour in the Iverson home. Nick made certain to put her things in the office. The weather was being its usual December blend of everything awful about winter. Not to mention there could be some sticky fingers wandering around in parking lots. He wouldn't put it past a family of raccoons to make off with her clothing.

It didn't hurt if he didn't think about it. Why should it hurt? He'd known her since Tuesday. That's a general acquaintance, not a person to get bent out of shape over. He finished putting down the chairs and unlocked the front door. Not even the mistletoe latte horde would stand outside in this weather. They'd been calm at least thanks to her coaxing them into trying anything else.

Funny how much brighter everything was. The café always felt like a lighthouse beaming against the darkness of five a.m. But the light felt warmer, like a fireplace flickering in a hearth instead of the dentist's office about to rip out a tooth. Yellow and orange stars made of tinsel hung from the pipes, turning the inhospitable light friendly. The menu that used to be white jagged lines on the blackboard now boasted pastel pink and purple text. Instead of his chicken scratch, the letters looped like they were done properly, along with drawings of donuts, coffee, and Christmas trees.

Nick breathed in, expecting to smell the familiar mix of grinding coffee beans, scalding milk, and floor cleaner. But the scent of pine struck him and tears beaded in his eyes. He forgot about the tree. It'd only cause a bigger mess in the already messy café. Nick flicked the closet branch, watching the homemade yarn ornament dance.

The employee door opened and the air changed to an intoxicating aroma of crisp dough and tart jams. Nick closed his eyes to breathe it in when a soft chirp broke him. She blushed bright pink and almost dropped the tray of donuts and pastries to the counter.

"Here's the first round. I hope they're okay."

Before he could answer, she dashed back to the kitchen. She'd changed that too, rearranging the storage boxes to form a makeshift counter to make it easier. It could all be returned to what it once was. Put the boxes back, shove the shelves against the wall, erase the drawings on the chalkboard, take down the decorations. It'd be like she was never here.

The bell jangled for their first customer. A familiar truck driver whose name he never got stomped his feet on the floor. "It's cold out there. Do you have donuts?"

Nick snickered at the childish joy in the fifty-something man's face at the prospect of sprinkles and fried dough. He slipped behind the counter, falling back into the pattern of the jaded man who owned a coffee shop. But before he went, he plugged in the Christmas tree's lights.

EMMA'S PHONE BEEPED. She reached for the towel on the counter to wipe off her hands, except it sent it tumbling to the ground. Her phone beeped again, sounding annoyed. A thick paste of flour, egg, and water had built up on her palms. If she touched anything it'd be ready for the deep fry.

Dropping carefully to her knees, she reached for the towel. That part was easy. It was the standing up that caused her to smack her head on the counter. "Damn it," she cursed, about to rub the spot when she remembered the flour.

"A damn from you…"

Her heart plummeted and she spun on the floor. Nick finished placing a box on the shelves. He cast his blue gaze to her struggling to stand without touching anything. "It must be serious."

"I dropped the towel, and my hands are covered." Emma held them up as if that would explain the bump on her head. Her phone once again beeped at her. "And this thing. Would you mind?" She turned her back to him and raised her back pocket while scraping the flour off her fingers.

"Uh…" It wasn't until Nick stood directly behind her, the heat of his body radiating from how close his hand swept above her back, that she realized her mistake. There were a lot, but pushing her butt at a man was the new one.

She felt the phone slip free. He didn't round his palm over the pocket where it'd been. Nor did he run his hand over her hip or slide his chest against her back to show her the phone. Like a gentleman, he held it out for her and waited. Emma tried to peel away the mess when the phone buzzed and the screen revealed a notification.

"Is it my sister?" she asked.

"Says…" He sounded near a laugh at her fumbling when his voice deadened. "RentaRoom."

Giving up on getting clean, Emma scooped her phone away. She put in her passcode and opened the app. Nick remained, nervously clawing his scruff. "You got it all figured out?"

No. She was on a wait list. Every time it moved her up a spot, her phone beeped at her until she accepted that she wanted to stay on it. If she was a minute late, they'd send her to the back of the line. But it wasn't his problem to solve. Putting on a smile, Emma pressed her phone tight to her chest. "Yep. It's all good."

"Good. That's…" Nick stumbled back. He picked up the box he'd just put down and muttered. "It's good."

Her phone beeped again, and she secured her spot in the line. After washing her hands and loading up the lone tray, Emma emerged into the café to find the windows splattered with snow.

"Ooh, whatcha got this time?" Sam asked.

"Bear claws, and I wanted to try an eggnog eclair."

"Gimme." He snatched up the eclair and nearly had it to his lips before Nick coughed and pushed a button on the register.

After the drawer shot out, he said, "That'll be four-fifty."

Sam grumbled and slapped a five into his hand. "That's highway robbery, that is."

Emma dropped her eyes, too nervous to see what he thought, but if she really didn't want to know she could have run into the back.

"Oh, oh goodness."

Was that bad? Good? She'd used too much nutmeg. Not enough?

"How is it?" she asked. "Can you taste the rum?"

Sam placed his wizened hand on hers and patted it. "Round of applause for the bandits. This is the most eggnog-y thing I've ever had, and that includes the nog my sister makes that the revenue men don't know about."

Emma smiled brightly at the compliment as Sam took a bigger bite than before. She glanced to Nick, who'd turned away to write 'Eggnog Eclairs' on the menu. He hadn't shown any interest in trying her eclairs, donuts, or even the tarts. Save for one kiss, he didn't seem interested in anything of hers.

All the drawings from Skylar were still up, the tree too. Though a single blue snowflake kept catching on a small breeze. The end flapped as the tape came undone. What if she pointed it out? Would he slap it down? Get a stool for her? Or lift her up into his arms again?

"What is this angel creating tomorrow?" Sam shouted for the whole café to hear.

Emma blinked rapidly and focused on the old man. "Ah, well… The thing is."

"Nothing," Nick said. He met only Sam's eye but—as he turned to stare at the front door—Emma caught a flash of pain. No, she was imagining it. He obviously didn't care if she came or went.

"Are you out of your mind? You don't keep Sinatra from singing and you don't stop this lady from baking."

Oh, dear. Emma's entire face burned red hot. It reached the tips of her ears, and she bent lower to hide it. But nothing, not even a nuclear meltdown of shame, could stop the old man.

"Look at this place. It ain't ever looked this nice and you can thank her for it."

Nick sighed and punched keys on the cash register just to spit out blank receipt paper. "Uh-huh."

"Not even Rachel could have turned it around like this."

Emma stared at the old man at the same time Nick jerked upright. He slammed his palms to the counter and dug in, the veins on his neck thickening. Instinctively, Emma took a half step back, when Sam said, "You've got everyone tiptoeing around like she's dead. It ain't right."

Only the dulcet tones of an unaware Dean Martin filled the air. Nick glared at Sam like the two were facing off for high noon at the OK Corral. The tension was thicker than cream patisserie. Sam reached for a second eclair without taking his eyes off of Nick, while the coffee-slinger folded his arms.

A loud beep sent Emma leaping into the air. "Oh jeez!" She fumbled for her phone, nearly tossing it twice before getting a grip. They'd moved her up another spot in line. She was only one behind securing a room.

"If anyone needs me..." Nick yanked his apron off and tossed it to the counter. "I'll be in the back."

The burgeoning anger transformed to sorrow. His shoulders slumped, and he shoved one into the door to slip away. Emma gulped and looked at her phone. Her thumb had pressed the accept button when she'd clasped it to her chest. But that was a good thing. She should get out of here. The last thing she needed was working in another powder keg restaurant.

Right?

Sam sighed, took a long drink of his coffee, and said, "That boy needs to get laid."

CHAPTER SIXTEEN

IT'D BE EASIER if she'd died.

He knew he shouldn't think that. Some of the old ladies who drank coffee for hours after church would tan his hide for it. But Nick couldn't escape the fact that if she'd left in a pine box maybe he wouldn't keep trying to rewrite that last Christmas.

A knock startled him, and he jerked up from his desk. Absently, he wiped at his cheeks as he looked to the only person daring enough to find him after that. Emma had no idea what she'd walked into. It was no wonder she wanted to walk back out.

"There was a weather announcement over Sam's…

the scanner. Sounds like a blizzard's starting up."

Nick waved it away. "They say that every December up here."

"You're not worried?"

"It's why I've got snow tires."

"Oh…"

God, she reminded him of Snow White. Not just because she had skin as white as…okay, not snow. That'd make her a zombie. And her hair was more of a dark brown than as black as whatever Snow White had. But her heart was so gentle and kind it'd cause a dozen woodcutters to fall to their knees and beg for forgiveness.

It'd certainly be a beautiful view.

Nick stood up fast, smacking his knee into the desk. That was gonna hurt come tomorrow. The kindhearted princess gasped at his folly and almost ran to tend to it, but he couldn't hide his reaction to her on her knees. Turning away, Nick rolled his knuckles along the dusty desktop, then pounded them once.

"What'd Sam tell you?"

"There was a terrible storm in the sixties that knocked out all power to the town for two weeks. And something about a donkey in the church's bell tower."

He laughed at the same old wives tale he'd heard as a kid. "Can I ask you something? Why'd you work in a restaurant if you just wanted to make desserts? Why not start your own bakery?"

Emma tugged her ponytail forward and twisted the end. "That needs money, which I didn't have after school."

"Work for one, then?"

She pursed her cherry lips and stared upward. The solitary flash of discomfort in her doe eyes made Nick want to stop this conversation, but Emma sighed. "I guess I…maybe I should have. I should. The truth is, I wanted to be the one to decide what was made. Not to create the same thing day in and day out to fit a set menu. To let my imagination run wild and craft new desserts out of old favorites and make something never seen before."

Emma swayed as she confessed to him. "I thought if I made it up the ladder, I'd be the head dessert chef. But I couldn't even hack the vegetables."

"I didn't want this place." Nick flicked the stack of forms, watching them fly up like bureaucratic snow. "Not at first, anyway. Dealing with people is not my forte."

She started to snicker before holding a hand over her lips. Nick wanted to pull her palm down so she could laugh at the truth, but he stayed put.

"Things in the plant weren't going well, downsizing, and my back was only getting worse. So we…so she thought the answer was our own little coffee shop."

Rachel had been damn near skipping with excitement when she'd found the old place. They'd been working tirelessly to change it over from a failed craft brew to their quaint and quirky coffee shop. All the while, he'd get up at four a.m. and perfect his newest blends.

"I was like you. I loved playing with flavors, there were so many syrups out there to mix and match. Beans from across the world. I thought I'd never get bored of it. Now there's just four things on the menu."

"What happened?"

He snickered at his folly. "She didn't want kids. I was fine with that. Chasing after a toddler and changing diapers wasn't up my alley. It was all going great, perfect. Then…the shit hit the fan."

They'd been running around like mad decorating the café for Christmas when he'd gotten the call. "My brother Pete was...in a bad spot. I had no money to throw at him. And he couldn't stay here, not after what he...what happened. That left Skylar in the lurch."

Emma pulled in a breath. "What about her mom?"

"She was gonna stick by Pete, but he fucked that up too. After a year or so, she ran off to Florida. Skylar heads down there for every other holiday." When her mother cared enough to send a plane ticket, anyway.

He didn't realize Emma had moved until her tiny fingers brushed over the desk's fake wood grain. "Losing a job is hard."

"Yeah, that's...that's true." Nick let his hand fall beside hers, their fingers pointing toward each other. He stared at her nails painted baby pink. His were gritty from the coffee grounds, the edges worn and splintered. It'd be nice to feel soft hands again.

"I couldn't let my niece suffer, not for what her dad... happened." He'd thought Rachel would understand. It was only for a few years. And Skylar wasn't a baby. It was family. "But when Rach said no kids, she meant it. Christmas day, Rachel moved out and I got a nine-year-old girl drawing all over the walls with glitter pens." With time, Nick was able to laugh at the memory of a confused but certain Skylar, five pens in hand, creating a rainbow in the living room. Back then, he'd shouted himself hoarse outside screaming at the world.

"Like an idiot, I tied every cent in my name to this place. If I couldn't keep it afloat, I'd drown. Luckily, there are enough people coming off the interstate who love overpriced caffeine."

Nick waited for a laugh, or for Emma to dash for the door. Maybe grab her things and run to that rented room. But she stood beside him, the tip of her index finger almost glancing against his.

"I can't imagine how much that must have hurt."

Like a cinder block to the chest. The pain lessened but the memory, the possibility of what could have been, stuck to him like boiling sugar.

"You gave up so much for Skylar when she needed you the most."

Nick flinched at the praise in her voice. He wasn't a hero, he wasn't hoping for valor. "I did what I had to." Rather than face her eyes, Nick looked at their hands. Both clung to the desk, fingers curled under the edge. But her pinkie began to slide closer and his did the same. He traced through the air almost caressing her skin, running up the knuckle to the edge, when Emma placed her little pink nail on the top of his.

The tiny comfort drew Nick to look up. He'd stooped from so much history that he was on her level and left adrift in her vast mocha eyes. She parted her lips, and he reached to hold her cheek, to brush his thumb down her jaw, and kiss her. Nick turned his palm and threaded his fingers through hers.

A beep burst from her phone. Emma's cheeks pinked, and she slipped away, her hand falling from his. "It's the…" she said, lifting her phone.

"Yeah, of course." The reminder that she was walking out the door smashed into his gut. Out of sorts, he reached for his phone to not look like he was watching her secure her room. *How is it already three?*

Nick texted his niece to ask her where she was. He didn't expect a response, only for her to get her ass in gear, and put the phone on the desk.

Finishing with her appointment, Emma slipped her phone into her back pocket. She'd made it all the way to the door but seemed stuck in the threshold. "I should head out front. It's been abandoned for a while. Oh, dear."

"Don't worry." Nick tried to excuse her away when his phone rattled across the desk. As he scooped it up, he mumbled, "Sam's probably already finished off the whole pot." It was from Skyler.

At Abby's. Studying for finals.

What about work?

Wasn't school more important?

Damn it. She'd twisted his logic back around to stab him in the brain.

Fine. But no later than five. Weather's bad.

Nick placed his phone upside down and wrung his palms over his cheeks. Whatever excuse Skylar came up with didn't matter. He'd have to make it through the rest of the afternoon without wrenching his own heart when another woman walked out that door.

SHE TRIED TO not stare, but it was growing harder with every inch. No one had walked through the door in fifteen minutes, and the last one who did brought in a pile of icy snow that melted into a puddle. The buildings were gone, eclipsed by the gray-white fog sleeting from the sky.

"Welp, looks like I best be heading home." Sam stood and bundled away his police scanner that'd gone dark after the storm announcement. He patted his pockets, tossed a couple of dollars on the counter, then stuffed on his mittens. "You got somewhere warm to stay?"

She had no idea. The app could cancel for inclement weather and this little storm was looking more like a blizzard with every minute.

"Cause I got a place perfect for a woman of your sophistication." Sam waggled his eyebrows and Emma tried to not cry out in shock. She'd thought of him as a grandfatherly type.

"That's very kind of you, but…I'm…I mean…"

"She's fine, Sam," Nick spoke up, stepping through the employee door.

Had he been listening? Or was he used to the old man hitting on every woman who walked into the café?

Showing more signs of the latter, Nick hefted up Sam's winter coat and helped the old man into it. "Better head home before this gets worse."

Sam gave in without a fuss, slipping his bag over his shoulders and hustling for the door. "You too," he said when he pushed on the handle. Freezing air blasted inside, nearly sending the old man toppling. Snow pelted his cheeks and wrinkly face. He pressed his hat tighter and shouted, "Unless you want to be stuck here all night."

With that, the last of their customers left leaving Emma alone with Nick. He stood next to the door, arms crossed while watching Sam teeter down the road. "There's a damn ice patch," he whispered, looking ready to run out and help. Sam must have navigated the path well enough as Nick turned away.

"It's looking bad out there," he said.

"It could be as much as nine inches." Emma held up her phone with the emergency weather app blaring about the blizzard warning.

Nick rubbed his chin. "You know the weather, always bragging about its nine inches when it's really six."

She laughed before she knew it was a joke. Emma pursed her lips tight to keep another giggle at bay when the stoic Nick gave a little smirk. "Might be best to close up now but wait out the storm. Unless you...?" He pointed to her phone, and she frowned. The app hadn't canceled yet, but it was only a matter of time.

"No. I mean, waiting sounds smart."

"Warm, at least." He stomped a foot and stared at the windows. The rising wind whistled through the panes, rattling the glass in the frame. Nick flipped the open sign to closed, but he didn't reach for the deadbolt. "I'll leave it unlocked in case some damn fool's out in this," he explained as if she needed to know.

Emma nodded at the sense that made.

"But I don't want to give them any ideas." Nick turned off the main overhead lights. Only the faint glow above the back wall, a halo around the employee door, and the twinkle of Christmas lights cut through the darkening gray air. Without the jangle of bags, customer murmurs, and hiss of steam, the music throbbed through the café. The intimacy overwhelmed Emma.

The yellow glow of the Christmas lights outlined Nick's cheeks, the spread of his shoulders, curve of his biceps, and line of his forearms. Her foot took a step forward, drawn to the light, while her heart feared the dark.

"It's..." Emma breathed, a chill racing through her

body. She shivered at the heat of Nick's body blocking off the cold. Slowly, he unfolded his arms, letting both rest on his thighs. She'd nearly held his hand before, wanting to comfort him. Now, she wanted to take it, wrap his arms around her, and kiss him. "Quiet in here."

"It is," he whispered. Nick raised his hand. *To hold her? Lift her up and kiss her?* It dropped, the knuckles banging on the table. "Seems a good time to clean up." With that declaration, he walked to the side to find the broom.

Emma closed her eyes, trying to shake away the goosebumps running the length of her body. Getting control of her voice, she said, "I'll wipe off the tables."

NICK NEARLY JUMPED at the buzzing from his pocket. He stared around the café that damn near sparkled and fished out his phone.

"Am I supposed to be walking to the café in this, or do you want me to not die?"

Skylar? Did that mean...? Nick groaned at the clock—sure enough—ticking over to five. She must have been waiting to call him with her smart-ass comment in mind. Instead of calming, the blizzard was picking up steam for round two. He stared at the snow building to the flower boxes and climbing.

"Stay put," he said. Emma looked up from a little table by the window. Moving the phone away, he whispered, "Skylar," to her, then continued with his niece. "It's best if you spend the night. Let me talk to Abby's mother."

"Okay."

Night had fallen hard, the normally blazing street lamps little more than distant stars in the storm. Nick began to pace and the walls tightened in around him. There was never much light—a handful of lanterns, equipment dots, and… The hazy glow of the Christmas lights pulled him out of the cave in Afghanistan. He wrung his neck, shaking away the jitters when a familiar voice spoke up.

"Nick. Hello."

"Uh, hi Mrs…" His brain blanked before the name came back. "Wilkins."

"Are you coming to get Skylar?" She sounded curious and excited. God, how badly did his niece wear out her welcome?

"That's what I wanted to talk to you about. With the storm—"

"It's a brute. Maybe it'd be better to not risk heading out into it."

Whew. Nick sighed at the mother instantly understanding. "Yes, thank you."

"There's plenty of space for the girls downstairs, which would leave the upper floors all to us," she said.

"Uh. I'm stuck at the café. I was hoping you'd keep Skylar and I'd pick her up bright and early in the morning."

A long pause followed and Nick frowned. He moved to see if the storm might have knocked out cell service when Mrs. Wilkins spoke. "Of course. I'm sorry you're trapped. How will you keep warm?"

Emma swept her hand down her hair, twisting the ponytail until she reached the tip and cupped her palm around the thick locks. *That hand would be a tight fit.* The heat from a thousand filthy thoughts burned in Nick's gut, but he couldn't shake them. Emma must have felt him staring as she put down her pen, raised her eyes to him, and smiled.

"I'm good," he squeaked. "I mean the place still has power and heat. I should go. Please keep Skylar alive until tomorrow."

"No problem, Nick."

Oh shit, she was standing up. "Yeah, goodbye." Nick ended the call and used the excuse of putting his phone away to try to tuck his erection into his belt. Jesus, it was like he was sixteen all over again. Just because a pretty girl stroked her hair and looked at him didn't mean... Fuck, he was making it worse.

Dropping an elbow to the counter, as if that'd hide the obvious tent in his jeans, Nick said, "That was Skylar."

"Is she okay?" Emma sounded concerned.

"Yeah. She's at a friend's. I told her to stay there for the night."

"With that Mrs. Wilkins." Her concern for Skylar pivoted to a strangely sly statement.

"Uh-huh. Do you know her?"

Emma laughed and shook her head. "No. She seemed nice."

"I think she's a real estate agent." Nick shrugged. He was probably supposed to talk to Skylar's friend's parents, but he didn't have time for his own friends never mind putting together play dates with adults. Emma laughed like a fairy tale princess singing to a bird and Nick followed suit, though he felt like a braying ass in comparison.

"It's getting late," she said, staring up at the clock.

"Yeah," he whispered. *It's dark and we're all alone.* "You...you need to be getting to your new place." He needed to get that fantasy out of his head. She was leaving, plain and simple.

"Um...well, it's. It's not available." Emma held up her phone, her eyes bigger than before. She looked near tears as she lowered the screen. "Maybe I could stay —"

"Dinner."

Her full eyebrow quirked up and she stared at him.

"We need dinner. I should make dinner. For you and me." Of course. It was so simple. With a jaunt in his step, Nick tugged off his apron, tossed it into the box behind the counter, and walked to the door. Rather than slip in, he held it open for the lady, who was blushing pink. He breathed in the scent of her walking past him. Sugar and cream, just as he expected.

"You really don't have to cook for me."

"Of course I do. You've been doing all the hot oven slaving. It's only fair."

Even though Emma was in the lead, Nick flipped the light switch for the storage room/kitchen and walked up to the oven with purpose. He rolled up his sleeves, gathered a pan from the sink, started up the lone burner, and paused. Bags of sugar and flour sat in the makeshift pantry. There was a noticeable lack of filet mignon and stuffed mushrooms to impress a lady. "I could make eggs?" he said, finding a carton in the fridge and the butter.

Emma smiled. "Sounds delicious."

"Oh." There was one thing he knew to make to show off. "And fat crêpes."

"What are fat crêpes?"

He laid out his tools, cut the pat of butter with a chef's knife, and — using the tip — drew it around the pan. In a bowl, Nick combined the flour and sugar. "It's kind of a long story," he said while whisking the batter.

"We've got time." Emma jumped off the floor and landed on a pile of boxes. She crossed her short legs at the ankles and waved them about.

Nick dumped the batter into the pan while watching her feet hover above the floor. At that height, he could drop to his knees, straddle her thighs across his shoulders, and… "Shit. Sorry." He raced to pour the excess batter back into the bowl while the bottom of his fat crêpe burned.

Scraping it off, he flipped the crêpe and waited for the sizzle before speaking. "Back in the Marines, there was one day of leave when a bunch of us found ourselves stranded. Nothing too dire, but we were all nineteen and starving. My buddy found a bunch of baking stuff, and I said I could make crêpes."

He shook the first fat crêpe onto a plate, then started a second. "Pretty sure I meant to say pancake, but my mouth said crêpe. They gave me so much shit for it, and I had to save face without having a clue what I was doing. So I made skinny pancakes or…"

"Fat crêpes," Emma said, laughing.

"Here, they're best eaten warm." He passed her the plate.

She struggled to roll up the severely caramelized bottom and the soggy top. But as she took a little nibble, her eyes burned bright. "If I made anything like this back in Portland, they'd have blackballed me from every restaurant."

Damn. Why did I think this was a good idea?

"Which is stupid because these are amazing."

"Really?"

"I love the surface area ratio with enough spongy interior to give a blast of…cinnamon."

"And a touch of ginger," Nick said, growing cockier

with his cooking.

"Ooh, you know what these need?" Emma leaped off the boxes and bent over to tug out a jar. She dropped it to the counter, her smile widening. "Honey butter."

"That's a great idea. I could have used you at basic training."

"I don't know about that." Her joyful stirs of the spoon to blend in the honey stilled. "I hate being shouted at."

Nick wanted to point out how everyone hated that, but from how low her chin had fallen and the nervous scratching of her leg, a tiny part of his brain told him this was serious. "Tell you what." He dropped another crêpe onto her plate and caught her eye. "You do the recipe making and I'll take the yelling."

"Deal."

CHAPTER SEVENTEEN

"THAT WAS DELICIOUS," Emma exclaimed. They sat in the café, all the chairs turned up except for theirs. The snow dampened the sounds of traffic, and the night darkened the air so the entire world vanished. Only the flicker of the Christmas lights and the nostalgic carols broke through their romantic shelter.

"It's all thanks to your butter idea," Nick said. He swept the last of his skinny pancake through the melted butter and sticky honey before popping it in his mouth and smiling. He'd left his sleeves rolled up, his naked forearms resting on the table. Emma bounced her fingertips on the table, trying to distract herself so she didn't run her nails up his arms.

Blushing at the thought, she slipped back and picked up her notebook. "Your fat crêpes were the real star. And the scrambled eggs with half and half. Genius."

Nick shrugged and looked pleased with himself. He leaned back in his chair and stretched. Emma piled up her plates with one hand and jotted down another idea with the other. *Cinnamon bun crêpes. Either crêpes rolled in cinnamon filling and topped with icing, or cinnamon bun dough rolled in crêpes. Have to think.*

"What's that?"

On instinct, she cupped a protective hand over her notebook. "It's my...my recipe ideas. Whenever inspiration strikes, I jot it down, then try to figure out how to make it work."

"Can I see?"

Emma thumbed the edge, her heart pounding. This was more precious than a diary, revealing all of her failures and limited successes. Slowly, she placed it in Nick's hand and girded herself for mocking.

He drew a finger down the pages, humming and nodding along before turning back. "Mistletoe desserts? Trying to steal my idea?"

"No!" she gasped, before catching a small twinkle in his eye. "You inspired me." Emma rose from her chair to lean closer and point at the ramshackle list. "The idea of a mistletoe theme for an entire dessert tray seemed like a fun challenge." It sounded stupid the moment she said it. Emma glanced up and realized she was nearly pressing her forehead to his.

Nick kept reading, unaware that she was staring in wonder at his thick eyelashes and the peek of blue below. The curve of his cheeks became rough from the rising beard and called for her hand. And his lips...

instead of the flat scowl, they were lifted, revealing the sculpted cupid's bow.

"Mistletoe trifle, mistletoe cheesecake, mistletoe tiramisu. You've covered a lot of bases. There's just one problem."

He looked up, and she nearly jerked back, but the roughly hewn charm radiating off of him shook away her panic. Nick reached over the table and swept his palm against the back of her hand. "How can you do a dessert take on something you've never tried?"

"Well, I'm not…" The hand around hers closed and he stood. Emma followed without pause as Nick guided her behind the counter.

He flipped the button on the machine and hunted under the counter for various syrups. "Hm. I can almost make a mistletoe latte again, but it'll be missing a secret ingredient."

Emma laughed. "Good. That way I won't have to worry about…"

Abandoning the stock of bottles, Nick looked at her. "About what?"

Falling in love.

She gulped and worried the hem of her sweater as she lost herself in his eyes. "Accidentally copying it. I don't want to steal a recipe, even by mistake."

He laughed hard and returned to gathering his material. Suddenly, he looked over his shoulder at her. "If that's your concern." Nick picked up a clean towel and folded it lengthwise, then again. He took a step closer. Emma was pinned between him and the counter. Her heart flitted in her chest as he reached up and slid off her hat.

The weak ponytail gave out, causing her hair to tumble to her shoulders. Nick was so close she breathed in the scent of his body. He dropped the cap to the counter, then lifted the towel to her eyes. There was a question in his, but Emma didn't understand until the terrycloth became flush with her face. Darkness fell. She placed a hand to the blindfold to keep it in place as Nick reached around her head to tie it off.

The naked forearms nearly against her cheeks caused her to gulp. She couldn't see him but felt the heat of his body almost pressed against hers.

"There," he said. His fingers slipped through her hair as he stepped back. "Now you can't steal my recipe."

The clink of bottles and hiss of steam filled the air. Without her sight, she was vulnerable, but she wasn't scared. Heat rose around her as Nick bustled back and forth.

"I'm guessing that it requires…coffee?"

"Ha. I'll tell you another ingredient."

Emma froze when his warm breath tickled her earlobe.

"Milk."

She knew she was supposed to laugh at the obvious answer, but her throat was struggling to swallow a moan instead. "Can I ask you about the latte?"

"I'm sorry, but that's all I'm willing to give away." He sounded like he was smiling.

Emma turned her head in the direction of his voice. "The legend about the whole—"

"One true love thing? It's not real."

"I didn't think it was," she said fast because a grown woman shouldn't believe in fairy tales, magic, and one true loves. "I'm just curious how it came about."

"Stupidity. When it first went up on the menu, it included the tagline 'One kiss and you'll love it forever.' Meaning drink this and you'll want more. Thanks to a bunch of coincidences, people took it literally, and this dumb myth was born."

He sounded like he regretted letting them run with it even though most places would probably kill to have that kind of a legend. Emma could guess why Nick wasn't as enthralled.

Silence, save the Christmas carols, fell. Emma grew more aware of how awkward, worthless and blind she was while someone else worked around her. She was about to start rocking on her feet when a hand pressed to her stomach.

"Excuse me," Nick said. With a gentle touch, he guided her to the side. The drawer behind her was pulled open and another clink of a bottle, but all Emma cared about was that palm sweeping around her hip. Once he was done, he helped her right back to where she'd been. God, she had to be blushing as red as a firetruck.

"One last little...there."

Standing up straighter, Emma asked, "Is it ready?"

"I used to do a milk pour in the shape of holly, but that doesn't seem important. Hold your hand out."

She did as asked when a curved and warm mug pressed to her palm. Nick helped guide her thumb into the handle then asked, "Do you have it?"

"I think so," she said. Taking in a cleansing breath, Emma tried to clear her palate before she took a sip. The heat rushed up her cheeks and nose first, followed by a dark, almost chocolatey roast. A nuttiness danced in the middle, sharper than pecans. Chestnuts? Emma blinked when the final note announced itself.

"Juniper!" she cried out in surprise.

"Damn, most people miss the gin syrup." Nick sounded impressed. He took the cup out of her hands and placed it beside her.

She tried to play through the flavors on her tongue while thinking. "It's more complex than I expected."

"I am a simple man."

Emma gulped. "That isn't what I—"

"It's okay. I know what I am."

"Any dessert requires nuts. Perhaps a combination of pecans and walnuts to mimic that. And I'd have to keep the sugar low or miss the depth of the rich coffee liquor."

Nick whistled and she froze in speaking her thoughts aloud. "Color me impressed. Your tongue's amazing."

Oh, boy. She licked her lip at the compliment. Instead of the mistletoe latte, all she could taste was hard flesh as her mind filled with the memory of him in the bath. Wrapping her tongue around that would be...

Emma tried to shake it away. She raised her hand to ask, "Could I have another taste?"

"No problem."

She heard the rattle of the mug gliding across the counter and raised her chin. A moment passed when nothing filled her palm. Emma parted her lips in anticipation when a firm heat pressed against them.

God! A richness not from coffee but the body of a man overwhelmed her senses. Nick's kiss deepened, hotter than before. When a hand cupped her cheek, Emma rifled back through his hair. He nipped his bottom lip under hers and grazed his teeth against her tender skin. She moaned and parted her mouth.

He didn't plunge in with his tongue but showed care in lapping her lips before darting the tip against hers. Emma pulled herself tighter to him and a hand clasped to the small of her back. That thick cock she only got a peek at pressed against her belly. She wanted to run her fingers up it, to cup the base and jerk it just as he'd done in the tub. Her tongue swirled of its own accord, wanting to show Nick just how talented it was.

Pressing his pinkie into the hollow behind her ear, Nick tipped up Emma's face until she grew light-headed. "How was that?" he asked, the struggle in his voice causing her thighs to tremble.

Leaving soon.

My entire life is two states away.

As she thought, his palm swept under her sweater. The warm hand cupped her naked back, and he pressed his fingertips higher. Nick placed his other thumb on her chin and circled his finger around the edge of her lips. A groan rose from Emma's curled toes.

"I need more," she gasped.

Nick kissed her harder than before. She held on for dear life, fully diving in. Palms caressed her cheek, then her belly, before reaching over her sweater to cup her breasts. He took care in teasing them, a gentle squeeze followed by a tender sweep under her small tits. His hands were the angels to his devil mouth.

Teeth nibbled on her earlobe, then bit down. Emma squealed, and he slipped a knee in between her thighs. *Fuck!* She swayed her hips forward, grinding against the hard muscle. Wetness swept across the whole of her vagina, causing her to cry out.

Her skin prickled like a thousand volts ran under it. She arched her back, wanting to feel his hands on her bare flesh. Nick toyed with her nipples barely making it through the padding in her bra. He drew his nose down her neck, sucking on her skin as he went. She fought off a whimper and ran her fingers down his shoulders. Emma was about to dig her nails into his biceps when Nick caught both of her wrists.

He rose, pinning her hands together. Hot breath twisted in her ear. "Let me show you what I can do with my tongue."

Emma nodded greedily and parted her lips, but Nick didn't kiss her. He guided her hands behind his neck. Hands cupped her ass and heaved her up. She nearly knotted her legs around his waist when she landed on the counter.

Confused, she started to lift the edge of the blindfold when her sweater flew over her head. It caused a sliver of light to peek through the gap, but all Emma could see was a line of blond hair before Nick reached around her back.

"I swear I remember how to do this," he muttered. She breathed him in as he fumbled to undo her bra. Emma leaned her head back and reached out with a kiss. Her lips struck scruff. The bristles darted across her tender skin and she kept going, nibbling up Nick's jaw. At his chin, she added her teeth and swept her tongue down that little cleft.

He gasped at the touch, then curled his hands under her breasts. Emma cried out and thrust her chest back. She didn't have much to work with, but that didn't deter him. Pinching her nipples, he toyed with the hyperactive nerves. Emma couldn't stop from shivering, the whole of her body breaking out into goosebumps.

"Are you cold?" he asked, placing his wide hand over the entirety of her breast.

"N-n-n-oooh!" Her answer turned into a cry as Nick sucked her breast into his mouth. He swirled around her throbbing nipple with his tongue and pinched his lips around it. She clung to his hair and, when he'd pinch harder, would rake her nails over the nape of his neck. Her panties overflowed and she moaned. Nick ran the back of his hand over the tops of her thighs, then swept his palm between them. Emma twisted to follow each time he'd almost run his thumbs down her inner seam, then pull away.

A deep chuckle rumbled from below. Nick roughed the scruff of his beard between her cleavage and she gulped. He touched the button of her jeans and pulled down the fly. Emma jumped in surprise. Nick left her pants undone but on. He stood up, and she ran her hands over his cheeks.

"Are you...?" Nick asked before she wound her fingers around the collar of his shirt and tugged. Snickering, he cupped her chin and kissed her as Emma struggled to get the thick flannel unbuttoned. The chest part was easy, but when she tried to tug it off of his wrists, they caught. Nick's hands were too big.

He chuckled against her lips and, after gently pushing her fingers lower, undid the cuff buttons and slid his shirt off. Beginning at the wrists, Emma ran the tips of her nails up his arms. Hard as bedrock, the muscles shifted as she traced them. She swiveled to trail the vein up his biceps and reached for his shoulders. It was hard to guess what he looked like from touch alone.

Emma shifted, trying to catch a glimpse of him through the gap in the blindfold. The towel tightened, and he whispered in a breathy voice, "No peeking."

With his wide hands, Nick swept down her sides and tugged her jeans off. Her boots fell, leaving Emma completely naked save for her fluffy socks. Nick traced his nails up her left calf, then the right. She buzzed in anticipation, trying to keep from leaping on top of him. The trailing fingers dipped down and clenched around her ankles.

Emma slid across the counter just as her ankles landed on his shoulders. *What is…?*

Heat pulsed against her bare vulva—a warm wind from two lips almost pressed to her. She squirmed, terrified of what he'd think when Nick lapped his wet tongue over her.

Holy shit! The slick heat swerved all around her lips, trailing out and back in, taunting her clit with a momentary tongue tap before circling back. Nick clung to her outer thighs, pressing them tighter to his cheeks, and picked up speed. First, he sucked on her longer lip. Then he flicked his tongue against her clit's hood. The increasing vigor scraped his scruff against her inner thighs.

Emma tipped back on her elbows, straining to place her hips closer to his impossible mouth. With her previous lovers, this was a means to an end. They'd put in their two minutes of work in order to move on to something better. But Nick seemed prepared for a feast. He nuzzled her muff with his nose then pulled his chin down her. When that dimple cupped around Emma's clit she cried out.

"You like that?" Nick asked. Rather than switch to another move, he brushed his chin back and forth. It should hurt, the tips of his whiskers poking into her throbbing flesh. But the image of the chin she'd nibbled on grinding against her chased away any pain.

Her back began to arch, sending Emma falling to the counter. A warm hand swept behind her, keeping her in place. Teeth nibbled on her inner thigh, and she spread her legs wider.

"Damn," Nick sighed. He worried his thumbs up the creases of her thighs and panted against her wet pussy.

"You taste incredible. I've never been so hard just…"

The hot tongue swept over her clit. Emma's head fell back, her neck a noodle as pleasure chased through her body. She struggled to breathe, her entire lower half on fire.

"Nick. Please…please…"

He sucked her clit into his mouth and Emma lost control. The balls of her feet slammed into his shoulders, forcing Nick deeper into her. He wrapped his arms behind her thighs, using his biceps to tuck her closer, as his tongue swept and swirled over her clit.

"I…I…" She panted, swaying her hips to compliment his licks. With one last swirl of his tongue, Emma collapsed into orgasm. Flames swept from her pulsing thighs up to her chest. She gasped, fighting to drink in oxygen. Her head grew fuzzy and the whole of her lower body clenched around him. Nick kept licking until Emma wrapped her legs around the back of his neck. With one final move, he planted his chin on her clit, and she pressed back, riding the echoes of pleasure storming through her.

It had to be an hour before Nick slipped her legs off of him. Slowly, she sunk towards the floor, all of her limbs jelly. Warm hands caught her naked hips, keeping her upright. "That was amazing." In her state, she couldn't think, only say the first thing in her brain.

Nick undid the knot in the towel. Sharp light cut into her eyes, but as she blinked it away, she stared in awe at the naked chest before her. Strong and trim, Emma's heart skipped a beat at his physique. He didn't need the six-pack abs of a twenty-year-old gym rat when he had the tongue of a god.

After tossing the towel aside, Nick cupped her chin. He brushed his thumb over her lips and smiled. "You nearly made me come in my pants." The dreamy look in his eyes snapped to panic.

Emma slipped her hands behind his back, holding him in place. "That's the nicest thing anyone's ever said to me," she declared and kissed him. The remnants of her orgasm coated his scruff, scenting the air with sex. As she parted her mouth, willing his talented tongue back inside of her, Emma felt the proof of how hard his cock was.

Slowly, she traced her fingers down his chest. Her pinkie found the scars on his stomach, and her index followed that treasure trail like Indiana Jones. "Ever since I saw you in the bath..." She cupped around his rock-hard erection. Nick gulped, his eyes closing as his head tipped back. "I've wanted you to fuck me."

CHAPTER EIGHTEEN

WHERE THE HELL did I put it?

Nick left a naked, beautiful woman who couldn't stop reaching under his pants in order to find a condom. There was a ninety-eight percent chance he didn't have anything in the back office, but he needed to cool his head before he did something amazingly stupid. Emphasis on the amazing. The way she'd curled her legs as she came was…

Not helping him.

He rifled through the desk, hurling stacks of folders to the ground. It'd be romantic if he wasn't in a panicking hurry. There was the drawer full of old rubber bands and tape. *Do not make your own.* What kind of a man didn't carry at least one on himself at all times? You know, in the rare event a bus full of supermodels broke down and they needed a strong man to give it a push.

The idea sounded damn near as ludicrous as a bedroom-eyed Emma waiting for him on the counter. Nick was tempted to throw a coat on and brave the blizzard for a pack when he yanked open a drawer in a dusty filing cabinet and a tampon rolled out. Underneath was the permission slip for Sex Ed and a...

"Yes!"

A single plain white square still in the packaging sat above the notes. No doubt it was meant to be used on a banana and would feel like a rubber glove around his cock, but he didn't care. It wasn't expired, it'd work.

Proud of his find, Nick dashed for the door and paused. He took a deep breath to calm himself and combed his hair. The throbbing between his legs slowed. *He could go all night, no problem.* Wringing a hand over his chin, the scent of Emma filled his nose. His cock hardened back to his early twenties in a heartbeat.

Pushing open the door, his jaw nearly hit the floor. Her mahogany hair draped across one shoulder, obscuring one petal pink nipple while the other was in full display. The warm lights of the Christmas tree highlighted her smiling cheeks as she crossed one foot in front of the other. Her short legs were as lean as a faun's. Nick feared he might break them if he wasn't gentle. But as he watched her run her hand through her hair, her thighs crossed to form a tantalizing t, the blood surged in him.

Nick took her in one arm, curled around her waist,

and pulled her onto her tiptoes. Her little hands landed on his chest for leverage, and he raised her off of her feet. "There's nothing hotter than a woman in socks," he growled before kissing her harder than ever. Emma's little yelp drew out the primal need he'd been beating into submission.

Wrapping one forearm under her ass, Nick pressed her back against the counter's edge and swatted a buttock. She cried out in shock, her eyes opened wide. *Oh shit, was that too much?* He kissed her lips in response and tenderly brushed his palm over the warm print on her ass.

"What do you want? The rough hair pulling or gentle screwing?" He panted in her ear, ready for either possibility.

Emma lifted her legs, her little feet tugging on his jeans. They slipped off his hips, hitting the floor with a thud, and she curled her toes around his freed cock. Impish mischief filled her sweet face. She nibbled on her lip while running her feet up him. "I want you."

Surging for her, Nick licked her ear and bit right on the edge. She squealed, and he jerked his hips. Emma clung to him, and she wrapped her palm around his cock. "I've wanted to ride you since I saw you."

"Even though I'm an old grouch who hates everything?" Nick groaned, giving in to her gentle sweeps up his shaft and under his balls. "Fuck, that feels good."

"Seems you like something."

Too much! He latched onto her wrist and yanked it away. God, how could she undo him so fast?

Struggling back a shudder, Nick caught both of Emma's wrists and spun her around. He placed her hands to the counter and kneaded into her hips. Her heart-shaped ass bounced, the pale skin crying to be pinked. Nick gave a sharp slap, louder than it was painful. Instead of gasping, Emma groaned. Her head bent lower and she shivered back against him.

He took his cock in his hands and guided it to the small of her back. The heat of her skin ignited him. She leaned up and Nick curled a hand around her breast. Slowly, he pulled back his hips, sweeping the shaft and head down her spine and in between her inflamed buttocks.

Nipping at her ear, Nick said, "I've wanted to see your ass turn red since you walked through that door." She moaned and opened her thighs, clenching her buttocks around his cock. It took everything in him to not thrust.

Emma turned, her brown eyes bigger than ever. In a pleading voice, she asked, "What's stopping you?"

Nick jerked away and slapped her just hard enough to leave a stinging handprint. As Emma cried out, he pulled her to him. The top of her ass pressed around the base of his cock while he ran his hands over her. First, he traveled over her stomach, then her breasts where he teased her nipples. He tugged back her hair and ran his teeth up her neck. Emma clung to his head, pressing him closer as he lined up a shot and slapped her ass again.

She clenched even tighter around him, her moan thickening him until he felt her ass cheeks spreading from his cock. Fuck, he wanted to do this all night. But Emma slid up onto her tiptoes, gliding the whole of his cock down through her ass crack, and Nick lost it.

He had just enough brain power left to grab the condom and slip it on. His cock looked ghost white in the generic condom, but none of it mattered. Nick swept his nails up her thighs, first the tops, then around the back and up under her ass. Emma trembled, her head bent as she bit down on her finger. Gently, he massaged her buttocks. The pink hand prints waved to him as he did, tightening the already snug fit in the latex.

Guiding his cock, he widened Emma's stance and slipped his fingers through her pussy. Wet and willing just like he loved. He pressed her wider and thrust inside.

Oh, fuck! Nick dug his nails into her soft skin at the squeeze and Emma cried out. Her pussy clamped on even tighter and the breath caught in his chest. Taking her hips, Nick raised her ass and spread her legs. Another inch of him slipped inside and he thrust deeper.

Emma gasped, and she tried to jerk back to meet him, but he had her suspended off of the floor. Nick began to thrust faster, his arms crying out as he pulled her back onto him. She yelped, clinging to the counter's edge with her nails. Her pinked ass pressed against the base of his cock, setting off a multitude of stars. This was perfect, fucking her from behind on the…

No. Nick released her to the floor and slipped out. When Emma's feet touched the ground, he wrapped his palms around her breasts and pressed his lips to her ear. "You're beautiful when you come."

"Wh…?" Before she could ask, he turned her around and raised her onto the counter. She wrapped her lean legs around his hips, and he thrust inside. Thanks to her tiny height, Nick could kiss her lips, toy with her nipple, and cling bare-knuckled to the counter while he fucked her. He meant for this to be slow, the tender side of him, but the way her skin burned red and glistened from his touch sent him spiraling.

With each word, he thrust harder, the whole of him plunging deeper inside. "The. Way. You. Fuck. Is…"

Emma cried out. Her eyelids closed and she arched back to the counter. Nick pressed against her spine as her pussy pulsed around him. The sight of her falling into orgasm set him off. He dug his toes in and clamped tighter to her skin as his semen gushed with enough force to break a wall. Luckily, the condom was thicker than a brick, not that it did anything to cut down on the rush of pleasure. He pulled harder on Emma, savoring the heat of her around him as the last of his cum spurted out.

She began to slide, her ass slipping off the counter. Nick ran his hands over her hot cheeks when gravity took hold. With all of his strength drained, the two of them tumbled to the cushioned floor mats below. His body took most of the blow. Nick groaned at the pain seizing up his back and tailbone. But when Emma landed, her hair sweeping off her shoulder to pool on his chest, any pain was forgotten.

"Smooth as ever." Nick groaned.

Her laugh brought one to him, and he wrapped his hands around her waist. Rather than try to get up, they stayed on the ground entwined in each other. She rested her cheek on his sternum and placed her palm on his pec. The steady pulse of her heart echoed through his cobweb-choked chest until his heart began to follow it.

"Is what?" she asked, confusing Nick. Emma tipped her head to look up at him. "The way I fuck is…?"

Jesus. He blushed from her saying fuck. How was the crotchety old coffee guy becoming such a softy? "I think I was gonna say amazing, but my brain melted to my feet." Nick kissed the top of her head, breathing in the exotic shampoo he'd smelled in his bathroom every night.

Behind the counter, the lights dimmed and even the music dampened to a distant melody. It was almost like they vanished into their own world. He ran his hand up her arm, exhaustion taking hold fast after the long day. The woman in his arms… Holy hell, he never thought he'd think that again. But the woman in his arms laid back down. How could someone so beautiful and sweet want his busted ass?

"I guess whatever you saw in the bathroom didn't completely turn you off."

Emma jerked as if his words pulled her out of sleep. She danced her fingertips across his stomach.

"Here I figured the sight of my gray hair was what sent you packing."

"No." She shook her head and beamed her big doe-eyes up at him with such fervor, Nick cupped her cheek. "I thought…it's silly." Emma buried her face against his skin. He ran his fingers through her hair, willing her to keep talking. It took a few more passes before she said, "I thought you didn't like me."

"What? How?" He'd been struggling to not get caught staring at her from the second she'd walked through his door.

"You were…I don't know. It's stupid."

In trying to piece back together the past few days, a few dozen moments struck back at him. Every time he'd catch himself thinking about Emma's legs, or her fingers, or lips, he'd lash out. As she was the only one in close proximity, all that self-loathing fell on her.

"The kiss by the tree…"

"That's…that one's on me." And then some. She was so young he didn't think she'd want him for anything other than shelter and money. "You blew in here like a ray of sunshine." Nick squeezed her. "Like cream and sugar into a cup of bitter black. I thought there's a girl with her whole life ahead of her. No chance she'd want to waste any of it on this broken-down husk."

Emma fell quiet, only the tip of her pinkie tracing down his rib. "I've already made a mess of my life."

"No, you haven't. So you had a setback, that happens to everyone."

"Lost my apartment, lost my job. Spent so much time at my job I didn't have any friends to lean on. And all because I couldn't hack it."

The tears running in her voice socked him in the gut. Nick brushed her hair behind her ear and swept the side of his finger down her cheek. "At eighteen, I joined the Marines. Thought that'd be my life. At twenty-one, I was discharged. Off to college I went…and dropped it two months later. Every time I thought I knew what I wanted to do with my life, life swerved. Working odd jobs, relying on charisma and the appeal of hiring a veteran got me a little farther, but…" He hadn't planned to own a coffee shop. That was Rachel's dream, one he'd been happy to cling to and call his own. Then she ran out leaving him with a business he'd never wanted.

"I'm never going to be a chef." Her dejected voice stung him.

Nick sighed and dropped his head to the floor. "They always say chase your dreams. If you want it, it'll happen. But I don't think anyone gets what they wanted at eighteen. Maybe the dream job turns out to be a nightmare. Maybe the wife…leaves. Maybe the kids never happen. There's no shame in changing your dream."

"That's not what any self-help guru would say."

"Yeah, well, if we were all perfect those leeches wouldn't have anyone to mooch off of," he grumbled, causing Emma to laugh. God, the soft flutter of her giggle almost made him want to break out into song. Nick gulped and clenched a fist until his nails dug into his skin. "Besides, don't you have a new place, a new job out east?"

She went quiet. Only her cheek swaying up and down answered him.

"Who knows? Maybe you'll become a fantastic chef out there and create the next cronut."

"I'm sorry."

"For what?"

"For flirting with you. For wanting you so badly even though I'll be leaving like…"

Rachel. Nick squeezed his fist tight, then opened it. The cold air stung his palm, but he swept it over Emma's warm ass. "You got nothing to be sorry for. I knew same as you did." *I tried to fight it because I knew.* "And there's no reason we can't have fun."

"Really?" She pushed up on her palms and the brightness in her eyes melted his cold, dead heart. Oh, he was in deep trouble if he wasn't careful. But as he ran his hand back through her hair, Nick didn't care about the end.

"We've got until, what, Tuesday?"

She nodded.

"There's so much more I can do to your perfect ass."

Four days left. Enough time for him to get infatuated but not fall any harder. Perfect. It'd been far too long since he'd been with a woman, even longer for it to go past one night. A chill wound through the cozy café. Nick reached for the first bit of cover he could find and slung an apron over the two of them. As he guided

Emma back to his chest, he held onto her and closed his eyes. Frank Sinatra sang them to sleep on the floor of his café.

For the first time in five years, Nick took a breath without a weight crushing his heart.

CHAPTER NINETEEN

COLD CRAWLED UP her leg and ripped Emma from her dreams. She shifted and tried to pull her freezing toes back under the covers...only for a naked man to cling to her. He groaned and turned to his side, taking her with, but it sent their apron-blanket tumbling.

"Damn it," Nick croaked, and he risked opening an eye. "Well...good morning." A lopsided smile grew across his lips. He massaged her shoulder and chilly back before draping a hand across her ass.

"That was quite a night."

"You're telling me. I am too old to sleep on the floor." Despite his protesting, he didn't sit up. Emma straddled his thigh, the tip of his cock resting on her skin. As Nick blinked and glanced down her naked body, his manhood started to rise.

She nibbled on her lip and drew her leg higher, brushing her flesh against his. Nick's eyes rolled back. He wrapped a hand around the nape of her neck and pulled her up for a kiss. Emma slipped her hand from his chest down the soft trail of hair on his belly and reached for the hard cock.

"Good morning!" The shop bell jangled the second a voice bellowed for them.

"Fuck!"

"Hello? Iverson, you old grouch, where are you hiding?"

Nick sat up the same time as Emma. He craned his head back and caught the clock. "Shit, it's seven."

She tried to wrap a hand around herself, but there was too much to cover with too little. Nick picked up the single apron and dropped it over his neck. "Go, sneak out the back. I'll distract him."

"But...?" Emma started to argue when Nick popped up. The apron only hid away the edge of his nipples, leaving his shoulders, the sides of his chest, and whole back exposed. Gathering up their lost clothing in her arms, she tried to push Nick's pants at him, but he was too focused on the interloper. Emma skittered on her knees for the employee door, well aware there was a gap between it and the counter where anyone could see her.

"Sam," Nick said, his voice dropping. "What are you doing here?"

"Getting a cup of joe," the old man said. "Found these fools out in the snow."

Oh, god. A gaggle of people quietly took umbrage

with being labeled fools.

"The sign said we're closed," Nick explained. He sidled to the side, bent down, and hefted up a huge box from behind the counter. It blocked any side views of Emma. For only a second, he looked back at her and nodded. This was her one shot.

"Tried the door, it wasn't locked. So I'll take my usual and at least three of those lovely lady's donuts, if you please."

Crud. Emma pushed on the employee door, opening it as much as she needed to slip in. After she vanished without anyone crying out or hooting, she stopped directly inside and peered back out.

Nick rang Sam up and began to turn around to start up the coffee machine when the whole of his nude back turned beet red. With exaggerated movements, he stomped backward, never turning to show his naked derriere to the customers. Though, Emma got to enjoy one last look before she raced to the backroom. Thank god she'd left her luggage here. She changed as quickly as possible and combed through her gnarled hair with her fingers. After tying her apron on, she stuffed her ponytail into the hat and joined Nick at the front.

"Hey, how's it going?" she called cheerfully to hide away any panic.

"The lady of the hour! Here I feared the grouch had chased you off."

Nick stared sheepishly over his shoulder at her. As he caught her eye, his embarrassed frown softened to a tender smile. Emma placed a hand on his shoulder and helped to guide him to the employee door. "Why don't I take care of them while you...check on the fryer? It's been acting up."

"Sounds good." Nick eased around her, his naked ass

gliding across her belly as he went. She couldn't help herself and dropped her hand to cup the passing skin. He jerked in shock and slapped a hand to the front of the apron. With a wider stance, Nick took two steps, then dashed for the back room. No doubt he'd find his clothing in the storage room and hopefully no one would ask why it was the same thing he wore yesterday.

"Who's next?" Emma asked, trying to get into the swing of things. She managed to ring up and start the next person's praline mocha before Nick barreled through the door.

"I forgot to pick up Skylar!" he shouted, rushing past the customers. "You got this?"

"She's fine, you worrywart," Sam spoke for her.

Even with the regular's assurance, Nick stopped and gazed back. Emma gave him a little nod, and he dashed out the door straight into the snow without a coat on. A little chuckle grew in Emma's chest at how frantic he was, but she couldn't deny how adorable it was either.

"Excuse me, ma'am?" One of the older ladies approached the counter, her face knotted in concern.

"Yes?"

"I found this on the floor." With a delicate touch, she dropped Emma's black bra onto the counter.

HOLY SHIT, IT'S cold. Nick stomped straight into a snow pile, the frozen slush winding up in his jeans and shocking his calves. Sure enough, at that moment the town's only plow rolled past shoving all the street snow onto the sidewalk for the shop owners to deal with. He gritted his teeth and was about to raise a middle finger in a wave, but he shook it off. Even with a crick in his back and snow in his socks, his good mood couldn't be broken.

Of course, there was a damn good chance his bare ass would be the talk of church tomorrow, but that was a problem for another day. Skylar's last message came in a half-hour ago and was just the word, "Now." That couldn't be good. Nick checked his phone one last time, making certain nothing changed, and he barreled ahead…

"Ah, shit!" He nearly walked straight into Mrs. Wilkins who had his niece in tow. "Sorry." A blush burned on his cheeks as he realized he almost plowed face-first into her chest range. To his surprise, she didn't step away in horror but moved closer.

"Nick."

"I was just coming to get her. Skylar?"

"What?"

Pink covered the bottom quarter of her hair, but Nick didn't have the wherewithal to turn that into a fight. She had an arm wrapped around Abby's, the two chittering together. At least she had her backpack on, so maybe there'd been some studying in between the surprise slumber party. Girls did that, right?

"Get to the café and clock in."

Skylar groaned. "But it's Saturday."

"I know, which means school won't interfere with you making up your missed shift." He tried using authority, but the lip on her wasn't budging. May as well try a different tactic. "Thanks to the blizzard it was a late start, and Emma could use your help."

Her eyes opened wide, then that know-it-all teenage grin took over. "So she didn't leave." Skylar turned to her friend and they both giggled.

God, he did not want to know. "Yes, she's inside, alone, fighting off Sam's conspiracy theories. So if you like her more than me, get going."

"Come on," she said to her friend, the two of them arm in arm. As she walked next to Nick, she bumped her shoulder into him and whispered, "You know your shirt's inside out?"

He couldn't react. He sure as hell couldn't curse, then try to fix the problem. All Nick could do to not feed her ego was grunt and vaguely shrug. Even still, Skylar cackled like all her evil plans were coming true.

With the girls gone, he focused on the woman that saved his ass. "Thank you for bringing her. Keeping her overnight and bringing her. I'm sorry about..." He waved his phone as if that could get him out of breaking the guardian code. The next time Skylar had girls over, one was guaranteed to stay two to three hours late. Great.

"It was my pleasure. She's a fantastic girl. You've done wonders with her given her father."

Nick jerked at the unspoken threat that Skylar's best friend's mother knew what really happened with his brother. Even if he wanted to run back inside and get to work, he had to play nice. "It's a challenge."

"I know. I've only been raising Abby alone for the past few months and some nights...let's just say they don't make a wine glass deep enough."

He put on a vague laugh and fell back to one of his rote talking-to-parents phrases. "Kids are a handful."

She leaned closer and almost pressed her chest against his arm. "The days are long but the nights... they're even longer."

What in the hell is she going on about? Nick didn't have

time for this. "Tell you what, why don't you get a drink from the café? On the house."

Mrs. Wilkins beamed at him. "That sounds delightful." Much like Abby and Skylar, she wound her arm around his. He blinked and, feeling like the mouse the fairy godmother turned into a footman, Nick led Mrs. Wilkins to the café. At the door, he tried to wiggle out by holding it open. She gave a hard squeeze of his biceps but had to let go to walk in.

From behind, Nick shouted, "Sky, get your friend's mom whatever she wants."

His niece turned away from her friend to give him the mile-long stare. He met it, and she gave in first, walking over to take the order. With all of that solved, Nick's gaze broke through the crowd to find the one lighthouse in the storm. Emma's smile was his northern star, brighter than anything in the sky. She finished with the customer and looked over. For a moment, she bit her lip and blushed before her eyes opened wide, and she pointed at his collar.

Nick finally glanced down to find the shirt's tag flopping out below his neck. No wonder. All he could do was shrug.

"I'm afraid the parent's skating party had to be postponed due to the weather."

The what? Nick stared at Mrs. Wilkins when it dawned on him. Oh right, the party to help get Skylar back into skating. "That's too bad."

"Hey." His niece damn near ran across the café to poke him in the chest. "I'm leaving early."

"Says who?"

"My hair appointment, remember?"

Jesus. If one more person asked him to remember something he was certain they never told him, Nick was gonna check himself for a concussion. "Yes, hair, dolled up, dance. Got it. What do you even need your hair done for? It looks fine."

Skylar stared him dead in the eye, then rolled hers. With a beleaguered sigh, she skipped back to Emma and the two fell into dangerous chatter. Nick scratched at his shirt tag, reminding himself he needed to get to the back and fix that when Mrs. Wilkins leaned so close her blond hair swept over his shoulder.

"Home all alone, you must have something special planned."

"Not really," Nick said even as he put together that it'd be him and Emma in his house with no fear of innocent eyes catching them. Ideas floated in his mind of the two of them curled around each other before the fireplace. No, her perfect white ass propped up on the kitchen table before he took a spatula to it.

He was so far gone he barely heard Mrs. Wilkins whisper in his ear, "Well, I could think of a few things."

"Sounds great," Nick mumbled, his cock half-hard as Emma innocently licked whipped cream off her thumb.

CHAPTER TWENTY

"ALLOW ME…"

Emma paused in tugging her errant suitcase out of the backseat of the truck. Holding out his hand, Nick gazed at her with a sly smile.

"You don't have to," she said while slipping to the driveway. They'd had a long day. Emma's feet and legs ached from racing to keep up with the requests for donuts. But once the lights were off and the chairs stacked, she'd sat beside him and all the pain faded away.

Nick managed to lift her heavy luggage with one arm and drape his other over her shoulder. "But I want to," he said.

Four days...dropping down to three with the sun.

The reminder barely made a dent in Emma's mood. She jumped up and kissed him, most of her lips pressing to his cheek instead. Nick laughed and bent over. His nose pressed into her cheek as he parted his mouth before her lips. The heat of his breath chased away the winter chill, and he kissed her. All the quick glances over the day, the intimate grazes, and the fact she'd stuffed her bra in her pocket reached a boiling point. Emma clung to his cheeks and rifled her fingers through his hair. His tongue, tasting of caramel and pecans, swept over hers.

She had to break away as another biting winter wind cut through her jacket.

"You're freezing," Nick said. She wanted to argue but her teeth chattered in response. He pecked a quick kiss to her forehead, then hefted the suitcase up with a groan. "What do you have in this thing? Pirate gold?"

Together, they stumbled for the front door instead of the side. The place was cool after hosting no one for two days. Emma shivered and rubbed her hands while abandoning her shoes. Nick was a gentleman and took not only her coat but her scarf as well. "I was thinking, since the corn dog and macaroni kid's gonna be out tonight, how's lobster ravioli sound for dinner?"

"Like you're trying to get me into bed."

Nick chuckled and swept her up into his arms. "It doesn't have to be the bed." With his kiss, heat rushed through her.

Her thighs clenched and an urge to tug off his clothes overcame her. But the ache in her empty stomach calmed her enough to think clearly. "Are you going to have to pick up Skylar?"

She'd been at her hair appointment for hours. The girl could pop in through the door at any second and catch them in the act.

"Her friend's gonna drop her off. They'll get dressed. I get at least three embarrassing pictures, then she's off."

Sounded like a good plan. Emma nodded and the two trekked into the kitchen.

"Can't say I miss that high school mess," Nick said as he flipped on the kitchen light. "The damn tie choked me the whole night."

"I bet you were handsome." She found her way into the fridge and, sure enough, there was a packet of 'real lobster meat' in the drawer.

Nick barked out a laugh and dropped the flour canister. "I looked like a bull with a rope on my neck. But you made all the jaws drop."

She gulped and touched her cheek. The divot from an old scar yanked her heart back to the trauma of high school. All she could do was shake her head and focus on creating the filling.

"Well, I'd kill to see you in a dress." Nick swept a hand around the back of her waist and pulled her close. "Or nothing at all," he whispered against her cheek.

The storm in her stomach settled. She turned to him, but he stared at the bowl and blinked. "You've already got that made up?"

"It...sorry, was that wrong?" Her years of training had kicked in without thinking. She knew what needed to be prepped and did it.

"A beautiful woman whipping food together for us? That's never wrong."

"But you...you were going to..." Emma abandoned the spatula and slipped away when a hand caught hers.

"Hey, I like cooking beside you. For starters, you know what you're doing."

Her cheeks burned and she smiled. "So do you."

"Uh-huh." He dumped the ingredients into the stand mixer and turned it on. As it kneaded the flour into pasta dough, Nick chuckled. "My food's edible, yours is... I think the last customer called your eclair divine."

"No, they didn't." Oh god, she was blushing to her knees.

"Like heaven inside pastry," Nick kept on. She tried to shake away the compliments, but they lightened her heart. His jovial laugh faded and, in a serious tone, he said, "The best thing to ever happen to Brew 4 U."

Four days…

She'd never been the best thing anywhere. Emma looked up at him and found herself falling into a winsome smile that spoke novels. Her hand abandoned the bowl and reached for his cheek.

Why not stay longer? Make divine eclairs, help Skylar with young womanhood, fall into bed with this impossibly sweet and gruff man every night. She pulled Nick closer, the idea perched on her tongue.

The stand mixer beeped in pain and he jerked away. "Ah, shit, where'd I leave that pasta roller-outer thing?"

As he hunted for the missing attachment, Emma returned to stirring, terrified of the want growing in her heart. She dipped a spoon into her lobster filling and held it up for Nick. "What do you think?"

He leaned over and curled his lips around the silver metal, about to swallow it down, when the walls rocked from a great blast. Nick spun around, the lobster tumbling to the counter. Both dashed into the living room to find the source of the explosion and spotted Skylar flying up the stairs in a panic.

"I'm not going!" she shouted.

The front door she'd slammed shut opened again and her little friend walked in more cautiously with a dress bag on her arm.

"Hi, Mr. Iverson," she said.

"What's wrong, Abby?"

He was answered by the double slamming of Skylar's bedroom door. Nick tipped his head back and groaned just as the touchy-feely woman from the café walked in.

"Hello, Nick," she purred. Even for ferrying around two teenagers, she was dressed to the nines in a sharp blouse and trousers with a blowout and modest makeup. Emma wiped her dirty hands on the back of her jeans that hadn't seen a washer in over a week.

"Hi. Can you give me a minute? I have a major drama incident to deal with. Skylar…?" He shouted into the air while taking the stairs two at a time. "What the hell are you doing?"

"Leave. Me. Alone!" she screamed before cranking her music. Nick banged on the door, but his thumping faded into the bass.

Uncertain of what to do, Emma glanced back to the kitchen, then at the young girl with her hair in an updo standing on the snow mat. "Would you like something to drink?"

"Ah, water would be nice. Thanks."

Emma smiled and was about to get it when the woman stepped in. "Let me get it for you, dear."

"The kitchen's right through…"

"I know," she said, claiming her territory with claws out.

Abby stared forlornly up the stairs, so Emma followed after the woman. She'd found the old pizza place glasses and had one under the tap.

"Seems you were planning a little dinner." She slammed the faucet's handle down and jerked around so fast that a droplet splattered on the stove.

Emma tried to maintain eye contact, but it was a losing battle. "It's all Nick's idea…"

"Nick?" The woman left her daughter's glass in the sink and stepped closer. The clip of her heels caused Emma's jaw to clench. "I'm afraid we haven't properly met. I'm Desiree."

"Emma." She held out her hand and the woman clasped it tighter than a cobra at an arm-wrestling match.

"You're the girl who does the donuts."

The dismissive tone sent a rare ripple of anger through Emma. "Among other things. I'm a trained chef."

"That so? You're staying with the Iversons to cook for them?"

"No. Nick was kind enough to give me a place to sleep while I work for him."

"Ah yes, for, not with. Wouldn't do you well to forget where you sit, dear."

On his cock twenty-four hours earlier.

"Mom?"

Emma's face burned hot at her witty comeback being interrupted by a concerned teenager. Poking her head in, Abby looked at her thirsty mother, then the glass of water in the sink. It was Emma who scooped it up and handed it to the girl while Desiree flexed her talons. No doubt she wanted to impale all ten acrylics into Emma's liver.

Needing air, Emma said, "Why don't we wait for Skylar in the living room? I think Jeopardy is on."

"Uh…sure," the girl said carefully.

They made it to the couch when Nick shouted, "Fine! Be that way!" and stomped down the stairs. He wrung a hand over the banister, looking ready to snap it off, when he caught the three ladies' eyes and froze. "I don't know what her problem is. She's mad about something…probably stupid and won't go."

Oh no.

"That's a shame," Desiree said, all sweetness as she rushed to Nick's side. "Is there anything I can do to help?"

He snorted and shook his head. "She'll tear your head clean off. You're better off going to the dance without her."

"Alone?" Abby squeaked.

Pity swam through Emma for the poor girl who'd no doubt been planning on spending the night dancing with her friend. "Why don't I try?" she offered.

Desiree snickered, but Nick tapped his lip. "That might work. She likes you. Just…" He reached over and took Emma's arm. Lowering his voice, he whispered, "Don't look her in the eye, or she might charge."

Emma laughed and strained for his fingers to give them a squeeze. The side of her face burned from Desiree's death glare. Not wanting to get in the middle of the divorcee dance, Emma hightailed it up the stairs.

Before she was out of earshot though, Desiree struck. "I didn't know you were hiring people from AARP. That's quite generous."

"What? Emma? She's not even thirty."

"Really? She wears more makeup than a grandmother in a beauty pageant."

That one struck deep. Emma clenched a hand over her chest and ran up the last of the stairs. She missed whatever Nick said, her heart unable to take it. Skylar's angry music thumped the door on its hinges. Carefully, Emma raised her fist and gave a soft knock.

"Skylar?" she called to her. "Do you want to talk?"

"Is *he* out there?" she snarled.

"No. It's just me."

Only the screaming singer filled the air. Emma shifted, uncertain what to do, when Skylar said, "It better be." The door flung open. Her pink and blond hair was done up at the front and waves cascaded down the back. Unfortunately, her eyes matched her dye job—the entire area pink and inflamed from the tears still on her cheeks.

"What's the matter? Why don't you want to go to the dance? Is it about…Antonio?"

Skylar screamed, "No! It's because I'm ugly!" She flung herself onto her bed and buried her face into the mattress. Emma took a quick look down the hall, then stepped in after.

"You are not."

"Yes, I am," she mumbled into her comforter before turning around to show her. "Look!" Skylar pointed to two relatively small zits on her chin. "They're hideous and massive! I can't let anyone see me like this."

"Oh." Emma wanted to laugh at the minor problem, but she knew better. This was life and death after all. "Dear, no one will—"

"Don't say they won't notice. They fucking will. They'll call me ziti face until the day I die." Skylar slammed her face back down into the blanket and moaned.

Dropping to her knees, Emma gently rubbed a hand over Skylar's back. "What if we cover them up?"

"There's not enough concealer in the world!" she screamed to the sky. Emma looked to her desk to find small tubes scattered across it. "I tried everything and nothing works."

Rising, Emma inspected the drugstore makeup. It wasn't the right color and looked chalky on the applicator. No wonder. Poor thing, this stuff was ancient.

"Let me get my kit," she said and dashed down the stairs. Nick and Desiree sat on the couch while Abby was forced to stand. At the sound of Emma getting into her luggage, he looked over.

"How's it—?"

"Working on it." Once equipped with her arsenal, Emma rejoined Skylar who was at least sitting up. "Don't pop it." She warned. "Trust me, it'll only make it worse. You're pretty light, so I might have to mix in some highlighter to make it work." When Emma cracked her makeup case, Skylar's eyes opened wide.

"Wow, that's...I don't know what half of this stuff is." She picked up a contour stick and a brow gel.

"I can show you later," Emma said. "For now, let's make you look as beautiful as you are." As she went, she explained the steps. "You want this to last for the whole night, so we'll start with a primer, then the foundation."

Emma worked fast, hiding away the two pimples. "You're probably going to want to toss most of your makeup. It's too old to work right on you."

"Okay," Skylar said. Her voice was rough, but she wasn't crying anymore as she held herself steady on her bed. Emma's knees were already aching, but she kept it up.

"You must be excited about the dance. Did you talk to...?"

She paused with her blush brush as Skylar's cheeks

pinked on their own. "I did," she gasped out with a giggle. "What you said worked. We talked for fifteen minutes about coffee, and he told me all about Italy. And..." Skylar lifted her phone and waved it around. "He gave me his number!"

"Congrats."

"He said he'd save me a dance tonight. It has to go perfect."

No wonder she was in such dire straights. Emma focused on blending. After adding a dash of blush and bronzer, then a hint of highlighter on Skylar's enviable cheekbones, she lifted her apple-shaped hand mirror.

"Holy hell." Skylar raised her chin and whipped it back and forth. "You can't even see it."

"Why don't we do some eye shadow? To compliment your dress?"

Skylar pointed to the dress hanging off her closet door. It was adorable and young, with a high neckline, no sleeves, and a poofy skirt. Emma zeroed in on the crimson belt around the black satin. "A cranberry with a dab of white on the corners should work perfectly."

The girl dutifully closed her eyes as Emma got to work. She wasn't as well-practiced in elaborate eye looks and had to concentrate. While she was tracing the black eyeliner across Skylar's lids, the girl suddenly asked, "What'd my uncle say to get you to stay?"

Her hand jumped at the end, giving Skylar a severe cat-eye. Emma clasped her wrist to keep from accidentally dotting fake beauty marks on her cheeks as well.

"We, uh, talked about dessert and coffee."

"And then you smooched," Skylar said with a laugh.

Damn it. Emma tried to laugh it off, even lie, but her throat caught, and she couldn't. "Hold still, please," she said instead, focusing on the girl's eyelids. Emma finished as quickly as possible, then gave one final spritz of a setting spray.

"How's it look?" Skylar asked.

"See for yourself." Emma held up the mirror and the girl squealed.

"Oh my goats, this is amazing. I look so…Antonio's gonna love this. Eee! Thank you, thank you, thank you!" She wrapped her hands around Emma and squeezed hard.

With care, Emma replaced her makeup tools and closed the box. "You're welcome."

Skylar was busy posing in her mirror, trying out various pouts with her reflection surrounded by cutout pictures of boys. She batted her mascara lashes and tested her lips before snatching up a lip gloss and coating her mouth. Even in the fancy dress and makeup, there was so much kid inside.

"How are you so good at this?"

Emma paused in the doorway. She could give any number of reasons. But as she dug her palms into the leather handle of her makeup kit, the old shame roared back. "When I was your age, I had bad acne. Not a couple of zits here and there, it was cystic." Emma brushed a finger over her cheek where the worst of the scars remained. She put on a smile even as the pain bludgeoned her self-esteem. "I taught myself to put on my face from magazines and some old MUA training vids. It gave me back my confidence."

It was the only way she was able to survive high school. Even now, if she didn't wear her full coverage, people would gawk. Coworkers would ask if she was sick or infectious. She'd wake before dawn to put on her makeup and wash it off at two a.m. so no man would know.

"That's bullshit," Skylar said. "Sorry, but...no one should be mean to you for things you can't control."

Tears built in Emma's eyes. She blinked them away before they could fall. "Thank you. You should get back to your friend."

"Oh, shit! Abby!" Skylar dashed down the stairs and grabbed her friend's hand.

"Does this mean you're going to the dance after all?" Nick asked.

His niece stuck her tongue out, which he laughed off as the two girls ran to get dressed. Standing by the door, Emma caught his eye. He smiled and whispered, "Thank you."

CHAPTER TWENTY-ONE

"WAIT, I NEED one more," Nick ordered the two girls. Skylar tossed her head back and groaned.

"We already took like two hundred pictures."

"It was five. Now stand next to the fireplace."

Abby carefully sidled near the brick while Skylar threw her entire arm across the mantle and leaned in. Before she fell into the flames, Nick pressed the button and his niece was off. "Okay, we're leaving now," she declared after snatching up her coat. She tugged on her friend's arm and the two of them ran for the front door.

"What else?" Nick asked.

"Uh…bye?"

"There will be no drinking. There will be no leaving the dance until it's over. Then you will text me."

"God, you're so embarrassing. Fine, yes, all of that."

"Sky?" He caught her flustered face quickly tipping into teenage anger. "Have fun." Her response was to grumble and run out into the cold for the Wilkins' SUV.

Mrs. Wilkins took a little longer to gather her coat. "It's going to be a long night," she said. "Any chance I could tempt you to join me for...?"

"The ravioli are ready to pop!" Emma called. She emerged from the kitchen with the pot in her hands.

Nick felt the same expectant energy his niece had as he stared at not only the pasta but the woman holding them. "Thank god, I could eat a horse. " He started to follow her when a cold draft caught through the living room, and he glanced to the open front door. "Uh, rain check."

"I'll hold you to that, Nick," Abby's mom said just as the horn blared. Sky was impatient as hell to get to that dance.

Laughing, he joined Emma in the kitchen to find her pouring a buttery cream sauce on the ravioli she'd also finished. "You are amazing."

"It's nothing special."

She held out a plate, but Nick filled his arms with her. "You took a door-slamming, wall-kicking teenager to bubbly and excited in two minutes. Then you made this fancy dinner with barely any help. How?"

With a shy giggle, Emma bit her lip. Nick's hands slipped off her waist to wrap around her hips. In a low, husky voice, Emma asked, "I thought you said you were hungry?"

He swept his palm farther, rounding over her ass. When he clenched where he'd spanked her earlier,

Emma gasped. Their dinner could wait in the oven. Nick curled under her ass and started to lift her up when his stomach growled loud enough to shake the copper cow mold on the wall.

"Seems I am," he had to admit, done in by his body. He took both plates and laid them on the table where they settled in for dinner.

The ravioli was better than anything he could have come up with, especially the butter sauce. They talked about nothing in particular, but he hadn't laughed so hard in his life. Her quiet demeanor did him in. Every time Emma set up a joke, he wouldn't see the punchline coming. He'd swear he could sit on that hard, wooden chair for hours on end just listening to her talk.

Emma reached for the empty plates the same moment he did, their hands bouncing off each other. That innocent touch charged through Nick, making him feel all of fourteen himself and working up the courage to sit near the girl he liked. Maybe she felt the same, her cheeks burning as she dropped her gaze.

Standing up, Nick reached for her. "Why don't we—"

His offer to leave the dishes for later and take advantage of the fire was thwarted by his phone. It buzzed across the table, hellbent on smacking into a glass. When Nick looked at the notification, he tried to fight off a groan—Pete.

"I've got to…"

"I'll wash these up."

"No, leave them to soak," he said while placing his phone to his ear. Nick walked to the living room, turning in a circle to catch a glimpse of Emma. "I can do it… Hey."

"What are you doing, little brother?"

"You called me."

"Right. Just wondering why you sent me these pictures. House looks good."

Jesus, did he even open them or only look at the thumbnail? "It's Skylar in her dress for her winter dance thing. I thought you'd want to see." Being her father and all.

"Oh...? Oh. Wow." His excitement dropped and melancholy slipped in. "I didn't even recognize her. She looks so grown up."

Probably because she had grown without him seeing her more than twice since he'd left.

"You let her out of the house looking like that? She's got enough makeup on to be the town bicycle."

For the love of... "Maybe if you were here, you could have had some say in how much makeup she has on." Not that it was bad. All Nick cared was that it got her to stop scream-crying, and he'd seen thicker on toddlers. "I'm doing the best I can."

"And when she gets knocked up at sixteen by some smooth-talking, motorcycle riding brat with a wispy mustache...?"

"You mean how Skylar was created in the first place?" Nick volleyed back.

People didn't like to talk about how her mom just made it out of high school to give birth. People preferred to pretend it was young love while Nick ran off to the Marines to escape their shouting matches. His pacing led him to the wall with the pictures his parents had put up. In an eight by ten-inch frame, Pete at age nine stood on top of a six-year-old Nick. He looked so proud with a pixie stick clenched between his teeth like a multi-colored cigarette.

Even though his brother had three years on him, it became Nick's job to keep him in line. He thought he'd escaped that role until the whole family came crashing down. He couldn't protect his brother, but there was one person he could save.

"Skylar's got a good head on her shoulders...more or less." For all her bitching, she put in the work and got good grades. Better than her father and uncle. All he had to do was guide her past the sea of hormones to college, and he was home free.

"I can't believe what you've done to her. I should take her instead."

For five years Nick raised her. The sobbing fits shifted from skinned knees to bad selfies. With no one else, he'd had to take her bra shopping and tried to not get beaten to a pulp while standing anywhere near the lady's underwear. He'd comforted her as best as he could despite barely understanding any of it. And now his brother wanted to swoop back in.

"Maybe you should," Nick said, strangling the phone. "Get a god damn place of your own. Bring your daughter home. Do literally anything beyond blame me and everyone else for you landing your ass in prison!"

"Uh..."

Ah, shit. Nick lowered the phone to his shoulder and turned. Standing in the living room, Emma looked ready to scamper away. She held up a dish towel and whispered, "They're ready to be dried."

How the hell am I going to explain this? Nick put on a smile and nodded, placing the phone to his ear. She took the cue and returned to the kitchen. Nick stared along the photos. They grew crisper as the date increased. Next to one of Nick in his fatigues posing by the grill with Pete and their dad was a baby picture of Skylar tucked inside a milk crate. The wall shifted to nothing but Skylar—pigtails, sidewalk chalk, school plays, Santa Claus. Her whole short life was up there, and Pete had missed a third of it.

"Come home for Christmas," Nick said.

"What?"

"Come home…or I'm telling Skylar the truth."

Before his brother could weasel his way out of it, Nick ended the call and set his phone to silent. He pulled in a steadying breath and joined Emma in the kitchen. She was already wiping down the plates she'd put dinner on and cleaned.

"Wait, I can—" Nick called before he slumped his shoulders. "Let me do that."

"It's all right. I've nearly…"

He slipped in beside her and took over. "Doing things with my hands helps."

"Oh. Okay." Emma skittered away, pressing her back to the counter.

Here he'd been hoping for a romantic evening alone with her. Instead, the family hydra reared its heads. "He was caught embezzling." Nick placed the glass on the drying rack and reached for a second. "From the same damn plant we both worked at. I was 'let go' just in case." It was what had pushed him to the café, much to Rachel's delight.

Emma didn't respond. She had her arms crossed in a self-hug, but any questions remained locked away so Nick kept talking.

"He didn't move away for a job. He got two years in the state pen once they caught him. Would have been even worse if they'd found the Oxycontin on him." It'd started thanks to an accident at the plant that became a full-blown addiction.

"Skylar was just six when he was arrested. Took them two years to get to trial and convict him. At first, it was easier to not tell her what happened. Daddy stole money so he could buy pills wasn't exactly show-and-tell material."

Their father had to cash out his pension to afford a lawyer who kept telling Pete to take a plea deal. But Pete admitting he was wrong was like asking the sun to burn cold.

Emma shifted in the fallen silence and asked, "If he was only away for two years…?"

"There were a few cycles of addiction, sobering up, then falling down the rabbit hole. We kept hoping he'd finally kicked it. Once you hit rock bottom you either bounce back up…or go six feet under. He's in a halfway house now, with some other guys getting off shit. Basically, the worst place for a teenage girl to be. So I've kept Skylar fed, clothed, safe to the best of my ability."

"That's…"

Nick shook his head hard. "Don't call me a hero." He bridled at the word tossed at him like a milk bone to a starving dog whenever people heard about his service. All he'd done was guard over munitions and watched the skin peel off a friend's face when a car bomb went off. That wasn't heroic, it was surviving.

She gulped and shifted. "You deserve a world's best uncle mug."

"Ha! Skylar'd lose her shit if I had one of those at the café." He laughed at how many shit kittens she'd have, then sighed. "I can't tell her. She was so young when it happened she didn't understand. Then when Pete got out, he begged me to keep quiet. Said if his little girl lost her admiration for him, he'd fall."

"I can't imagine how hard that is to keep."

"I used to think it was for Skylar's sake, so she'd feel pride in her parents. But now, after all this time, it's

Pete refusing to face the consequences of his actions. If he doesn't see them cry, then he didn't do anything wrong."

He dropped the soggy towel to the counter and wound his hands around the edge. Her mom had tried to tough it out living near the penitentiary to support him, but that bubble finally burst, and she'd run. Skylar got to see her on vacations and trips to Florida at least. What did her father send her? He hadn't even bothered to mail her a birthday gift in three years. Nick took to adding his name to a card to keep up the charade.

"Maybe it's finally time you told her the truth?"

She made it sound so simple. Emma was an outsider unaware of the mess of trauma lurking below those happy family portraits. If he told Skylar there was a good chance she'd hate him even more than her dad. And he couldn't handle that.

"Do you know what I need?" Nick slipped a hand around her waist and pulled her close. He aimed for a kiss to give this night hope, but his chin collapsed to her shoulder instead. Wrapping himself in her arms, he listened to her heart pounding against his chest.

"What?"

For you to stay in my life.

He almost whispered that against her neck, his lips moving but no sound emerging. Nick blinked away the thought and leaned back. "A shower. I don't know how you can stand me."

She smiled sweetly. "It's not so bad."

Cream and sugar... Nick cupped her chin and brushed his thumb over her cheek. "Why—" He traced her lips, mesmerized by the soft skin. "—don't you join me?"

CHAPTER TWENTY-TWO

THE TWO TRIPPED over each other as they climbed the stairs, alternating between kissing and racing to catch the banister. She wanted to join him, but the closer they drew to the bathroom, the greater the dread grew in Emma's heart.

"Let me get that," Nick said. She expected him to flip on the light, but he pulled her sweater off instead. "Much better." He ran his hands over her chest and reached for her pants when Emma jittered away.

"Maybe some lights would help." She laughed to

explain her strange reaction and turned them on.

The harsh glow gave no quarter as it cut across Nick's grizzled cheeks. It would be less kind to her. He roughed a palm over his stubble and turned on the tap. The water ran down the drain as the two people who'd shared each other's bodies tried to not grow awkward.

"Here." She caught the hem of his t-shirt and lifted it over his head. He had to duck to help, and before she could pull it off, he kissed her. All her pent-up energy siphoned elsewhere. Emma dropped his shirt to the ground then went after his pants.

"Whoa." Nick scrambled, clinging to her hips as she undid his jeans. "I'm gonna have to up my game to keep up with you."

He cupped her chin and held her, staring into her eyes. She clung to the same boxers they'd tossed into the box of straws. Nick brushed his thumb back and forth, a serenity washing across his face. Emma reached around his back, pulling his hips to her belly. More bubbled in her mind, words she ached and feared to hear.

"Baths require water, don't they?" Nick said. His gaze drifted to the open drain, and he dropped in the plug. As the water splashed into the tub, the two of them stripped off haphazardly. She took off her jeans and socks and put them on the sink, leaving her in her underwear. Nick pulled everything off himself at once and stretched.

"God it feels good to be out of those." As he raised his arms over his head, giving in to the strain of his muscles, he looked overjoyed. Slowly, his eyes opened and traced down her body. First, her face and neck. As they traveled, his cock surged halfway up.

Emma reached behind to the hooks on her bra. She

bit her lip, watching his erection bounce, then harden to steel as she lowered her bra. Slowly, she tugged the straps down—trying to act provocative—when Nick leaped for her. He kissed her, his tongue sweeping in to toy with her lip, and pulled her panties off.

"Please, you're gonna drive a man mad. Me. You will make me coo-coo bananas if you don't take a bath with me."

How can I say no?

Emma nodded. Taking her hand, Nick stepped into the tub. He gasped at the hot water slopping up his calf, then guided her to join. While he sunk in, his long legs slipping down and feet pressing astride the faucet, Emma took her time. The lukewarm heat of the tub surprised her. As she started to lower herself, she slipped.

Nick was quick to catch her, helping to guide her legs and press her back to his chest. She bobbed between his thighs, sweeping her buttocks against his cock. He nibbled her neck and ear as he ran his palms over the tops of her thighs.

The water splashed and Emma shied her face away. Nick bent over to pick up a washcloth and catch the floating bar of soap. Placing his hands before her, he lathered up the cloth. She watched the bubbles rise across the surface, hiding away her pale legs. Nick let the soap go, and she expected him to begin washing.

One hand swept under her breast and another drew the warm washcloth over her chest. She leaned back in surprise, wrapping her arm around the back of Nick's neck. "I thought you'd go first," she gasped. He took his time, caressing the cloth across her breast, down her wide cleavage, and over her pooched belly.

"You know what they say about ladies," Nick mused.

With his free hand, he pinched her nipple while the washcloth dipped farther between her thighs, straining them apart.

Emma tried to help him, but her legs were trapped. She raised one up, the cold air nibbling on her wet skin. Nick cupped her jaw and began to scoot the two of them lower. At first, she welcomed the warm water, before realizing it was coming for her face.

Lighting quick, she sat up, landing her ass on his thighs. The washcloth floated away, and only the panicked splashes filled the air. Nick had one hand placed almost chastely to her belly. The other hugged the lip of the tub, seeming uncertain where to go.

She couldn't get out of this.

"How do you…what do you think about makeup?" Emma asked fast and clenched her eyes.

Nick snorted. "Since it got her to stop crying, I don't care."

What? "No, not about…" Okay, maybe she should have asked him if Skylar was allowed to wear makeup. Men could be rather opinionated about it, especially when they didn't use any. "I mean, do you think, if you see a woman wearing it, do you call it…" Her heart galvanized and in a dead voice, she finished, "…false advertising?"

She'd heard it often. *Men, beware women wearing makeup. They're lying to you. First date you better take her swimming to see what she really looks like, or you could wake up next to Quasimodo.* Avoiding the trap had seemed easy enough until the handsome man invited her to take a bath with him.

Nick scratched his graying temples. "Like when it's a scam that claims it'll make you twenty years younger?"

All she could do was shake her head. Emma turned

in the bath, her skin blistering even though the heat had waned. There was no escaping it now. It wouldn't help for him to be surprised by the scars and texture of her face. Better to rip that Band-Aid off and be done with it.

"I…" She couldn't face him and stared at the wall. On the tile was a small drawing of a star done in marker which was probably permanent. "I wear makeup."

"Uh-huh. Figured that out when Daryl was laughing at me for having lipstick on my neck. Good thing he didn't see the other spots." Nick smirked at the memory, but Emma couldn't escape her spiral.

"I've got scars. From when I was Skylar's age."

"What happened? Did someone hurt you!" He pivoted from pain to anger so fast, Emma feared he'd leap from the tub to chase down the imaginary villain.

"No, not like that. Acne. It's cleared up for the most part." *Accutane, a blessing and a curse.* "But…"

He steadied himself and swept both arms across the lip of the tub. "You're worried about something I can't understand."

She nodded then shook her head. "Let me show you." Turning around, Emma placed her back to him. Nick took care to hold her, sweeping his palm over the top of her arm as she cupped water and washed away the foundation, the bronzer, the blush, the primer. Her armor floated away in the bubbles. What would she do if he panicked? If he called her a witch and threw her out of the house?

Okay, that probably wouldn't happen. But if he didn't want to touch her or kiss her? *I'll be fine. Get my car back, go to my sister's, live with a desiccated heart for the rest of my life. No problem.*

Emma didn't realize her hands were shaking until Nick took both. They stopped slapping the water as he rubbed them together. "You don't have to do this."

He was a man she'd known for five days. They'd only slept together once. He took her into his home, gave her a job when she was desperate. Made her feel safe and whole. She had to know.

At first, Emma shifted and turned the side of her face. He couldn't have seen much through her hair, but years of scrutinizing pictures had taught her he'd see something. When Nick didn't leap out of the tub in a panic, she did the whole one-eighty. Her eyes stayed downcast, zeroing in on the combat scar across his stomach. As she finished her spin, her knees bent, her hands flat in the water, she waited to be struck down.

A warm hand cupped under her chin and began to raise her eyes up. She blinked, fearing to find his gaze wandering anywhere else, but he stared her right in the eye. "Would you believe me if I said you're beautiful?"

"No." She gasped at the truth slipping out, but to her surprise, Nick laughed.

"Two years in pre-teen hell has taught me to ask that. Though it's hard to not fight against it. Can I say you're sweet?"

"Yes."

"Can I call you adorable? Can I say you have the biggest, prettiest eyes I've ever seen?"

Said eyes began to tear. Emma had to blink them away as she nodded. Nick swept his thumb across her lip. "And if I said I want to press your thighs apart, pink your ass, and bite your neck while you scream my name…would you believe that?"

Emma's mouth fell open to gasp, but Nick's lips plunged to hers before she could. The way he held her cheek so gently while kissing so dirty made her heart flutter and toes curl. She ran her hands through his hair, tugging on the locks to get him to cry out as he pressed a hand tighter to her breast.

"It was you," he moaned in her ear before running his nails down her side and rolling his palm over her butt. She clenched her thighs in anticipation, but Nick didn't slap it as he'd wanted. Instead, his fingers glided from the crest of her ass down to the tickling underside, then he pulled on her inner thigh. Emma slipped lower into the water. She flailed a hand out in fear of cracking her skull, but he grabbed her palm.

"When you caught me in here." Nick traced a nail down her lifelines, following each one until they met at the heart. Looking her dead in the eye, he guided her hand to his cock. Half of Emma's hand submerged as she folded her fingers around his giving girth.

Brushing back her hair, Nick whispered in her ear, "I was thinking of you."

An alien sense of power overcame her. She wrapped her thumb around the base and reached under to cup his balls. Nick strained for her wrist, but Emma caught it and placed it on her breast. He sighed while toying with her nipple, tugging on the tender skin until she wanted to cry.

"You're filthy," she said, growing more certain with every heartbeat.

"Do you want me dirtier?"

"I'm going to wash you."

"Oh…" He sounded defeated until she cupped both her hands around his cock and jerked them counterclockwise. "Oh, fuck!" Nick jumped, splashing water out of the tub.

Emma watched him squirm, just as she had *that* night that felt months past. To think, she'd nearly run away from him without doing this. She slipped back, Nick's hand falling off her breast and smacking the water. Just as he was about to follow her, she bent over and placed her lips to the head of his cock.

She swirled her tongue over the top, tugging back the pliant crown so the opening widened. Nick brushed a hand back through her hair. He tugged the sopping locks up and wound them around his fist like a rope. She was at his mercy, while he was at hers.

Opening her jaw, Emma sucked him in. The tip of her nose bounced against the water's surface as her tongue reached an inch lower. Nick began to pant, begging for more. She managed to press his cock deeper, the crown plunging against the back of her throat. Slowly, she worked her jaw up and down, tugging on the skin with her tongue then sliding it back with her hand. When she'd reach the tip, almost slipping off of him, Nick's grip on her hair would slacken.

Emma smiled at how much he was enjoying this. She opened her mouth and took him back in. This time, she worked her hand into the rhythm. With a loose fit to her mouth, she lazily swirled her tongue, then cinched her palm and jerked up his cock. Nick reached behind to dig into the shower caddy, scattering shampoo and body wash bottles.

As they plunged in, the water level rose into her nose. She tried to pull back, but a whimper from him sent her diving underwater to suck his cock. Holding her breath, Emma licked down the full length of his shaft, trailing the vein. His cock pulsed in her hand, getting harder and more difficult to take in by the second. He had to be getting close. She cupped her palm behind his shaft, ran the head over her lips like a balm, then opened her mouth for one last run.

Her hair tugged, pulling Emma back. She sat up and

found the wild eyes of a man about to blow. He caught her wrist and pulled it away, both of them listening to his ragged panting. "You…you won't get away that easy."

"Oh?"

Nick unrolled his grip on her hair, letting the coil fall to her shoulder. He reached forward and caught her ass in his hands. "I want to fuck you in here until the tiles crack."

Damn. Emma clenched her thighs, every reverberation from her clit echoing deeper inside. A hard slap to her ass jerked her to attention and Nick groaned in her ear—a hard, barely-keeping-it-together groan. "But the damn tub's too small."

With no effort, he hauled her out of the bath at the same time he stood. She swayed her hips against his. The hardness of his cock turned her butterflies into tap-dancing elephants. Emma wanted to leap onto it, then and there. She lowered her foot to the ground and yelped.

"It's cold," she tried to explain. Nick glanced down at her legs, and he scooped her up in his arms. Wrapped around him, Emma was carried to the bedroom she never thought she'd see again. He kissed her hard and hot, his tongue rolling with hers before he pulled out her bottom lip and bit it. When she yelped, he tossed her onto the bed.

Emma's wet skin struck the sheets, but Nick didn't care. Growling, he paced about the room turning on a single lamp. The air flickered like candlelight. "I've wanted to use that for ages," he admitted.

Bending over, he cracked open the military trunk at the foot of the bed. "You ever look in here?"

"No." She shook her head. She'd never.

He snickered. "Course not, cream and sugar. Well… how about this?"

With loving precision, he laid out a menagerie of toys. Emma recognized the paddle, the flogger, two sets of cuffs, and a long line of rope. There were others she couldn't make heads nor tails of. She'd swear one was a pasta crimper.

Nick ran a hand over her cheek and dug a knee into the bed beside her. "It's a lot of options."

"You're…very thorough."

"Are any of 'em scary?"

"No."

"Are any of 'em…exciting?"

She hovered a hand over the rope but wasn't certain. Instead, she picked up the padded cuffs with red leather wrapped around the metal and placed them in Nick's hands. He undid the latch, then raised an eyebrow. "You sure? You don't have to pick—"

Emma kissed him hard and latched the first cuff around her wrist. "I'm sure. Oh, and…" For a moment, she reached for the flogger, but the straps looked heavy. Instead, she went for the lighter paddle that wasn't wider than a hand.

When Nick held that, he shuddered, weighed it, then nuzzled against her neck. "God, you have no idea how badly I've wanted to do this." As he kissed her, he closed off the cuffs, then slipped away to return the rest of the toys to the chest.

"There were a few hints," Emma said. She sat on her knees, uncertain what to do. As Nick swung the paddle absentmindedly, her eyes grew bigger.

He caught her staring and stopped. "If it's too much, if you want to stop at any moment…"

"Shout kumquat?" Holy hell, was she really going to

do something that required a safe word?

Nick laughed hard. "Ya can if you want. Stop works too. I'm not into any of that forcing stuff, even for pretend. And don't hold back on my account. You get uncomfortable, you need a break, you want a snack…"

"Nick." She clung to his shoulders, the chain of the cuffs cutting across his neck. Holding him closer, Emma whispered, "Pink my ass, already."

"Yes, ma'am."

She puckered for a kiss, but Nick scooped her entire body up and hurled her onto the bed. Before she could wiggle, he grabbed her cuff's chain and looped it over a hook hidden in the headboard. "So you don't fall off," he said.

All Emma could see were her stretched-out arms and the pillows she'd curled up on for the past nights. Nick took one and guided it under her stomach. He swept his palm down her back, then he did the same with the paddle. Gentle, calm strokes of his hand were followed by the warming leather.

When he reached the small of her back, Emma started to moan. His hand cupped over the top of her ass, and a kiss landed on the middle of her spine. It was so tender, she sat up on her elbows when a swat struck her ass. Barely even that, he'd used almost no force, but the feel of her cheeks bouncing caused her to groan.

"More."

Nick answered with two swats to her other buttock. Emma curved her back, thrusting her ass up to him. Her wet hair slipped off her shoulders, exposing the whole of her naked back. A low moan broke from Nick and a heavy palm landed on her skin. He raked his fingers over her, serpentining down her body until he swerved around her ass and smacked it. This one rang out and Emma gasped.

"Too much?"

She struggled to glance over her shoulder, finding Nick straddling her on his knees with one hand clenched to his raging cock. *Fuck*. Emma jerked her hips, the slippery pillow gliding against her clit. She had to bite her lip to keep from moaning and fought to keep her voice level. "It could go pinker."

His wicked smile caused her to gasp. She reached up to the chains and gripped them. Nick slapped her ass three times with the same force. He had a well-practiced hand. With each one, she jerked at the sting, then gasped out a moan. God, she'd never felt so turned on without anything touching her clit before.

Nick bent over her, his moans of pleasure kissing up her back. He took care to not touch her stinging ass no matter how much Emma kept flexing it up.

"Should I try the paddle?"

Yes!

What if it hurts?

What if it hurts right?

Biting harder onto her lip, Emma looked back. "Maybe be gentle?"

He smiled patiently. "We can save it for later."

"No! I mean, I want to try. Please?"

Nick placed the paddle against the small of her back, and he kissed her. As he trailed lower, he brushed his cheek after so the scruff prickled her skin. Emma shivered and clenched tighter to the chains. The edge of the paddle trailed over the top of her ass. He flipped it to the flat and swept it across the swell of her buttock. It was long enough to swat her entire ass in one go.

What did I get myself into?

When the paddle left her skin, she arched her back

and readied herself. It swung with a crack of thunder, but when it struck, Emma glowed. She wiggled her ass, begging for more because her voice was lost. All she could do was gulp in air and pant it back out, her body in flames.

Nick gave another swat with more force. Emma rocked forward, nearly dislodging her chains from the hook. She adjusted, ready for the next round when a great groan rose from behind. Just as she started to look, Nick's lips pressed to hers. His body eclipsed hers, his pecs coddling her shoulders as his cock bounced against the top of her hot, searing ass.

"I can't wait any longer," Nick moaned against her mouth. He sat up and tore open a condom. When he returned, he pressed the torn wrapper into her hands, then clamped his hands to her wrists. Using his legs, he pushed her ass up. It stung when it hit his pelvis. Emma gasped then cried out as the pain switched to a scorching pleasure.

He plied her thighs apart with his knees, then thrust himself in. *Holy shit!* Even with his cock ready to explode, he slipped right in. She'd never been this wet in her life. Emma gasped at the pressure quickly racing through her veins.

Teeth nipped at her ear, and Nick's controlled panting swept across her cheek. He jerked slowly, fighting to keep it going, but she ached for a release. Emma raised her ass, smacking it against him.

"Fuck!" they cried out together.

Nick pressed her lower into the mattress, his thrusting speeding up. The cuff's chains rattled like a ghost in a whirlwind. Emma thrust back, her clit finding the pillow and his cock plunging straight into her g-spot. Whiteness enveloped her.

Her body went numb. For a brief second, Emma feared she'd stroked out. Then all the pleasure hit at once. It boiled over through her, racing her heart, tickling the entirety of her chest, and clenching her vagina into his cock. She groaned at the tight fit, and Nick pulled her hands close to her chest.

He cried out, "Emma," thrust once, then collapsed on top of her.

Time stopped. The world stopped. All she knew were the jagged breaths slipping from the lips pressed to the nape of her neck.

"You are…" Nick pulled himself from her. He took care of the condom and undid the cuffs. As Emma began to turn around, she watched the man with a huge smile and wild eyes struggle to comb his hair. "You're beautiful," he said. "I'm sorry, but…it's all I see."

"Well, I guess I can't stop you." She winced when her pinked ass grazed the bed.

Nick raced forward. He guided her back to her belly and rolled her hair in his hand. "Here." A cool lotion struck her ass. With gentle strokes, he soothed it over her buttocks. "Let me take care of you."

CHAPTER TWENTY-THREE

EMMA FINISHED THE last of her makeup and gave a cursory glance. After she wiped down the packaging and put it all back in her bag, her phone vibrated. *A new voicemail?*

"Skylar!"

She walked out of the bathroom to find Nick holding a cup of coffee while banging on the girl's bedroom door. Emma wasn't certain when she came home, only that in the early hours, Nick had returned to bed grumbling under his breath. It'd stopped when he'd curled her in his arms and fallen asleep.

"Come on. Breakfast," he kept on, a wicked smile rising. Slowly, he took a sip of his coffee, then caught Emma's eye. Abandoning his quest to wake the teen, Nick reached over and pulled her close. "I got pancakes in the oven."

"Sounds wonderful. What about…?" She glanced to the mug in his hands. He passed it over to her, and she took a quick drink. The hand Nick had around her waist drifted lower. He watched her intently as he brushed his palm over the brunt of his paddling.

"You need any pain killers?"

"No. Though, some cream and sugar in this would help."

He laughed hard. "How could I forget?" Nick leaned closer when the bedroom door flew back.

A hundred pounds of teenage rage stuck its head through the gap and shouted, "What?"

Nick and Emma stepped apart simultaneously, looking like two normal friends and nothing more. "There's pancakes and…" He coughed and slapped a hand over his mouth, but it barely stifled the laugh.

Poor Skylar looked like she was hit by a runaway train. Her elaborate updo had fallen in pieces, leaving the pink ends standing straight out. Worse was the makeup she must have been too tired to wash off. The cranberry eyeshadow was now more of a hangover red and smeared clear to the right side of her face.

She looked at Emma who found the bitter coffee and her phone very interesting. Then she zeroed in on her uncle who finally got his shock of laughter under control. "You said I didn't have to work today."

"I said breakfast, not work. Café's closed today."

"What?" Skylar's eyes bulged. She stampeded out of

her room to stare at him. "You never close. Like ever."

"Well, I was thinking maybe we all take a break. There's a fresh patch of snow on the ground and a sled in the garage."

"Sledding. You closed the café to go sledding?" She kept looking at Emma as if she was waiting for them to shout 'got ya!' "How's anyone even know? What about the regulars? Sam?"

"He'll be fine." Nick waved it off. "I updated the website so people can…"

"You know how to use the internet?"

He glared at her. "I'm not eighty-five."

"Uh-huh. Sledding? Really?"

Nick shrugged. "Or you could go ice skating. I think the rink's open today."

"A day off. A Sunday, when the church crowd gathers up the tables and leaves those bible quotes printed on fake dollars. You're not opening for them?"

"Stop making a fuss. You can go back to sleep or join us in the kitchen. There's pancakes."

"Okay. Okay…" She stepped back into her room and closed the door without answering.

Emma stopped fussing with her phone and handed the coffee back to Nick. "She didn't seem excited."

"Oh, I think that'll change." Nick took a deep drink and smiled at her.

Her thumb moved on its own and started playing through her voicemails.

"Em, it's your sister. Good news, the local pizza place is hiring. You just gotta walk in for an interview, then do a drug test."

A loud crash broke from Skylar's bedroom. "Uncle Nick?" the girl shouted. "Where are my skates?"

"In the closet," he said.

"No, they're not."

"Let me look…"

The next voicemail rolled over and it wasn't from her sister. "Hey, Kia Soul. Good news, I got the part early. All I need to do is…"

Skylar popped her head out wearing a great grin as she extended a pair of worn and yellowing ice skates. "Found 'em!" She nearly danced in a circle with excitement.

"They're gonna need sharpening."

"Yeah, yeah. Do you skate?"

Emma silenced her phone, skipping the rest of the mechanic's voicemail. "Ah…no. But you could teach me."

"Okay, but there's a lot of falling on your ass."

She and Nick both winced at the thought. He reached for her waist but paused at the curious eyes of the teenager. Instead, he wafted his palm just above her arm. "Don't worry, you can join me on the sidelines. They have outrageously priced hot cocoa."

"Can we go to Gio's Pasta too?" Skylar asked and Nick shrugged.

"Sure, why not. What do you think?"

An entire day with just the three of them… No job interviews for minimum wage pizza parlors, no mechanics calling about her car. Emma shut off her phone and the rest of the world. "Sounds perfect."

HE'D NEVER FELT so energized while flipping on the café lights. The sky may be dark as pitch, but Nick felt light as a feather. They'd had one nearly perfect day of snowball fights, and warm lasagna, and Emma resting on his lap as she read. Even Skylar was up earlier than usual, weakly smiling on a Monday morning. It felt like his entire life had reset, and he was going to get it right this time.

"You know what?" He slapped his hands together while gazing back at the café. Emma and Skylar paused in laying out the chairs to look at him. "I think today's the day the mistletoe latte comes back."

"Really?" Skylar leaped up and squealed. "Are you just saying it?"

Nick picked up the sign that'd been sitting by the door since December started. With his sleeve, he wiped away the "No" and added "Please ask for" before the mistletoe latte.

"Yes!" His niece shouted, pumping her fist in the air. "This is perfect." With that, she ran away.

"Never thought she cared what we serve here," he said, surprised at her reaction.

"Maybe she's curious too." Emma finished adding the forbidden item to the large menu and looked over her shoulder at him. "It is really good."

With a lightness in his steps, Nick vaulted over the counter. Luckily, they hadn't put anything out yet or his foot would have sent it flying. He wound a hand around Emma's waist even as she strained to finish the looping E. Brushing his lips to her neck, he whispered, "Wait until you try this version."

"Oh, yeah, that missing special ingredient."

Nick smiled. "I've got a better idea. You've inspired me."

Her cheeks lit up red, and he ached to see the same across her buttocks. "I don't know how."

He pressed his lips to her ear, darting the tip of his

tongue against her lobe as he whispered, "Yes you do."

"The oven's making a weird noise and…"

Nick walked away and flipped off the espresso machine. Emma tried to pick up the chalk in her fingers. Both looked completely guilty as Skylar stared at them.

"Weird noise, yes, that's… I mean, I assume it's normal. I'll go check. Maybe I could whip up a mistletoe donut for the occasion." She said that to Nick, but it was Skylar who perked up.

"Ooh, can I have one?"

"Do you have five bucks?" Nick interrupted.

"Don't listen to him. Of course, you can have one. There's always a few that don't make it to the tray," Emma whispered to Skylar as if he didn't overhear. The two, thick as thieves, slipped into the back room.

A soft twinkle of Jingle Bells filled the air and Nick breathed in the crisp cut of snow. Not even a week ago, he'd been tempted to abandon this place and go back to building tractors. Now, he'd never known such serenity. Emma was the piece he didn't realize was missing.

Nick stared at the gin syrup he'd mixed up himself for the latte. "I wish this thing actually worked." If all it took was one sip of his brew to keep her in his life, he might start believing in fairy tales and Santa Claus.

The bell jangled, surprising him. Nearly no one stopped by until after five. Shaking like a wet dog, a woolly coat shivered the snow onto the black mat, then a head raised up.

"So ya didn't die after all," Sam said. "Did you know this place wasn't open yesterday? Do you know what yesterday was?"

"Morning, Sam. Usual?"

"It was Sunday! That's crossword day, which means

my old lady is spitting hot tacks over the damn thing. Where am I supposed to go, Nick, if your place is closed?"

He started up the pot of black coffee. "How about the library?"

Sam shooed away that suggestion. "They chase me out the second I turn on my scanner. Hey, is that right? You got the mistletoe latte back?"

"Sure do."

"Are you Nick's evil twin?" After a second's pause, Sam asked, "The nice twin?"

"I'm the exasperated café owner about to toss you back out into the cold."

"So you weren't replaced by lizard people. Good. I'll try that thing then. And put me down for three donuts."

It came back to him like a musician picking up their instrument after decades of abandonment. After the gin syrup, walnut and pecan flavoring, he added a dash of peppermint, then the milk. Instead of shoving it over, Nick took his time, pouring off a sprig of holly design and dotting three berries in the milk. Pride swelled in him as he passed it to Sam.

The old man raised it to his lips. He looked up at Nick who couldn't stop hovering, shrugged, and drank. "Not bad. Prefer my usual, mind. But not bad."

The bell jangled again, people taking care to wipe their feet as they gazed around the warm and bright café.

"Come on in. This crazy bastard's brought the mistletoe whatever back," Sam shouted before he took such a long sip the foam left a milk mustache on top of his salt and pepper one.

"Really?"

"You can tell whoever that Miss B lady is that Brew 4

243

U is serving mistletoe lattes."

The exhausted people gave a minor cheer but it was enough to invigorate Nick. He reached for the mugs and the beans, before remembering most were still in the grinder. "Give me a second," he said, walking to the back room. "Sam, watch the counter."

"Aye aye, captain. So, any of you hear about the next snow storm?"

Nick wanted to whistle and almost did as he approached the storage room. He pushed on the door, and Emma's voice struck him.

Instead of sounding delighted, it was hushed and sharp. "When's the interview?"

Interview? Nick froze, his breath shallowing.

"That's really soon. What if...? Uh-huh. Okay. Yes, it sounds like a good job."

He spun around and slammed his back against the wall. A job interview. Emma was...of course she was. She had her whole life ahead of her working in fancy restaurants and becoming a dessert chef. He knew that.

He knew they didn't have much time left, and that one day she'd walk out that door. Emma was never meant to be permanent, a warm breeze after the blizzard. Nothing more. Nick had prepared for that, told Skylar when she'd asked. He was ready for the return to working the rush alone and the lack of donuts to delight the customers. The business could survive without her.

He just wasn't so certain if his heart would.

"YOU CAN'T TELL him."

"I won't," Emma promised. Internally, she chuckled at the ecstatic girl acting like a boy slow dancing with her was scandalous gossip. "Did anything else happen with Antonio?"

Skylar whipped her head around as if she feared ears listening in, but the sizzle of the deep fryer easily covered over anything. "Yes. He held my hand. And he got me some punch."

"That is serious."

"Then he said he'd call me later."

"Has he?"

Her spirited dancing stopped and Skylar pulled out her phone. "Not yet, but we were so busy yesterday, and the dance went really late. Like, I hadn't been up that late since I forgot to finish my science…er, I mean in forever." She darted her finger over her phone, raising the keycode screen. "I'm gonna text him. Tell him about the miracle happening in there. Can you believe it?"

She could, but Emma put on a careful smile. "Not at all."

"Eee!" With that, Skylar rushed off, leaving Emma to tend to her dough alone. She was about to roll it out when her phone went off.

"Hello? Oh, hi sis."

"I've been trying to get you for days. Why was your phone off?"

"Low battery," Emma said instead of 'I wanted to spend the day being someone else.'

"Look, the pizza place I mentioned, they need people now. Like now, now. Something to do with a Christmas parade. I've set you up to meet with the boss."

"I don't know. I mean, I'm still trapped here."

"You know, there's this German couple that's been

looking for a room. I'd get a nice Christmas for my kids renting yours out…"

Emma sighed and gulped. Steadying the phone to her ear, she asked, "When's the interview?"

"Wednesday."

"That's really soon. What if…?" *I'm still here.*

"This is the best I can do for you."

"Uh-huh. Okay," Emma let her mouth respond as she punched down the dough. Instead of donuts and pastries, she'd be spinning pizzas or putting frozen, pre-bought crusts in the oven. That sounded more likely.

"No one's hiring 'cause the holidays, and it's work."

"Yes, it sounds like a good job." Emma lied through her teeth. She didn't want it, but she'd need it. These past few days with Nick and Skylar had been better than anything she'd dreamed. But would he want to keep her on as a baker? As something more?

"Look, I've got to go. Things are really piling up here."

"Em? Emma, what are you — ?"

She killed the call and slipped her phone to airplane mode. No doubt her sister would call back and leave numerous voicemails to remind her how important the pizza job was. Maybe the place was nice, but there was no way it had a sweet and excited teenager learning about life, or a handsome and occasionally gruff owner that made her body sing with his touch.

Emma punched the dough harder, trying to beat down her dreams that'd slipped away from chef whites and banquet halls to a tiny kitchen and the smell of coffee in her hair.

CHAPTER TWENTY-FOUR

SHE WALKED OUT with her tray of fresh donuts to a smattering of applause and a loud cheer from Sam. "Let me help you with that," he offered by taking two of the eggnog donuts off the tray. One went straight into his mouth while he left her to place the rest on the counter.

"Anyone else pre-order?" Emma asked. People dashed forward, clearing out the tray in record time. "Guess I'll go make more."

The café was packed with nothing but smiling faces, every person taking their time to sip their coffee and chat. Nick closed the register, handed over the receipt, and reached for a mug.

"This place is hopping," Emma said, holding the tray to her chest. "They must really love your latte." She wasn't surprised. At long last, they could enjoy the fabled drink.

Nick snorted. "All they keep talking about are your donuts and eclairs. I think that guy wants a pop of cake?"

She chuckled at the mangling of a cake pop. An awkward jitteriness rose between them. He had a line stretching out the door, Emma had rows of doughy circles ready for the fryer, but neither could move. It was the worst time to do it, but Emma had to know if... if he wanted her around as much as she wanted to be around.

"Can I talk to you about something?"

Nick's palm fell from the espresso machine handle. He jerked to her, then to the coffee. "You...you need to try this."

Emma looked to the line of warm but uncertain customers. Nick glanced too, but after tossing a mocha at a woman, he got to work. "Take a seat."

This was silly, but she hopped onto the stool next to Sam. It was the same one she'd sat on for her first day in Lake Holly. "You see the weather out there?" Sam asked. "They say it's another blizzard."

Emma glanced over her shoulder. White splashed against the window. "I think it's just the old snow blowing in the wind."

"What's taking so long?" Skylar asked. She dashed from cleaning up an abandoned table to standing right behind Emma. "What are you doing?"

Nick moved with confidence, dropping in his

mystery ingredients so fast she couldn't even see them. "Our resident pastry expert needs to try the new mistletoe latte before she…before she can make her version. Right?" He stopped his java dance to look over his shoulder. A treasure trove of questions lurked in those sky blue eyes, but Emma didn't know how to open it.

"Ah." Skylar snickered and stepped back. "Got it. You two enjoy your…*latte*. But then the table by the tree is waiting on their americanos."

Emma turned to follow when Nick placed the mug in front of her and began to pour in the milk. As the coffee line rose, a white image emerged. Not of holly and ivy, nor mistletoe—it was an unmistakable heart with a wreath surrounding it. Nick topped it off with a sprinkling of green and white sugar, and he handed it over.

"Here you go."

"It's almost too pretty to drink." Emma turned the mug around to slip her thumb into the handle, but she froze as the beautiful heart he'd poured began to shake. Luckily, she stopped before it broke.

"Please." Nick's simple plea wrenched her up into his eyes. "I want to know what you think."

Closing her eyes, she took a deep drink. *Oh, it's hot.* Emma tried to keep from reacting in surprise as the familiar coffee roast blended with the nutty and juniper syrups. It was sugarier than the last one and… She licked the edge of her lip and stared at him. "Is that sweet cream?"

Nick's smile rose, his eyes gleaming. "You found me out."

"It's wonderful, richer than before, and…" Every sip reminded her of him. Dark, occasionally bitter and abrasive on the first note, but with each new taste a surprise opened of split pines, a little nuttiness, and a tender vein sweetness winding deep within. Emma didn't want to stop drinking it, but she feared what would happen when it was gone.

"Looks like you've got a little..." He pointed to her nose. *Oh, dear.* Emma moved to wipe it off with her thumb, when he—in front of everyone—cupped the back of her neck. He leaned across the counter and she stood on the stool's footrest to reach him.

Emma closed her eyes and she parted her lips.

"Hey, Soul? I've got good news."

Nick retreated his hand and she dropped to the floor. The mechanic hustled over. "Morning, Nick. Usual?"

"Uh," was all Nick said, but he didn't rush to the cash register. He stood close, listening in.

"Did you get my messages?" the mechanic asked. "Never mind. I got the part in early and just finished installing it. Your vehicle's all ready to go. Even got it cleaned up. It was brown, right?"

"Gray?" Emma squeaked. It was finished? Already? But there was at least another day to go. How could it be done?

Daryl laughed. "I know, Soul. That's mechanic humor for you. Don't worry, it's in tip-top shape."

"That's...good? I mean, thank you for getting it done early."

"Didn't want you to be stuck here under his growling mug any longer." Daryl jerked a thumb to Nick and laughed.

Emma looked over, but Nick had his back turned to them both. All she could see were his shoulders hunched in thought. He wouldn't have to house her anymore. Not have to feed her. Not wake up next to her in his bed and swoop his fingers down her back until she gasped.

He was free.

"What do I owe you?" she asked.

"Well, I've got the invoice back at the shop, but with parts and labor, it comes to about three grand and change."

"Three…! That's a lot of money."

"We do take credit cards."

Maybe there was hope after all. Maybe she'd have to stay here to work off her debt for another week. Help out with the Christmas rush and become so invaluable Nick would want her to stay.

With certainty in her steps, Emma walked around the counter to the man hunched over the coffee. "Double espresso with…oat milk!" he shouted to the room with a growl. "Why is that a thing? Oats don't have udders."

"Nick…?" she started, before her voice dropped to a squeak.

He glared at her and all her nerve fled. "Yeah?"

Emma tried to not look away, but she couldn't help it. A softer voice asked, "What do you need?"

I wish I knew.

"I guess my vehicle's done, but the bill is…" God, her chest ached and her jaw clenched shut. She couldn't force it out no matter how hard she tried. It wasn't that she thought he wouldn't let her stay for another day, or five. Deep in her soul, Emma didn't think she was worthy of an extension of his kindness.

"So I heard. Highway robbery, but that's mechanics for you. Let me talk to him. I can get it down to something reasonable."

Emma placed her hand to his arm. He paused in walking away to berate Daryl and looked back at her.

"It's not that." She swept her hand lower, tracing the heavy flannel until her fingertips glanced against his skin.

Nick was the one to take her fingers and hold them safe. He turned her away from the bustling café as if they were alone in the middle of a blizzard all over again.

Biting her lip, Emma forced out the courage. "It's... well, I was wondering if —"

The shop bell jangled, cutting her off. She breathed deep, prepared to ask him to let her stay when Nick's eyes darted to the crowd and his jaw dropped.

"Rachel?"

CHAPTER TWENTY-FIVE

IT'S NOT REAL. That's just a tall woman with brunette hair and sharp blue eyes. There has to be tons of those in the world. He'd blink and the face from his memories would fade.

"Nicky."

Pain shot up his arm, and he stumbled back, his heart awash in the sticky and stinging memories.

It was her, five years later out of nowhere. Out of all the coffee joints in all the world.

She was dressed the way he'd remembered, professional but with a skirt. Always with a skirt. Rachel stared around the café, then she met his eyes and smiled, "This place hasn't changed a lick."

"Neither have you," Nick said.

Her response was to smile as if it was a compliment. "Is that the same chalk you stole from the hardware store?"

"I didn't steal it. I borrowed it." He picked up the white nub and cradled it in his palm. Rachel laughed the same way she had used to while laying beside him. "Besides, that was a lot of chalk pieces ago."

Five years. He felt every single mont while rising at four in the morning. Read every lonely day in the crow's feet and laugh lines etched into his face. But she looked like none of it happened. Had it all been a waking nightmare?

Nick's gaze darted beyond the returned ghost to find Skylar glaring at the back of Rachel's head. She wasn't a buoyant kindergartner about to draw all over the woman's financial papers. The five years hit him across the face, five years both of them spent struggling without help until…

He caught Emma, her head low and gaze darting to Rachel. She looked spooked as if about to run. Nick wanted to take her hand and protect her, but that was silly. Rachel wasn't some wicked witch.

"What are you doing here?" he asked.

She shrugged. "The mistletoe latte."

"Of course." What else could it be but that damnable drink? "Did you want one?"

Rachel smirked. "I think I can make it myself." Before he could argue, she slipped around the counter and hefted down a mug. "You still keep them under here? Of course you do." She bent over and busied herself in the cupboards, no doubt looking for the good syrups.

He felt boxed in, the espresso machine shooting out

hot steam on his left, Rachel bouncing her ass on the right. Nick kept walking backward until he hit something and it cried out. He spun around to find Emma. She held one of Skylar's old snowflakes in her hand.

"This fell. I was going to fix it. Unless…?"

"Oh, you hired someone?" Rachel stood up and stared Emma down. "Can you tell me where the milk is? He's always leaving it places."

Her big brown eyes darted up to him before she pointed to the carafe he'd left on the counter. "Right there."

"Thanks, dear." After topping off her coffee concoction, Rachel took a quick sip and sized up Emma. "Do you do anything more around here or just clean up?"

Emma wafted the blue snowflake around before tucking it behind her back. Her mouth opened wide, then she closed it.

"She makes donuts, and pastries, and other delights Sam keeps bogarting." Nick pointed to the old man whose entire muzzle was coated in sugar.

"You got the oven running? Oh my goodness." Rachel dropped her coffee, a drop splashing out. She latched onto Emma's hand and tugged. "You have to show me."

The girl looked over at Nick but gave in to the pull. That was Rachel, harder to argue with than a brick wall. They vanished into the back room, leaving Nick staring at the two cups. Rachel's was barely touched while Emma's… Only a drop of his coffee remained in hers, but it was the pink lip stain that entranced him. Nick picked up the white mug and turned it in his hands until the imprint of her pretty mouth faced him.

"Why is she here?" Skylar fumed.

Nick shook out of his funk. He dropped Emma's mug into the wash bin without looking. "I don't know. The mistletoe latte, I guess. Maybe she saw everyone talking about it." *Or maybe…?*

"Are you freaking kidding me." She gripped her broom like a ninja about to beat a man to death.

Nick held up his hands, not needing an all-out war. He tried to take the potential club from his niece when Daryl stepped up.

"Look, I don't want to get in the middle of this domestic whatever, but I'm gonna need my coffee."

The ex running around the back of his café vanished from his mind. A colder wind cut through his chest as he stared at Daryl. Three grand was a lot, and Emma sounded in dire straights. Icicles plunged into his heart. She had a sister to get to and a job interview. It'd only been a week, after all.

"Skylar? Get him his coffee. Black and cream." He grabbed her arm as she walked past to whisper, "But make sure it's non-dairy without him knowing."

"Okay. Where are you going?"

Rachel. Emma. Dozens of out-of-towners chanting for the mistletoe latte to spice up their 'gram. He didn't have a clue how to make any of it right. "Gotta check in the back," Nick said, and he vanished through the door.

SHE WAS BEAUTIFUL. Not like Desiree who had that perfect-ice-princess look going on. Rachel was the "it girl," the coolest queen bee in school. She'd get straight A's, have all the guys chasing her, be captain of the volleyball team, and not even sweat while winning state. If Emma wasn't so in awe, she might think to feel jealous.

"Wow. I can't believe you've got all of this running. Bit of a tight fit though." She had to hunch down to avoid the boxes that poked from the top shelf. Emma was so tiny she didn't even see them while she worked.

"I made due as best I could."

"I'm sure Nicky didn't make it easy for you." She elbowed Emma in the stomach and laughed as if they were best friends. "Do you mind if I fry up one of these donuts? I've always wanted to try."

Emma nodded and watched her lower the dough without splashing a drop of oil. No wonder he'd been madly in love with her for five years. She was perfect.

"Have you been working here long?"

She shook her head. "Only a few days."

"A few days? Why the way you took charge, I'd have thought you'd been here for years. He must have been desperate."

Her heart plummeted. Of course he was. Why else would he have given her work? Given her a bed? Kissed her under the mistletoe?

"Hey!"

Emma leaped at Nick's voice. Was he about to run in and declare his ex was wrong? She picked at her apron pocket as he skidded a halt and scratched his jaw. "Can I...? Emma, can I borrow you for a second?"

Maybe he didn't hear Rachel. Maybe he didn't care. Her head jerked in a nod, and she glanced back to the beautiful woman browning another donut. Before she went, Emma scooped up her recipe notebook, then followed Nick to the office. He didn't say anything, just pulled open a drawer, tugged out a checkbook, and began to write.

"You wanted to talk to me?" Emma began.

Nick nodded, dropped his pen, and tore out the check. As he held it to her, she caught the three thousand on the amount line.

"I can't accept that."

Instead of tearing it up, he wafted the check. "Daryl should know I'm good for it."

"No, that's not…that's too much money."

"You more than earned it."

No, she didn't. Not at the rate they'd worked out. Not in the small time they'd had together. Emma couldn't stop shaking her head, wishing the check would vanish into thin air.

Nick passed it to his other hand and tried again. "The business is booming, customers are happy, and you got the oven working. Some of it's an advance for that. Please. Take it."

She gulped, staring at the thin paper with his signature. One last kindness that cut her to the bone. Emma fought back the tears with all she could. "Do you really want me to?"

He floundered at that, the offering hand drooping. Instead of answering, Nick licked his lips and his eyelids hung low. "Without this money, you're stuck here. You're trapped, right?" He raised his head, took a steady breath, and declared, "No one wants to be trapped."

All she had to do was take the check, get in her old car, take a job at a pizza joint and forget any of this ever happened.

Or…?

Emma bit hard into her lip, her eyes swimming in tears as she clung tighter to the recipe book in her pocket. It was stained not with steak sauce or aioli, but dough and sugar. If she left, she could return to her old life, keep her old plans, and chip away at the industry that ground people like her to dust.

And if she told him here and now that she wanted to stay?

Her heart pounded in fear, terrified that he'd wave the check at her again, but even more scared of what wanting to stay with him meant. "Nick, I…" Emma closed her eyes and a tear slid down her cheek. "I l—"

"Nicky, look!" Rachel breezed into the office and spun around, showing off the apron and hat for Brew 4 U. "It still fits." She gave another twirl and Nick watched. "Am I interrupting something?"

I'm an idiot. Why would he want someone as worthless as me when the one that got away walked back into his life? She pinched her thumb and forefinger to the check and slowly tugged it from Nick's hand. For a second, he tightened around it and jerked away from Rachel. But as he stared at Emma, he relaxed his grip, and let her accept it.

"Thank you," she said, holding the reminder that she didn't belong here in her hand. "For everything."

"Emma." He moved to chase after her, but Rachel was in the way, asking about the office. "No, that had to be moved after water damage. Wait…"

She'd already dashed down the hall, her heart tumbling with pain. If she didn't do it now, she never would. "Daryl?"

The mechanic looked up from his coffee and met her eye.

"Here." Before her heart stopped her, she gave him the check and didn't look back.

NICK SKIDDED TO a halt just as Emma handed over the check. Daryl took his time looking it over, then he stared over at him.

Is it genuine?

Did he want to give her the chance to fly away? Was he really willing to let her walk out the door and never come back? Did he, deep down, know that the best thing for a woman like her wasn't a broken man in a small town café?

He nodded, willing to let her go.

"Good. I'll finish the paperwork. Want me to drop your Soul off in the parking lot for you?"

She looked over her shoulder at him, her eyes wide and vulnerable.

Jesus Christ, man, tell her. Tell her you don't want her to leave. That she's the best damn thing to ever walk through that door. That you want to wake up next to her for as long as you breathe.

"What the hell's going on?" Skylar drifted over, looking wary.

All of Nick's turmoil snapped on her. "Don't fucking curse."

She glared with a full lemon-pucker at him, before looking to Emma. "You're not...are you leaving? Already?"

The employee door swung open and Rachel sauntered in. She held a fresh donut in her fingers and took a bite while watching. Skylar's eyes narrowed to slits at the woman before she wrapped her arms around Emma.

"You can't go. You were gonna teach me how to use primer."

Emma patted a hand against her back. "It's okay. There's lots of tutorials online. I'm sure you'll figure it out." Her drifting gaze skipped past Nick to land on Rachel. "Maybe someone else can teach you."

"My mom sucks at makeup. She thinks an eyelash curler is used on pasta," Skylar wailed, clinging tighter to her.

"So, do I move the car or what?" Daryl asked tapping his foot.

Emma peeled away from Skylar's crushing hug. "It's okay, I can pick it up after my shift."

She was leaving.

Of course she was leaving. That was what he wanted, after all. To go back to the way everything was. Him, angry at the world, fighting with his niece, wishing his brother would grow up, spending every day wanting to toss the customers into the street. It was perfect.

"Why wait?" Nick asked, fuming. "No reason for you to keep toiling away here. Don't you have an interview to get to?"

"An...?" Emma squeaked as if he shouldn't know about that. As if he wasn't helping her to move on to bigger and better things. "Okay." She undid the little bow on her apron and pulled it off.

"No, you can't go."

"It's okay," she assured Skylar.

Emma reached for her hat and Nick caught her arm. Her big brown eyes gazed up at him, pleading with him to do the right thing. "You can keep that," he said. "There's a ton in back."

"Thank you." She blinked her eyelids then wiped at the sides while handing him the apron.

Nick folded it up, watching Emma give Skylar one last hug, then banter with Sam. "I should get my purse from the back," was the last thing she said. He held tight to the apron still warm from her body and felt something hard inside. *Oh shit, her recipe notebook.*

Chasing after her, Nick called out, "Wait." She clung tight to her purse slung over her shoulder but turned from the exit to gaze up at him.

"Emma." *There are a thousand things I want to say to you. To thank you, to plead with you, to find some way to give us more time.* "You almost forgot this."

He handed over her recipe book and she gasped. "Thank you, I...I'd be lost without it. I can't believe I almost left it behind." She shook her head in disbelief while placing her treasured book in her purse.

Emma held out her hand. "Thank you. For giving me this...for everything."

Tendrils of her hair had fallen from the cap, two curls brushing against her cheek. Nick wanted to push them back, take her face in his hands, and kiss her.

He took her hand instead. "You're welcome," were his parting words to her. Smiling even as a tear slipped down, she turned and walked away from him forever.

CHAPTER TWENTY-SIX

SKYLAR DEATH-GLARED at him as he settled in behind the counter. She tossed her broom to the ground and began to stomp over when the damn Italian kid swept in. All her righteous anger transformed into girlish giggling.

"Antonio. Hi!"

Nick did his best to overhear while trying to not make it obvious. If that kid so much as looked below Skylar's chin…

The boy smiled at Skylar and greeted her in Italian. That did it. Her entire face turned beet red. "Wait right here." She ran for Nick, the righteous anger about

Emma forgotten. "I need a mistletoe latte."

"You do?"

Skylar blinked slowly at him. "And two mochas. For customers you ignored."

There was no arguing with that. Nick got back to business making the mochas first so he could keep an eye on his niece and the Italian stallion. She seemed to forget she was supposed to be doing a job, lingering way too close for comfort. Every time the kid talked with his hands, Nick was certain one would wind up on his niece.

"This is exciting." Rachel slid in beside him. She took one of the mochas and added a lid to it.

"Why are you here? Didn't you join with some co-op coffee shop?" Not that he was supposed to know that. Amazing what one could find while light Googling after a bout of insomnia.

"Yes. It's going well. The partners have expanded to include a tea room and bakery. Though, the donuts you have here are impressive. I might have to steal the recipe."

"Good luck." He laughed. "I've got two mochas and one mistletoe lat—"

Skylar dashed in and yanked the latte out of his hands. She gave him a quick smile, then ran back to the boy.

Oh no.

The customers quieted enough that Nick could hear her say, "I made this just for you."

Antonio at least took the cup, stared askance at the design, then risked a quick sip. Nick missed out on the snobbery dismissal of 'an American's idea of coffee' as steam shot out and the bell jangled. He noticed Mrs. Wilkins ushering in her daughter, who zeroed in on whatever Skylar was up to.

"Maybe I've just been thinking lately. About the old times." Rachel leaned closer to him and cupped a hand on his arm. Nick stared at her. He couldn't do anything else as his brain kept screaming at him about the old times.

Which bit? The part where I had to figure out how to get a kid to stop crying and eat dinner after working a twelve-hour shift alone? Or when I was up until two in the morning fighting with a pile of soggy paper-mâché to make the head of Lincoln? Those good times?

"Nick! You have an old ghost here." Mrs. Wilkins swooped in, adding more flame to the fire.

Rachel stared at her. "Desiree. You've dyed your hair."

"Don't be silly, it's natural." She fluffed her hair in response, then leaned closer to the counter. "Nick, there is a matter I wished to bring to your attention. We could perhaps talk privately…?"

He shuddered at having to return to his office. "Here's fine."

She shrugged. "My daughter told me that during the dance Skylar went missing…with the exchange student."

"Missing?" Nick looked up to find Skylar toying with the end of his scarf while Antonio took another sip.

"Now, I'm not one to pass judgment, but this could be a problem."

"No, it won't." *They'd never find the damn kid.*

"She's young, yes, but you know what they say about the sins of the father…"

Nick's heart stopped dead at the way Mrs. Wilkins' voice rose.

"…I mean, now it's just running off with boys, but

the next thing you know she could be drinking, cutting school, then wind up in prison just like your brother."

He gritted his teeth at the idea that flirting with a boy would lead to a life of crime. Skylar was a good kid, damn it. He'd made sure of it. "That is—"

"Your brother?"

Fuck.

Mrs. Wilkins leaped aside to reveal Skylar standing directly behind her. His niece clenched her fist and glared not at the one who'd dropped the secret like a bomb, but at her lying uncle. "What's she on about? Dad's not in prison. Right? Uncle Nick."

"He...he's not in prison. Now."

"What?" she shrieked, tears springing in an instant. "No. He can't be. He...he left for a job, for me, my future. He wouldn't lie to me. You're lying. You're all fucking lying." Skylar jabbed a finger at Mrs. Wilkins, then Rachel, and finally at him.

"Sky—"

"Don't tell me what to do!" she screamed and turned to flee. Unfortunately, her Italian heartthrob was right behind her. She barreled into him, splashing most of his latte into his face. Skylar didn't even slow down to see if he was okay but shoved open the door and kept going.

"Skylar, wait!" Nick jogged around the counter after her. "Here." He tossed a dirty towel at Antonio's head and ran for the door.

"Nicky." Rachel stopped him in his tracks. "She's just throwing a tantrum. She'll work it out herself."

Nick shook his head. "You don't know anything about her or me. Skylar!" Without a second thought, he barreled into the freezing cold in just his jeans and flannel.

Ah, fuck. The sleeting snow he'd been certain was a lie

pelted against his cheeks. Nick hoisted up a hand to keep his eyes from freezing over and shouted, "Skylar!"

There wasn't a response, but he spotted smaller footprints with hearts cut into the soles leading away. Why did she carve heats into her shoes? That was a problem for another day. Nick followed the trail, not to another alley or shop, but circling around the café and leading to his truck. Skylar didn't have the keys, so she'd slumped against the door and kept kicking at it.

"Hey. If we can't get that thing open later, we're stuck here," he called to her.

A tear-stained, red-faced Skylar looked at him, then kicked even harder before she turned her back on him. "It's not true. She's lying. They're all lying. He wouldn't…"

"Sky." Nick approached cautiously and placed a hand on her back. He expected her to shrug it away, but she turned and threw her arms around him. As she did, her phone nearly beaned him in the nose, and he saw an old article about Pete's arrest. There was no stuffing this toothpaste back into the tube.

Nick swept her up into a hug and she clung tighter to him, squeezing the air out.

"I. Don't. Under. Stand," Skylar hiccup-sobbed against his chest. "All this time he lied to me. He was supposed to move for me. He said it was for me. Every phone call, he'd… He stayed away because I'm awful."

"That's not true."

"He doesn't love me! No one does!"

Nick's heart couldn't take much more breaking today. Just as he had when Skylar was a slip of a kid running into the café with a skinned knee, Nick dropped lower to her eye level. "Your father loves you so much."

"Then why isn't he here? He's not in jail anymore. Why didn't he come back? For me?"

"Pete, your dad, was sick. He…suffered and it made him do bad things."

"Like steal from the payroll?" Skylar snarled.

"Like that. And other things. Even though he's out of jail, he's struggling to make ends meet, to…" Nick sighed, unable to hide this any longer. "To stay sober."

Skylar's eyes went wide. For her, drugs were orange-flavored aspirin or evil demons lurking in the hands of sketchy men in cities. Nick had done everything to keep it that way, but there was no running from the monster in the closet.

"Why didn't he tell me?"

There were a dozen good reasons Nick had heard from Pete's lips over the years, but none of them were the truth. "Because he's scared. Of you losing respect for him. Of you not loving him."

Skylar clenched a fist. "I'm so freaking mad at him."

"It's okay, you can curse."

"Shit!"

"That wasn't the one I expected, but—"

Skylar shook her head and stared at him. "All this time, he was supposed to be sending you money. He said he was."

Nick didn't answer but looked away, which told her enough. "Pete's in a halfway house, barely making ends meet. Even if he sent whatever was left over…"

"I knew the Christmas and birthday presents were really from you—"

"You did?"

Skylar stared him dead in the eye. "I see your handwriting every day, Uncle Nick. It didn't take a genius to figure out who put 'To Skylar' on them."

Damn, he didn't think of that.

She squeezed her eyes tight and slumped against the truck. "He really fucked everything up, didn't he? His life, mine, yours."

"No." Nick wiped his hand against her cheek, smearing her tears. "Pete made a lot of bad choices, and it's been hard fixing them, but having you in my life is a blessing."

She glared at him. "Come on."

"Okay," he laughed. "Some days it's a challenge, and others I want to ship you to the moon, but most of the time, I can't imagine being without you."

"Even if…you've been alone because of me?"

How is she this smart? Nick bit his lip and shook his head. "No, I haven't. And, anyway, maybe that'll change. She…she's back."

"Why?" Skylar's hopeful tears dropped to teenage sass in an instant.

Maybe the mistletoe latte had her thinking about the past? The latte…? Of course. "I bet she's Miss B. What if Rachel wrote an article about the old latte we'd invented just to see if I'd bring it back?" *To see if I still wanted her.*

His niece stared at him like he was the dumbest man alive. "No, she isn't."

"It all makes sense. She had the pictures. She knew the legend. She shows back up here. She…"

"It was me!" Skylar screamed to the snowing heavens.

"What?"

"I sent in those old pictures. I emailed a bunch of different food bloggers. It was me, not her. Not the woman that ran out on you. Me!"

Nick's tiny hope that Rachel came back for him

snuffed out in the snow. All he could do was stare at Skylar. "Why?"

"Because I needed you to make it again. I figured if I could get him to drink the latte, then we'd kiss under the mistletoe, and he'd...be my boyfriend."

"He who? That seventeen-year-old!"

"Oh my god, I splashed coffee onto him!" Skylar shrieked.

"It was more like a caffeinated baptism."

"He's never gonna want to talk to me again. What have I done?"

Nick hated the kid with all his being, but he swept a hand around Skylar's shoulders and told her, "If he won't talk to you for that, a simple accident, then he's not worth having as a boyfriend."

"So you're saying I date him?"

"For the two days he's remaining in the states, sure. As long as it's done in the café, with both of you standing at all times."

Skylar groaned and smashed her face into his shoulder a few times before she glanced at the passenger seat. "What about Emma?"

Nick couldn't hide the wince in time. "She's going home."

"But you like her. Don't lie to me. You've done enough of that."

Damn, she was going to use that one for a long time. Nick shook his head, trying to find a way to tell Skylar she was wrong, but... "Yes, I like her. A lot."

"So...?"

"So she has her life to live and...it wouldn't be right to stop her."

"Are you kidding me? That is exactly what you're supposed to do. Run to her, tell her you like her. That you don't want her to leave."

Just like that? Chase after the woman walking out his door? He almost had — taken her hand, held her cheek, kissed her, and begged her to stay. But his damnable pride and a fear of a second broken heart stopped him.

"Sky, what about…?"

"Forget Rachel. Forget Abby's mom too. They're not the one for you. Emma is. I can tell."

"Well, as long as I have the blessing of a fourteen-year-old." Nick tried to laugh it off, but his heart was beating faster in both fear and exhilaration. Take that tiny hand in his, look deep into her big brown eyes, and tell her everything. Tell her that he never wanted her to leave, that he needed her in his life. Not as a baker, not as a teenager wrangler, but…

"Okay. I'm going to find her." *Jesus. Really?* He nearly started giggling at the freeing thought. "I'm going to… where the hell do I look? The mechanic's. She's got to be there." Nick dashed out of the parking lot, no longer feeling winter's bite. His entire body glowed like the sun as he broke into a run down the sidewalk. "Skylar? No kissing that boy!"

Holy shit, he was really doing this. He was going to talk to her. What should he say?

Emma, I want you to stay in my bed and never leave. No, too kidnappery.

Emma, you are the light of my life and…I don't know how to do poetry.

Emma, let's shack up.

Dear god, he should have asked Skylar for help.

Nick shoved on the glass door, his sinuses filling with the stench of diesel and motor oil. The whirr of pistons fired through the air, and he hunted for Emma and her gray Soul.

"If it isn't my coffee supplier." Daryl pushed up his face shield and stared at him. "What are you doing here?"

"Where's Emma? The…the Kia Soul?"

"She left twenty minutes ago. Probably on the highway already."

No. Nick's chest caved in. He could have told her everything, could have held her hand and begged for her to stay. Instead, he let another woman—the only woman for him—walk out the door.

CHAPTER TWENTY-SEVEN

"LEAVING LAKE HOLLY" blew past Emma. The highway was nearly deserted from the winter storm. Ice and snow pelted her windshield, but she couldn't stop. If she did, there was no chance she'd be able to start again. She'd even left her luggage behind, too much of a coward to ask for Nick…

Damn it.

Emma wiped vigorously on the inside of her windshield, but this fog came from the tears in her eyes. She tried to shake them away while keeping her focus on the road.

It was what was best for him.

It was what was best for her.

What? Did she think he'd have fallen in love with this random helpless woman in a few days and refuse to let her go? That didn't happen in real life. No, Nick could get his second chance romance. Skylar would charm her Italian heartthrob and Emma... Well, she'd keep trying.

"This was supposed to be easy," she whined to her graduation tassel hanging from the rear view mirror. When she'd moved it across her cap, her dreams had seemed so simple. Work her way through the ranks in a kitchen. Become known for her delicious, innovative, and magical desserts. Get noticed by a world-famous chef and impress people around the globe.

Nowhere in there did she have 'fall head over heels for a small-town coffee man who made her toes curl and lips part.' Nor did she intend to care about a teenage girl who needed a woman's hand to get through this complicated life.

Emma's phone beeped. Her sister sent another text asking where she was and reminding her about the job interview. Was she really going to do this? Hide away in her sister's spare bedroom scraping by on minimum wage while washing off the stench of burnt tomatoes and mozzarella? Was that all she deserved in life?

The tears became wracking sobs. Emma's foot pressed on the brake, slowing her SUV until it crawled along the highway as she struggled to breathe. The snow built up on her wipers, smearing over the window while she cried her heart out.

This wasn't supposed to hurt. She knew she'd be saying goodbye. She knew it was only temporary. But the pain...it nested deep inside her chest. Spiny tendrils snaked out of her heart and choked up her throat. Emma reached into her pocket, hunting for a tissue to wipe away her tears.

A blue piece of paper tumbled to the seat beside her. "The snowflake," she gasped, picking it up. She slammed on the brake, her SUV skidding on the slick road. It came to a stop on the shoulder as she uncreased Skylar's snowflake over her steering wheel.

She'd never laughed so hard when he'd scooped her up off the ground. Then, when he cupped her face, brushed her hair back with his thumbs, and kissed her…

Emma traced along the edge of the snowflake with her finger.

Her shattered world felt whole in his arms.

All her life, she'd cowered when voices rose. She'd fled when the heat grew. She'd never thought she was strong enough to fight back—against abusive bosses, bullying classmates, flippant roommates…her sister. For the first time, she found someone worth fighting over.

She fully turned around on the highway, leaning into the skidding snow, and took off back in the direction of Lake Holly. Emma pressed a button on her phone. "Sis, I'm not gonna make it for Christmas."

"What? But the interview…"

"Isn't for me. I belong somewhere else." She smiled wide, her heart leaping about at the potential. Oh, she'd fight like hell for him. Tell him…tell Nick the truth. That even though it was a few days, even though she walked away, she couldn't escape how much she—

Emma shrieked as the front wheel hit a patch of ice and spun out. The wheel lost all control, the world of white blurring before her. The SUV pitches forward and careened wildly into the ditch. Screaming, Emma jerked as the front end crumpled into a cement barrier and her forehead struck the steering wheel. Blood dripped onto the blue snowflake and Emma blacked out.

HE TRIED TO not look defeated as he walked back into the café. Skylar stood up, but when he came in alone, she too crashed back into depression. Emma was gone and there was nothing he could do. He didn't even think to ask where she was headed, because deep down a part of him thought she wouldn't go.

Skylar dashed over and held up her phone. "You know I have her—"

"Get to school," Nick interrupted. "I mean, it's getting late and you have finals."

She ground her jaw but picked up her book bag. All he could do was hope to get back to what he'd been before Emma walked into his life. Skylar stomped to the door, but before she slipped out, she hugged him tight.

"It'll be okay," she said and headed out.

God, he wished he could believe that.

"Hey, is this the mistletoe latte place?"

Nick winced, his dour frown twisting into a snarl. But as he stared at the wide-eyed and curious face, the anger shifted to a deep ache. It swallowed him whole, dragging him into a freezing lake of endless black. He didn't want to take his rage out on anyone. Not the hapless customer needing caffeine. Not even Rachel, who'd swept in as if she owned the place.

She was the one who took the order, acting like the last five years never happened. But he couldn't pretend.

No, he wouldn't, not when he had just as many good memories with Skylar, and the café, and Emma as he ever had with her.

"Get out of here," he said calmly to the woman counting out change.

She smiled at him. "Don't worry. I remember how to do this." Rachel reached for a mug, but Nick took it from her hands.

"No. This isn't your place. You walked out, and you're not wanted here any longer."

"Nicky…" She placed a hand on her hip then reached for him, but Nick ignored both.

He placed the mug under the espresso machine and started the pull. "I don't know why you're here. I don't care. But this is my place."

"I helped build it. I painted it. Even if you've let it turn to shit," Rachel whined.

In his mourning, he'd forgotten about her grating tendency to turn everything back on him. *Why'd I even want to marry her in the first place?*

"I made it. Me, and Skylar, and…everyone in town. This isn't your café, Rachel. It never was and won't be again." It'd have been a good time for a round of applause, but the café was too busy enjoying the new improved mistletoe latte. Rachel fumed, but ripped off the apron she'd stolen along with the hat then threw both at him. Nick didn't even bother to catch them.

"I hope you fail," Rachel snarled as she stomped for the door. "And your donuts are flavorless."

"You bite your tongue," Sam shouted before he ate the last one left.

Nick should keep that up. Even if Emma wasn't… coming back, people loved the donuts. And he needed to paint that damn wall. Maybe a light green, or a happy yellow. Anything to get rid of the dour air in here.

When the bell rang to announce Rachel's second departure from his life, he looked up and felt nothing. It wasn't the real woman he'd been aching for all these years, but a version of her that'd lived inside his head. Even that was finally gone, erased by the tender fingers, big brown eyes, and gentle gasp of another.

Damn it. Nick swiped at his eye with his shirt, acting like he'd gotten coffee grounds in it. "Here you go. One mistletoe latte. Who's next?"

"Storm's really picking up out there, eh?" Sam asked, needing conversation. He kept fiddling with his scanner, finding nothing but static.

As Nick waited for the customer to decide, his gaze drifted to the wash bin. Mugs and spoons floated in the soapy water, but a single one hovered on the top. White as cream, it still bore the pink kiss from her lips.

"Reports of a crashed SUV on highway thirty-eight."

Nick wrenched away from Emma's mug to stare at Sam. "Thirty-eight? That's the one that head's east."

The old man waved a hand to get him to shut up. He fiddled with the knob and the police blotter continued. "Caller said it was a gray Kia."

"Hey, isn't that...?"

"Emma!"

NICK SPUN HIS truck around, nearly smashing into a tree. He'd been watching the side of the road leaving town and almost missed the tracks trailing off into the ditch. Snow blew in, wiping away any hint of the blacktop below. He took it easy for fear of hidden ice, but his heart would not stop pounding. Oregon license plate, a gray SUV nearly camouflaged in the sleet. It was hers.

"Emma?" he shouted. Leaping to the freezing ground, Nick shook off the shock of cold and ran for her. As he drew closer to the SUV, the front came into view. It was pulverized like a crushed pop can. *Fuck.*

"Emma!" he cried, running hell-bent to the driver's side. What if she was hunched over? What if she was hurt? What if she…?

The driver's side door was open, light streaming from the overhead bulb ripped off of the roof. But there was no one inside. Okay, she may have gotten a ride. Except he hadn't seen anyone on the road. And, for as bad as he'd fucked up, he knew she'd call him first.

There, in the snow. Footprints led away from the crash. Nick followed them down the ditch and into a field. She must be trying to get back to town. Why didn't she call for a tow or the cops?

How long had she been out in this? He shivered under his wool jacket. No chance her puffy coat would last long in the freezing wet storm. His jeans were already soaked through, then hardening to ice as he struggled through the snow drifts. What if she was hurt? What if she wasn't thinking clearly?

"Emma!" he tried again. "Please be okay." The wind battered at the prints. At the top of the hill, they vanished. His trail was gone.

Ahead was a stand of trees, but she might have veered to the right where a single light burned in the distance. *Damn it.* Nick cupped a hand to his mouth and shouted for her again. "Emma!" he tried to the right and struggled to see through the icy sleet stabbing his eyes.

There was no sign of her, but she could be farther on.

"Emma!" he called to the trees. Movement. A brown shape darted between the black and white trunks. It had to be her chestnut hair swaying in the wind. Turning his back on the farmhouse, Nick trudged after the momentary flit of brown in the sea of white.

The wind picked up, nearly tossing him back. He flung his hands out to keep from falling and snatched onto a branch. It shattered in his hands, and a brown head popped up from the snowy underbrush. Doe eyes stared at him all right, the kind that came with a white tail and antlers.

He'd followed a deer into cover. The creature shifted its ears, then darted away as Nick folded his hand into a fist and slammed it against the tree. "Damn it!" He couldn't stop now. He had to keep trying, to look in every drop-off and turn she might have taken.

And if I'm too late?

Nick opened his mouth to shout her name, but the pain clogged his throat. All his mind could conjure was her tiny body curled up in the snow, frozen and unmoving. Gulping in air, he coughed out the only thing that would get free. "Cream and sugar."

"Nick?"

It was the wind. He told himself that even as he turned around to find the sound. Then it grew stronger. "Nick?"

"Holy shit."

She raised her head, and he almost crumbled to his knees in prayer. Somehow, she'd wound up next to a tree, her small body blending in with the brush. Nick took her hand, wincing at how cold it felt even in his frozen mitts. She reached for him, patting his cheek, and he nearly burst into tears.

"I crashed my car," Emma said plainly, and he laughed. Not at her, but from the joy of finding her.

"Here." He scooped her up off the ground, his heart throbbing as he held her safe in his arms. She wrapped her hands around the back of his neck and snuggled her cheek to his chest. Fighting against the wind, he carried her back to his truck.

"How did you find me?" she asked, her voice soft and rippling in pain.

"Sam's scanner," Nick said, and he shook his eyes to clear them of the falling snow. "I owe that man free coffee for life."

She fell quiet, but he could feel the tender thump of her heart even through his panicking chest. When they got to the site of the accident, Emma frowned deep, but he walked her past her SUV and placed her in his truck. He knew she was safe, and about to be warmed by his heater, but Nick stopped from rushing to the driver's side.

Blinking, Emma looked up at him, and he tripped straight into her beautiful brown eyes. Nick cupped his hand to her cheek, his skin stinging from how cold it felt, and he leaned to her for a kiss. A shock of red stopped him.

"You're...you're bleeding," he gasped. A trickle of blood clung to her forehead.

"From the crash," she explained. "Guess my airbag doesn't work."

"I need to get you to a hospital." Which was a good hour's drive away on a sunny day. "Urgent care." He ran so fast around the front of the truck, the grill snagged on his jeans' pocket, but he kept going. "That needs to be checked out."

He expected resistance as he leaped in, probably

because he'd have argued it was fine and gone to sleep with a concussion. But Emma nodded meekly and placed her hands in her lap. She rubbed them together, then on her legs.

Nick started up the engine but didn't take it out of park. Instead, he cranked the heater to blast and cupped his hands over hers. As he rubbed them vigorously, she looked over at him and a tiny smile rose on her lips.

"Thank you," she said and the dam he'd been building cracked.

Fat tears rained down his cheeks as he kept running his hands over hers. "Don't say that. I don't deserve it. Not after what I…"

She slipped her hand out of his. He stopped warming her up, his head falling as he struggled to stop the damn crying when a cool palm fell against his cheek. Nick stared up into a tender and knowing look.

"I should have told you," Emma said.

"I never wanted you to…"

"It scared me."

He laughed. "It scared me too." His gaze drifted to her SUV and the mess of footprints. "But losing you scared me more."

He almost said it. The words were right there. They'd been screaming in his brain, leaping to his tongue, but at that moment, he froze. Instead of facing her, he stared at her SUV. Something about it was bothering him.

"There's not much ground tore up for you spinning a full one-eighty."

Emma swiped at her defrosting nose and a whiffling breath slipped free. "That's because I was coming back."

She was…? "I don't want you to leave, to leave Lake

Holly, to leave the café…to leave me. Because, I think I love you."

Her smile radiated warmer than the heater. "I think I love you too." She glanced down and snickered. "I know, a week."

"Not even that," he had to admit. He'd been debating the same, so little time and so many feelings.

Do this right. No more damn half-measures. "I know that a tiny café in a tourist town like Lake Holly can't compare to a fancy restaurant in a city, but I love what you do to me. To my coffee shop. To…everything in my life. You make me excited to wake up again, and I was a fool to let you leave."

"Nick." She cupped his cheek and drew her finger over his chin, playing with the stupid dimple. "I want to stay here. You're the first person to believe in me, to give me a place to create. To…to make me feel like I can do anything. Chef whites are nothing to a barista apron and a brown hat."

"I love you," he said. She smiled with tears in her eyes, and he held her face, guiding himself to gently touch her lips. Tenderly, sweetly, Nick kissed Emma with his whole heart, and she kissed him back.

As he pulled back, taking in her smiling face even through the tears, Nick shook off the rosy glasses. "I should get you to a doctor. Because I don't want anything to happen to you."

"My protector," she said, clinging to his hand.

He smiled. "Always." As he turned to the road, a metal tube clanged against his foot. He reached under to unearth a thermos. "Oh, I brought coffee in case you might need it to warm up. Here."

Emma screwed open the top and smelled the brew. "Did you add…?"

"Cream and sugar, exactly as you like it."

CHAPTER TWENTY-EIGHT

"THAT WAS SO good!" Skylar scooted back from the table and patted her stomach.

"You didn't touch your eggs." Nick jabbed at her plate which had half of her omelet but only crumbs from the cinnamon rolls.

She stared right at her uncle. "Like I said, so good, unlike Christmas Eve. It's too bad you didn't make dinner last night." For that, she looked to Emma who dropped her fork and smiled.

"I would have been happy to —"

"No," Nick interrupted, taking Emma's hand. "You're injured. She's injured. Besides, I thought I did fine with the roast."

Skylar stuck out her tongue and wafted her flat palm up and down. "Eh…"

"You know there are starving orphans who'd kill for that roast and my eggs," Nick argued back.

"They can have 'em." She folded up her napkin and twisted in her chair. Swaying back and forth in place, Skylar looked ready to bolt.

With a beleaguered sigh, Nick waved his knife. "All right."

"Presents!" Skylar squealed. All of her teenage angst vanished at the promise of gifts on Christmas morn. Her body blurred as she rocketed from her chair.

"Just…" Nick called, but Skylar was already through the door. Emma caught a hint of the girl in her fluffy bathrobe bent over by the couch, her hands around the biggest box. Sighing, Nick placed his silverware on his plate. "We'd better get in there before the teenage tornado devours the whole house."

Even though the accident had amounted to just a few butterfly stitches across Emma's forehead and a day's worth of headaches, Nick had and still was doting on her. He didn't just take her hand but swept his arm around her waist to help her up. Emma tapped her lips with her napkin, doing her best to catch any errant maple syrup. Pancakes, eggs, bacon, orange juice, coffee —Nick went all out for Christmas morning breakfast. And she'd gotten to enjoy the sight of him in just his fleece pajama pants whipping up the eggs before dawn.

"What about the dishes?" Emma asked.

"Leave 'em. I can chip off the leftovers with my chisel later."

She flinched at the idea. "It'd only take a few minutes to rinse…"

Nick took both of her hands, then he pressed them to his chest. "It's Christmas." He brushed his fingers around her face, nearly touching the lingering scars from the crash. "And you're…"

"A guest?" Emma guessed.

With a soft plea, Nick said, "Very special."

She couldn't stop her blush as he pulled her close.

"I don't want anything to happen to you," he declared, peering into her eyes.

Emma bit her lip. Her body both burned and glowed under the cute Christmas pajamas they gave her last night. "The chances of me getting into a head-on collision with a dishwasher seem low."

"Still…" Nick brushed his nose against the side of hers. "Why take the risk?" They kissed freely. Without the fear of a clock running down, Emma melted in his arms and Nick held her tighter than ever.

"Socks!" Skylar's displeased shout broke their moment. They both smiled at the teenage growl. "Who gets socks on Christmas?"

"You'll be sad when you stop getting those," Nick called back.

Her answer was a low grumble and the manic shredding of paper.

Holding Emma safe in his arms, Nick guided her to the door. She didn't need the help, but it was nice to be held. Besides, she suspected it was more for him to find any excuse to run to her side and carry her upstairs. As the door swung open to the living room, Emma brushed her hip against him. "What if I make dinner tonight?"

"Yes, please!" Skylar shouted from her sea of torn

wrapping paper. Stacks of cardboard boxes surrounded her as she went to work on the next present.

"No." Nick glared at his niece, then he looked at Emma. "I'll handle dinner. A traditional Christmas goose."

Skylar stuck out her tongue and crinkled her nose. "At least let her do dessert. That's your favorite, right?"

Smiling, Emma nodded. "Right."

"Fine, fine." Nick accepted defeat while he guided Emma through the mess of paper to the couch. As he sank in beside her, she placed her head on his chest. He draped his arm over her shoulder and sighed. "Am I always going to be outvoted going forward?"

"Yes," Skylar said. "You may as well accept the inevitable and… Oh my god. Holy…! You got it?" A mess of shipping pellets dumped out of a large box. Skylar raised a white box to the sky, her eyes nearly brimming with tears. "A new phone?"

"It's from your—"

Skylar stared at him and Nick sneered. He dug into the back of his neck and sighed. "Yeah. I did. But it's the same shitty plan so don't…"

The teenager blew to her feet, scattering torn paper in her wake. "I have to text Abby. She's never gonna believe it."

Sighing, Nick craned his head around to follow her, but Skylar was gone in a blink. "…use up all the data." Laughing, Nick shrugged and turned back to Emma. "Kids. What can you do?"

A blur blew in from the side. In a soft voice, Skylar said, "Thank you, Uncle Nick." Then she was gone.

"I think you're doing good with her," Emma said.

He looked about to argue before he snickered. "Yeah, I guess I am." Nick pulled her closer and she swung her legs up onto the couch. Both watched the fire dancing in the hearth. The scent of pine from the small tree Nick cut down yesterday filled the air with the Christmas spirit.

Every year since graduating, she'd spent Christmas working. The holiday had meant cooking dinners for other families to celebrate being together. For her, Christmas was a bowl of mac and cheese on the couch while 'It's a Wonderful Life' played on the TV.

"How are you holding up?" Nick asked suddenly.

Dreamy-eyed, Emma looked up at him in confusion. "I'm good. Great."

"You're not tired? You can take a nap upstairs, or here on me if you need—"

"Nick." She pressed a finger to his lips. "I'm fantastic. It's wonderful. You're wonderful. This whole day is…" Tossing her arms around him, she buried her face in his chest. "I'm so happy I'm here with you."

"Me too." He kissed the top of her head, then curled around her. "Oh shit, I didn't… Did I hit your wound?"

"No," Emma laughed, touched at his concern. "It's getting better. Really."

"Then…" Nick twisted in his seat causing Emma to sit up. He reached through the mess of scattered paper to pluck a small rectangular box from the tree's branches. Steadying it in his hands, he looked up at her from below his brow. "I hope you'll like this."

"Oh my gosh." Emma gasped, holding the box that didn't look like a phone. It could be a gift card. As she twisted it, something thunked inside.

Not a gift card.

It's not. It couldn't be. It's…

"A key?" She lifted it between her fingers, beyond confused. It didn't look like one for a front door or even the café.

"Here." Nick stood, holding out his hands. Emma pushed away the small bit of paper mess and rose. He didn't have to take her far. Just past the tree, Nick stopped and jerked his head to the office door. "Go on and try out your present."

Emma slipped the key into the knob and turned. The door swung open and Nick reached for the switch.

Waves of tiny Christmas lights came to life above a bed with an adorable pink quilt. Beside it was a small end table with a desk lamp and a footlocker sat at the end. Emma gasped in shock, then she brushed her toes over a fluffy white rug below the bed.

"What happened to your office? All your stuff?"

Nick swung his foot back into a sheet, hitting a cardboard box. "It's still here. But I'm going to try to get rid of it in time. Got to sort through what's trash and what's..." He looked at her and a dumbstruck smile lifted his lips. "What's worth keeping."

"How? When?"

"While you were resting, I brought in the mattress and had a little help sprucing the place up."

"Skylar?"

He shrugged. "She thought the lights would be 'whimsy core.' Whatever the hell that means."

Emma laughed but appreciated the soft touch that made the room glow.

"Oh, and Sam put the lock in so, uh, be careful you don't get locked in by mistake."

"You...you got all of this, for me?" She could hardly believe it.

"I know ladies need their space. Boy, do I know that." Nick rolled his eyes up to the second floor. "So this is yours. You can sleep down here whenever you want.

Um… I mean, this is where you'll sleep, not that I expect you to… In my bed. But you can. If you want. I mean…" He winced and clamped his hand to his temples. "This went better in my head."

Pulling his hand down, Emma gazed into his wonderful eyes. "I love it. Thank you."

His panicked exhaustion gave way to a genuine smile. "You're welcome."

"It's just, I wish…"

"What? There's a desk under all that junk I can clear off. Get you a better chair? Maybe a fan? Or a heater? Is it cold in here?"

Emma cut through his sudden offers by biting her lip and shrugging. "That I got you something."

"Oh, but you did." Nick swept his hands around her waist and pulled her close. "You got me peace of mind. You got me joy. Happiness. Those beautiful eyes and heartwarming smile." His lopsided grin shifted to a devious smirk. Leaning closer, Nick whispered in her ear, "And that little pink ass."

His palm clapped down on her butt. The force was minimal but the sound made her yelp in surprise. Liquid fire gushed down her core. Emma glanced back to his cozy setup and realized it wasn't just any footlocker, but the one from his room with all the toys.

"So, a bed down here." She fiddled with the tie on his pajama pants.

"Uh-huh," he whispered.

"With a lock." Emma glanced to the door then back to him. Wide-eyed, Nick swung it shut and bolted the lock in place. "As far from any prying teenagers as you can get."

She hooked her fingers into the waistband of his pajamas and started to walk backward. He followed like an eager puppy. "You are one devious man, Nick Iverson," Emma said. The back of her knees struck the bed and she bent down to it.

Nick caught under her and helped to pull her up the bed. That quaint, grandmotherly quilt rode up with their bodies. As she fell back into the feather mattress, he straddled above her. His eyes were heavy and breath straining. "Damn," he moaned, his lips against her neck. "You found me out...cream and sugar."

Before she could answer, he kissed her. She ran her palms over his chest, tugging on the cheap waffle weave of the top before reaching right for his pants. The cute reindeer print strained at his cock damn near forcing the fly open. Emma nipped his lip just as she reached for the button.

"Hey," Skylar shouted from outside the door. Both adults froze in place. "I'm going ice skating with Abby. See you later!"

As the front door slammed, and the sound of snow tumbling from the roof followed, Emma and Nick stared into each others' eyes and laughed.

"Merry Christmas," Nick said, the tip of his nose against hers.

"Merry Christmas, and a..." Emma clenched her palm around his cock, his moan rattling the lights above. "Very happy New Year."

CHAPTER TWENTY-NINE

ONE YEAR LATER...

Emma adjusted her hair part twice, flipping it from the right to the left, then back. What if no one showed? What if they hated it?

"I can't do this," she said to her reflection.

Hands slipped across her waist and clung to her fluttering stomach. When Nick perched his chin on her shoulder, she rifled her fingers through his hair. "Yes, you can," he whispered against her neck and kissed her.

A calm coursed through her veins at his touch and certainty, but Emma couldn't fully shake the jitters.

"And if no one comes?"

"Then…" He turned her around so that instead of her nervous wreck, she could lose herself in his handsome face. He'd been growing his hair longer, letting it fall wild to nearly his shoulders, while his jaw was clean-shaven. Emma bit her lip at the chin dimple fully on display before she gazed up into his patient eyes.

"…we get to eat twelve delicious soufflés for Christmas." Nick's simple answer to the problem made her smile. "Also a huge tiramisu and those espresso bonbons."

"Can't forget the lava cake pudding either."

He laughed and swept her up in his arms. "I'm going to gain twenty pounds over the holidays."

Emma squeezed him back harder. "And I'll love every ounce."

The bird clock in her makeshift kitchen tweeted to announce the hour. Showtime. "I suppose…"

"Wait." Nick presented her with a large white box sporting a red bow. "You'll need this first."

She wrinkled her nose, trying to keep from ripping into it in excitement. "Your gift's back at home."

"Don't worry…I already love it."

"But you don't know—" Emma chuckled at his smirk. With a deep breath, she pulled off the lid. A gleaming white chef's toque and jacket sat inside. "Oh my goodness," she gasped, taking out the coat. On the pocket, in beautiful red and gold stitching, was her name. Emma slipped it on and Nick placed the hat on her head.

"You look amazing," he said.

She squeezed his hand while staring at the professional chef in the mirror.

"Hey!" Skylar stuck her head through the door. She

wore a dark red party dress with the same crimson eyeshadow from her dance. "The crowd's getting restless. Are you coming or what?"

Emma smiled at her little family and nodded. "I'm ready."

"If I may…" Nick extended his arm to her. He was the only one still in the same flannel and jeans from earlier, but that felt right. If he'd put on a suit or a button-up, he wouldn't be the man she fell in love with.

Sliding her arm around his, Emma and Nick walked toward the café proper. Skylar took the lead, dashing through the door. The second it swung open, Emma's ears perked up with the sound of voices. At least someone showed up for this.

Nick held the door for her to walk through first. Emma clutched her fingers together once, fighting to steady her nerves, and she emerged into the café. Twinkling lights sparkled against the new paint, the reds and greens of Christmas catching on the sunny hue of the walls. Fresh greenery and candles sat on the tables that'd been pushed together to create a cozy, family-style atmosphere.

As she walked to the crowd, every chair claimed by an excited and hungry face, Emma stopped and looked up. Hanging directly over the gathering was a sprig of mistletoe. When she saw it, she looked back at Nick. As he lightly blushed, her heart melted all over again.

Raising her chin, Emma announced, "Welcome, honored guests, to Brew 4 U's first secret dessert tasting extravaganza."

The people who'd bought tickets to her event, who wanted to try her food, all clapped wildly. Some she recognized as regulars of the café, others came in just for this. Skylar sat at a table farthest from the action across from her father. She held up her phone and explained loud enough that even Emma could hear, "His name's Jeremy, and he goes to Bellview high."

"What happened to the foreign guy?" her dad asked.

"God, dad." Skylar rolled her eyes. "Antonio's like last year. Keep up."

Nick stepped in quickly to ask, "And how old's this Jeremy?"

"Sixteen!" Skylar complained before she realized everyone had turned to the momentary teenage drama. "So, it's fine that he's taking me to the rink tomorrow. Right?" She didn't ask the question of her father, but Nick.

"As long as you call me…"

"When I get there, yes. Fine." Skylar placed her phone screen down on the table and glanced around the room. "Where's the desserts already? I'm starving."

"Ah, yes…" Emma began before a familiar face interrupted.

"Don't tell me Nick had anything to do with them," Sam cracked before braying and slapping his knee. "Or we're gonna need a stomach pump to end the night."

Nick slipped in beside her and rubbed a comforting hand to her back. "You have nothing to fear. Every morsel was touched only by Emma's—" He leaned in and whispered in her ear, "—beautiful, enchanting, succulent—" Then he shouted to the rest of the table, "—fingers. You're safe."

Steadying her shoulders, Emma began her speech. "Tonight will be a celebration of the holidays with a caffeinated twist. We'll begin the first course with a quartet of bonbons. The first is inspired by a sleigh ride, peppermint twists with…" As she continued, explaining the dishes and their history, Emma felt like she was flying.

The secret dinner went better than she could have expected. Some plates didn't even have crumbs left. She'd bustled around the tables, talking with people, recommending wines or coffees to go with. Nick chipped in, playing surprise bartender, as he mixed up a few drinks for the people who wanted to stay and savor the atmosphere. Even as the clock struck midnight, no one seemed to want to trek out into the snow. It took Nick grumbling and pulling out the wash basin to get them to gather their coats.

Every single person asked for a ticket to the next one that Emma hadn't even planned. She wanted to squeal but fought to keep her excitement tempered to remain professional as she bid goodbye to the last of the guests.

"I'm gonna stay at Dad's tonight," Skylar said to Nick.

He stared at his brother before looking at his niece. "You're trying to get out of clean-up, aren't you?"

She laughed and nodded even though it was obvious she wanted to spend time with her father. They had a lot of catching up to do.

"I can't say I blame you." Nick groaned staring at the stacks of plates. Fancy dinners were great at making dishes. "How old's this Jeremy guy again?"

"Sixteen," Skylar said, before adding, "and a half. But that still fits the half plus seven rule. So…"

Nick tipped his head, unable to argue. Skylar giggled, then she ran over to hug Emma. "That was amazing. I got so many likes from your dishes."

"I love you, too," Emma said hugging her before the girl dashed for the parking lot, already texting her friends.

"You." Nick cupped his brother's shoulder and held him tight. Pete gulped when Nick pulled him in for a half hug and slapped his back. "I'm glad you finally got here."

"Me too. Though, if your lady keeps making chocolate cakes like that, I'll visit every weekend."

Nick put on a toothy grin to tell Pete he was testing him. The man laughed, called for Skylar, and left the two of them alone. Emma undid the snaps on her chef jacket to breathe in the cool air. She gathered up the first of the plates for the basin when Nick swept his hands around her stomach.

"Leave that," he said.

She abandoned the trash even while saying, "We'll have to clean it up eventually."

"That's for later. Right now…" He cupped under her chin and gazed down into her eyes. A heartwarming smile crossed his lips then he kissed her under the mistletoe. "You are the best thing to ever happen to me, Emma Belmont."

"I can't imagine my life without you in it, Nick Iverson," she said, feeling silly saying his full name. She started to laugh when Nick dropped to one knee.

For a second, she feared he'd hurt his back before reality caught up. "Oh my god!" she cried, clasping a hand to her mouth.

"Emma, you're amazing. You make life worth living. I want to wake beside you every morning. To stay up late hosting these secret dessert parties even if I drag ass and growl like a bear the next morning."

She laughed, tears falling from her eyes.

"Will you marry me?" Nick reached into a back pocket. Instead of a small box, he held up a stack of papers.

"Yes! A thousand times, yes. Only, what are…?" She took his hands and not the papers, fearful he meant for them to marry that moment. As romantic as that sounded, she was too exhausted to even think about it.

Nick rose and held them out for her. "You know that place next door that used to be a buffet with all the nice ovens?"

"Uh-huh."

"Instead of a ring, I bought you a bakery."

Oh my god. Emma stared at the deed to the retail space in disbelief. He did that for her? He believed in her enough to…?

Of course he did. She wrapped her hands around his neck, holding him close. Nick swept an arm under her butt and lifted her into the air. As she came eye to eye with him, Emma drew her nose against his and whispered, "It's perfect."

Alone in the café, with Sinatra singing them a Merry Christmas, Emma and Nick kissed under the sign for their seasonal mistletoe latte.

One kiss and you'll fall in love forever.

THE END

Enjoy this sneak peek of my Christmas romance
Pride & Pancakes

*When Beth Cho is tasked with interviewing elusive musician
Tristan Harty, it's hate at first sight. Despite his sapphire
eyes and lithe frame, he's got to be the most infuriating man
on the planet.*

*Tristan Harty is already sick of reporters and this one is
proving no different. Sure, she might be adorable with her
ebony hair and big brown eyes. But her incessant need to dig
into his past is dragging on his last nerve.*

*The bickering duo vow never to meet again, but Mother
Nature has other plans for them, trapping them in a Vermont
cabin via a blizzard. The more Beth learns about the
aristocratic Tristan, the harder it is for her to keep her
professional distance, just as Tristan discovers a familiar
heart beating in the beautiful reporter's heart.*

*But what happens when the snowstorm's over, and the
melted Tristan and enamored Beth are free to leave? Can their
reluctant attraction bloom into a deeper love with the thaw of
their judgmental ice. Pride & Pancakes is a sweet yet steamy
contemporary story inspired by Pride & Prejudice.*

Chapter One

Why isn't the car spinning out in the snow? Nothing
dramatic that'd require an ambulance or the jaws of life,
just a minor hiccup in her travel plans. Anything to
delay her from this coming storm. But, no, Beth couldn't
be that lucky.

Wringing her hands over the rented Civic's

steering wheel, she glared out at the stark white landscape. It'd started muddy and drab, dawn hours away when she'd left New York City. Six hours later, deep in Vermont's snow-capped mountains, the azure skies did nothing to evaporate the dread in her heart.

The road was little more than dirt and snow packed down by wide wheels, increasing the throbbing headache Beth knew wouldn't vanish once she reached her destination. At the sign for the Honeymoon Cabin — *charming* — she turned right to follow an even thinner trail. The tiny car barely made it into the ruts dug out by a monstrous SUV, Beth listening to every *chunk-chunk* of snow splatting out of the wheel wells.

As a twist of smoke pierced the snow-peaked horizon, her editor's parting words rang through her skull. *'Land this damn interview, Cho. If you don't…'*

He didn't need to finish his threat — everyone in journalism was well aware of the always-looming cutbacks. It didn't matter how much money their website pulled in, it was never enough for investors. And the easiest way to line their pockets was by sending yet another reporter to the breadlines.

While the six-hour-plus drive in inclement leaning to suicidal weather didn't endear her, it was the subject of the interview that had Beth chewing glass. If it had been a fickle actor known for being handsy, she'd have brought her friend Bruno as an assistant. If it had been a mealy-mouthed politician — not that her employer cared about politics beyond if one was caught without pants — she'd have kept a slew of previous soundbites at the ready.

But this? This was…

Her thought snapped away when the ever-rising ground finally leveled out and she emerged before a picturesque cabin. It looked like a Victorian Christmas card had come to life. The cabin of massive red logs boasted a single chimney puffing perfect clouds of smoke into the air over snow-capped shingles. Quaint green shutters hung off the three windows she could make out. There was clearly a picture window for the living room, but it was frosted over from the encroaching cold. Pine trees lined the driveway, each one dusted in white snow as if a designer had painted them.

It'd be a lovely place to vacation or hide away in for a week while trying to hammer a book out. But that wasn't what awaited her inside.

Pulling a cleansing breath into her lungs, Beth snatched up her purse and laptop and struck out into the cold. Her leg sunk a foot into the snow, the freezing air punching into her chest and a gasp escaping her mouth. Cruel, frozen water tumbled into her shoes.

Damn it! Damn it! Damn it!

With each step she took to the cabin, more plummeting snow filled her ankle-high boots. They were cute for the city in winter but pointless this deep into the wilderness. It was doubtful anything short of a whole bearskin would keep someone warm up here. Thanks to her having turned up the heat in the car, the snow quickly melted to slush, seeping up her socks and leaving her crankier.

Despite dreading what awaited her inside, Beth

dashed for the cabin. At least it'd be warm and snow-free. She grabbed onto the wooden railings with their woodland animal carvings and leaped up the three front steps. The door was a firehouse red with a wreath of cedar and holly hanging from it. Breathing in the smell of hamster bedding, she pushed on the handle and let herself in.

A flash of lightbulbs from by the fireplace interrupted Beth's entrances. Orange flames danced inside the stones there, three stockings without names dangling off plastic greenery above the fire. And standing beside it, an arm lazily draped over the mantel, was what had had her grinding her teeth for six hours.

"Tristan?" the photographer called the stone man glaring through space. "Can you turn and raise your chin?"

If he raised it any higher, all her shots would be directly up his nose.

Tristan Harty. Once a teenage heartthrob sporting floppy hair that dusted over those striking blue eyes, he'd climbed the charts with a handful of songs plucked out on his guitar. The trajectory of his career followed the majority of those who began in the same way. He'd grown older, teenage girls had moved on, his star had faded. Now, he was trying a comeback thanks to the rise in '90s nostalgia and his PR team had finagled an exclusive interview with her magazine.

Instead of the leather jacket overtop an expertly distressed T-shirt, they'd dressed him like Father Christmas. A black suit coat, tailored tight to his thin frame, lay unbuttoned over a crimson vest. A pocket watch, of all things, dangled off the vest. *Does he intend to recite some Dickens to the photographer as well?* Time had thinned the soulful mane of his younger years. Locks shorn to an inch revealed more of his forehead than any had seen in a decade.

While most men his age would have wrinkles piling up across that vast brow, the cold demeanor of Tristan Harty kept his face nearly as preserved as if he were a botoxed socialite. Somehow, his record company had convinced an entire generation of fifteen-year-olds that he was the deepest, most soulful man in existence. Beth wanted to laugh at the thought when the man in question focused away from his photographer to where she stood dripping at the front door.

Eyes bluer than a sapphire burned into her soul. She tried to swallow, but her throat constricted. Even turning her head was proving impossible as ten thousand watts bore down upon her.

"You!" a voice shouted, evaporating the confounding spell. Beth blinked, glancing back at the once bewitching man. With the glare broken, he transformed back into a snooty aristocrat hoisting up a guitar.

From the mess of photography equipment that claimed the cabin's entire living room bustled a wide man. He wasn't fat, at least not in that lovable oaf way, but his rectangular build easily fit into a doorway. He was the comedic opposite of the thin man pretending to play a song for the camera.

"Who are you?" he shouted at Beth.

She flexed her lips in a not smile. "The interviewer."

What had to be the manager scoffed. "You're late. What took you so damn long?"

"I'm afraid transporters haven't been invented yet, so I had to rely upon the old-fashioned horseless carriage," Beth snapped, in no mood to be shouted down by the reason she was in this mess. There were a dozen more interesting concerts and art house movies she could be reviewing at home instead of wasting an entire weekend in Vermont.

The manager pinged his beady eyes skyward. "What? You never heard of airplanes?"

She chewed on her tongue, keeping the caustic comment at bay. There was no chance of her company splurging on an airline ticket, seeing as how they couldn't ship their reporters as freight.

"Barry...?" A voice of reason stepped into the fray as the very subject of the interview spoke up. "Let it be," Tristan whispered. His speaking voice was soft and drifted in the tenor range, a surprise for anyone who knew his songs.

Barry the manager was in no mood to do such a thing. He was clearly incensed there was no underpaid intern to boss around and had to take all that anger out on someone. "Listen here..." Whatever derogatory term floated in his brain remained there, though he stared twice as hard at her eyes. "We ain't got time to waste here. So get this little Q&A session done fast. Got it?"

"Mr. Barry." Beth unlatched her purse, picking up her phone. "This little 'Q&A session' is part of the deal.

I have full access to your…talent, and we host a release for his album." She should have been surprised at having to remind him of the back-scratching contract, but it was a wonder sometimes that most managers had the wherewithal to work a bed.

His annoyance at her tripled in strength. Beth internally smiled at her barbs when Barry pointed toward an open room. "Fine! Set up in there. I'll send Tristan in once he's finished."

"Thank you ever so much." She hefted her bag closer to her side. Just before she turned her back on the primping and posturing, another cobalt glare burned across her sights. For a foolish breath, her cheeks burned.

So I'm to work in the bedroom? While grateful she wasn't being forced to conduct her interview in the bathroom, she'd done worse. Once, she'd had to question a football player while crammed inside a food truck while an untended open fire singed an inch off her hair. Though, as she gazed around the room, a new unease settled in her gut.

While the living room and small adjacent kitchen were rustic and woodland themed, this was where the honeymoon adjective came from. The bed was gigantic, with four posters painted like birch trees, and a damn canopy, of all things. Red and pink silks hung off the posts and a shimmery duvet covered the bed itself. Perched between the ordinary pillows was one in the shape of a heart. There were no bottles of wine in a bucket on the nightstand, but a remote sat there instead. Beth was both curious and terrified to see what it was for.

She glanced at the oval-shaped mirror set in the vanity, finding in the glass an exhausted woman who'd been awake since three a.m., driven up a mountain and still had to crack this damn introvert. At least she'd thought to check in at the hotel first, knowing she'd be exhausted by the time this was over. A warm bath and a night of typing in her terrycloth pajamas was as good a reward as she could count on.

Unbuttoning her blazer, Beth set to work. There wasn't much in the way of seating in the bedroom, so she picked up the vanity's chair and placed it in the center. Hopefully, Tristan would feel just comfortable enough to be uncomfortable. Laying out her tools of the trade the way a warrior would before battle, Beth inspected the batteries' lives. Her phone was holding strong—she'd learned to keep her apps to a minimum lest she miss a vital picture or be unable to record a pivotal quote. The laptop was at seventy percent. Not great, but she'd only crack into it once she was back at the hotel.

The room felt too bright and cheerful. For some subjects, that'd be perfect. The candy-coated-sprinkle types loved nothing more than to bake cupcakes and divulge all their secrets while frosting. But not Tristan Harty. He'd been in the spotlight for over fifteen years, then out for eight. In all that time, the most people'd gotten out of him was his name, date of birth and current hit song. He was a black hole of personal information, and in order to keep her job, Beth had to get this vacuum to sing.

Cracking her knuckles, she took one last look at her reflection. Instead of the fretting thirty-year-old reporter, she saw a little girl. With her neon-pink unicorn notebook in hand, that girl in pigtails had been prepared to ask dictators and humanitarians alike the hard questions, and wouldn't stop until she got them. This Beth could handle some has-been musician.

READ MORE IN PRIDE & PANCAKES

Scan this QR code with your phone to receive a free book and join my newsletter!

About the Author

Ellen Mint adores the adorkable heroes who charm with their shy smiles and heroines that pack a punch. From contemporary small town romances, to steamy reverse harem paranormals, her pen knows no bounds. Witty charmers, rule-stickler grumps, and shy nerds are all her book boyfriend type. She has a needy black lab named after Granny Weatherwax from Discworld. Sadly, her dog is more of a Magrat.

When she's not writing imposing incubi or saucy aliens, she does silly things like make a tiny library full of her books. Her background is in genetics and she married a food scientist so the two of them nerd out over things like gut bacteria. She also loves gaming, particularly some of the bigger RPG titles. If you want to get her talking for hours, just bring up Dragon Age.

Made in United States
Troutdale, OR
12/04/2023

15332090R00195